OASIS SERIES

Book One: Ascension

Jeannie van Rompaey

Clink Street

London | New York

Published by Clink Street Publishing 2016

Copyright © 2016

First edition.

ISBNS: 9781910782675 (paperback)
9781910782682 (ebook)

The universe is transformation;
our life is what our thoughts make it.
Marcus Aurelius Antonius(121–180).

Also by Jeannie van Rompaey

Novels

Life Drawing
After
Devil Face

Short Stories

Betrayed
Afternoons on the De Keyserlei
The Idealists
And her mother came too
Anna-Belinda
Swap
Recognition

Contents

Chapter One
Artefacts and painted nails
(according to Odysseus)

Isis bursts into the histo-lab, her three arms thrashing about like a crazed puppet on a string. 'He's at it again! Sacked half the workforce of Compound 33 today. Our turn next, for sure.'

I look up from the research I'm doing on art forms as political satire from Honoré Daumier to George Grosz. I must try to calm down my young assistant. She's just returned from the compu-centre where rumour is rife and panic spreads like the plague.

'And guess what?' she wails. 'His name is Ra. How pretentious is that?'

I put my docus on one side with an inward sigh. 'In point of fact, it's an appropriate name for the new CEO of Worldwideculture. The God Ra is traditionally identified with the mid-day sun, the generator of light, growth and creativity.'

Isis pulls a face. 'Thinks he's God all right, but if you ask me he's keener on destroying than creating.'

'We mustn't judge him too quickly, Isis. Time will tell.'

'We may not have much time. The compounds he's already visited reckon he's a monster, a devil, a mutant.'

'The last comment is redundant,' I remind her. 'We're all mutants.'

She rolls her pupils upward until the whites of her eyes illuminate her moonface. 'Whatever,' she says, and trips her way over to the caffeine dispenser. That's the tenth tab she's taken this morning. Since we've had our own dispenser in the histo-lab it's all too easy for her to help herself. No wonder she's so hyped up.

'We may consider ourselves normal,' I explain for the umpteenth time, 'but none of us are.'

I flick through some old photographs on my compu to remind Isis of the way humanoids used to look. Not that they all looked the same, but the distinctions between them were subtle. Everyone had one head, two eyes, a nose and a mouth, two legs and two arms, a measure of normality that we can never be sure of nowadays. Not that many humanoids – mutant or otherwise – have been born for years. As far as I know.

I consider myself fortunate to have been born with only one head and tell Isis she should be grateful to have been similarly blessed. The poor girl has three arms, two of the usual length and one half-size that flaps about in front of her body; but an extra arm is a better option than an extra head. The two-headed people of my acquaintance find it difficult to arrive at the most simple of decisions. I believe that I owe my responsible position within Worldwideculture to the fact that I'm a one-headed person. I may only have one eye but it is a large one in the centre of my forehead and I am therefore clear-sighted, able to make decisions easily without the distraction of an alternate self. I try to explain this to Isis.

'Get over yourself, Ody,' she says, popping another tab. She's taken to calling me Ody lately, a nickname I take to be short for my name, Odysseus, but yesterday she called me Odious by mistake. A slip of the tongue.

Or is it? She likes to tease.

Because of my position as chief chronicler, I'm privileged

to see authentic images not accessible to others. I slot a DVD into my compu. DVDs are obsolete, of course, but as my department is the histo-lab, I possess one of the rare compus fitted with a player. It gives me a good feeling to play a filmogram in its original format. This particular one, *Gosforth Park*, was made over two hundred years ago in 2001, a period piece even then. The actors walk in a more co-ordinated manner than our somewhat lumbering method of ambulation and they make gestures virtually impossible for us to emulate. Their speech, for the most part, is pleasant to listen to, a far cry from the habitual jerkiness, high-pitched squeaks or hoarse croaks typical of our attempts at personal communication.

Isis is only half-watching. After a few minutes, she leans over and ejects the disc. 'Got the picture, Ody. Trouble is, all these humanoids are dead. Dead boring.' She giggles at what she considers her wit. The fingers on her short arm brush my shoulder. 'I know you love these antiques, Ody, but not everyone's as sold on the past as you are.'

I can't really expect Isis to understand; a girl who has never had the chance to go to a museum, an art gallery or an exhibition of any kind. Not that I've been to such places either but my academic studies have helped me envisage them.

'The culture of the past provides us with a perspective that enriches our current lives,' I inform her.

'Yeah, yeah,' she yawns.

She seems to have recovered from her tirade about the new CEO, intent now on setting out a row of miniature bottles containing liquid gel in various colours. She reads the labels out loud to amuse me: grungy green, bubonic blue, rampant red, putrid purple, pandemic pink. Her creative task for today is the beautification of her nails. 'Now Ody, what do you think? A different colour for each hand or for each nail?'

She doesn't really want my opinion but I find myself smiling, indulging her caprice as she sometimes indulges mine. I've grown fond of this moonfaced girl and I like to think she has some affection for me. She's the nearest thing to the daughter I never had and I've not given up hope that, in spite of her youthful cynicism, some of my passion for the treasures of the past will rub off on to her. But perhaps not today.

Just as she begins to apply gel to the first nail, the door swings open and in storms Heracles.

'How dare you?' he bellows in that hoarse voice of his. His third leg, slightly out of kilter, grazes the wall. 'How dare you question my research?'

Isis doesn't look up. She's used to this brash young man and ignores him. Quite right. In any case, it's not Isis he is addressing but myself.

'It's my job as your mentor,' I explain, 'to check your work. Finding several errors, I felt obliged to point them out.'

'You pompous prick! You – you know-it-all,' he splutters, arms and legs flailing around like Don Quixote's windmills. 'I am the best researcher here. I should be in charge of this histo-lab, not you.' He holds the edge of my workstation to steady his clumsy limbs and sticks his huge square face close to mine. 'You're past your sell-by-date, old mutant.'

I'm a bit shocked by this outburst but have no intention of becoming embroiled in a shouting match with him. Diplomacy is called for.

Isis looks up for a moment and raises her "bubonic-blue" eyebrows – the result of last week's beauty project. 'Get over yourself, Heracles,' she says. 'The job's not yours yet. Never will be with a temper like that. Show a bit of respect for our mentor.'

I don't need Isis to defend me but I'm grateful for this show of loyalty. I try to express my thanks by catching her eye, but she's focused on her nails, the hand on the short arm splayed out flat on her workstation, as she applies the gel with long smooth strokes.

'Odysseus doesn't realise how lucky he is to have me in the department,' Heracles grumbles. 'Kali says my IQ is the highest in the compound.'

Not higher than mine, I think, otherwise why do I find errors in his work?

'If Kali says that, it must be true,' Isis snaps. Her sarcasm cuts through the air like the swish of a sword. I've never heard her voice so harsh. 'Kali, the dark witch. Just because she's got one more arm than me, and some lethal pets, you think she's something special. You should watch out.' Isis extends her little arm, circles an index finger tipped with its glutinous layer of rampant-red and jabs it at Heracles.

He flinches. A pink flush spreads from his neck to his cheeks, past his three eyes to his broad forehead.

Time for me to speak. 'Your work, generally speaking, is impeccable, Heracles, but when you do make an error – however high your IQ – it is my duty as your mentor to draw your attention to it so that it can be rectified.'

Heracles starts to protest but I pre-empt his objections. 'Now, let's put that little matter behind us and move on. There's something I'd like to show you. A painting that I believe to be authentic, but I'd value your opinion.'

I stand up and glide round my desk. I do not judder as I move. Or only rarely. I am one of the few mutant humanoids able to move about smoothly. I really do glide. It has taken years of practice to perfect this movement, but well worth the time and effort if only to see the looks of wonder on the faces of my colleagues. As I slide over to the art-cab, I note with satisfaction that Heracles can't take his eyes off me.

I pull out a canvas from one of the drawers and hold it up to the neo-lite. 'A genuine Grosz, I believe?' I know I'm right but it's politic to ask for his confirmation.

'*The Wanderer*, 1943,' Heracles says. 'The solitary figure is of course George Grosz himself romanticised as an old tramp. Just look at the depth of colour and the clear definition of those tortuous grasses. No way could a compugraph do justice to these effects.'

Heracles, his tantrum forgotten, almost sings with joy. 'It's genuine all right. Wow. It's totally fab.'

'What's fab about it?' says Isis. 'An old man wandering in the wilderness with mud on his boots, painted by someone called Grosz? That says it all. It's totally gross.'

'Give us a break, Isis. Do try not to be such a silly bitch.' With this parting shot Heracles strides out of the histo-lab and slams the door.

Isis gives a self-satisfied smile, pleased with the effect of her jibe. As for me, the longer I live the less I understand young folk. Why did Heracles leave so brusquely? And why is Isis so keen on riling him?

The fervour Heracles demonstrates for the painting goes some way to restoring my confidence in him, confidence that led me to employ him initially; but he hasn't apologised for losing his temper, nor for his insolence in suggesting it was time for me to retire. Neither has he agreed to correct the errors in his research. His high opinion of himself and his propensity to flare up whenever he feels undervalued make me doubt that he would be a good choice as my successor.

To my surprise, when I venture to express some of my concerns about Heracles to Isis, she defends him. 'You've got to remember, Ody, he's young, out to impress, wants us to believe he's Zeus's gift to the humanoid race. All young males are like that.'

Are they? I don't know, but apparently Isis does. I frown, not caring to dwell on the images that flit through my mind of Isis with a series of young male mutant humanoids out to impress her.

I look again at the painting by Grosz. He felt sorry for himself when his exile in the United States failed to bring him the acclaim he'd hoped for. His political satire lost its bite and he did not make the grade as a serious painter. Heracles is right. The old man in the wilderness is certainly Grosz himself.

I imagine myself outside these windowless walls abandoned in a similar landscape, the barren wasteland that Earth has become. I shiver.

Our planet is dead, or so we are told. No birds, no animals, no plants remain; buildings have crumbled into ruin. Only we mutant humanoids survive – our pitiful, distorted bodies the result of contamination from The Great Plague of the twenty-first century.

Unlike Grosz, I don't venture outside. None of us do. We are confined to these dome-like compounds, locked in for our own good we are told, so as not to breathe the polluted air. Each compound is a safe environment away from the contaminated area outside – a sort of oasis in the middle of a desert. It's unlike any oasis I've seen on a compu screen – no palm trees here – but it does provide us with some kind of sanctuary, some kind of life. Thanks to our scientists, we do have AES, Alternative Energy Sources, neo-electronic power and therefore neo-lites and neo-compus, which make our lives, if not enjoyable, at least bearable. We have scientists to thank for that.

As chief chronicler I've written many times about the reasons our planet died, but still can't pinpoint how exactly we came to this pass. I just can't make sense of it. Whether I try to compress the cause into one word or to indulge in long explanations, nothing seems to suffice. In the past a lot was talked and written about blame. Now the subject is rarely mentioned and much of the necessary data to research these causes seems to be missing from our compus. Censorship? If so, by whom? Worldwideculture itself, I assume. What else is there? Who else is there?

Blame. Who is to blame? We are. The human race. How did it happen? One word, I said. All right. Here it is: carelessness. We used up our world's resources and allowed our carbon footprint to destroy our world. Here's another word: greed. And its companion, power. And another: selfishness. And another: recklessness. And another: war.

Some say God ended what he began. A punishment for the misuse of the talents He gave us. You really can't blame Him if he did. We have behaved quite appallingly. But how can we put the onus on Him? Who believes in God any more?

Whoever or whatever the perpetrator, God or man, it is indisputable that the carelessness, the greed, the recklessness and the wars led to The Great Plague and thus to the death of our planet. And to our mutations.

I sigh. Does it matter who or what is to blame? Yes, I think it does. We must learn from the past to stop it happening again. I know that's what they said after the Nazi holocaust; yet more dictators and more atrocities followed. But I'm a historian and, oddly enough, an optimist. I do think it's worth looking back and reviewing our mistakes in the hope that we can do better. But enough for now.

I stare at the painting. It's melodramatic. Grosz is wallowing in despair. He feels sorry for himself. I am not like him.

What keeps me going is my joy in collecting artefacts from the past. Culture is the key to our continued survival. I'm convinced of that. I slide over to the art-cab and put the painting away in its drawer. I don't want to look at it any more. I don't want to be affected by the artist's obvious depression.

We are what we are. We live from day to day. We do the best we can, make the most of our skills and talents and endeavour to reach the monthly targets set by Worldwideculture. On a good day I believe my work is worthwhile, recording the past, preparing for a better future.

But for longer than I care to admit, very few paintings or other antique artefacts have come my way. I no longer receive packoids of treasures to open. Or very rarely. *The Wanderer* arrived this morning. Before that nothing for weeks on end, a sign that someone, somewhere, is determined to sabotage our heritage, to steal or, worse, destroy the little evidence still in existence. It occurs to me that Ra could be one of these saboteurs. I think of his reputation, of his cold-hearted dismissal of staff. It is said that he turns the sacked members of the workforce out into the wilderness. What happens to them there? Are they left outside to die or are they transferred to another compound and given more appropriate employment? We don't know and the not knowing is terrifying. For us the wilderness is a threat, the fear of the unknown.

Suppose Isis is right and Ra is not a creator but a destructor, his name a cruel irony. I shudder at the very idea.

Isis notices my concern. She doesn't miss a trick. 'What's up, Ody? You can't be worried about Ra's visit. Your job's safe. You're totally dedicated to your work. Everyone knows that.'

It's the nicest thing she's ever said to me, but if Ra is indeed a destructor who does not believe in preserving our heritage, my dedication won't count for much.

I start to retrieve a few of my favourite artefacts to hide them in my dormo-cube for safety. An old player with a collection of CDs, symphonies by Mozart and Beethoven, Mike Oldfield's Tubular Bells, albums of The Beatles and The Rolling Stones, DVDs of Fawlty Towers and David Attenborough's nature documentaries plus an early Picasso and a Royal Doulton plate. An eclectic mix.

These objects do not belong to me. I know that, but I must save them for posterity, just in case my suspicions about Ra are justified.

Isis frowns. 'What if he finds out you've got them? Then you'll be for it.'

She doesn't really believe that. She can't imagine why any of these things are worth saving.

A sudden whoosh and in dashes young Mercury. I'm pleased to see him. I was beginning to feel a bit maudlin and he always cheers me up. He bounds over to Isis, puts an open palm high above his head, inviting her to do the same, to slap their hands together – their usual greeting. High fives I think they call it.

But she cries out, 'Watch it, Merc. Can't you see I'm doing my nails?'

He looks at me shrugs and grins, indicating that he'll never understand females. I empathise.

'I've got a message for you Odysseus,' he says. 'From Kali.'

'Why can't she send an auto-mail same as everyone else?' Isis scoffs, holding her nails out in front of her to dry. 'Why does she have to use you as her little messenger?'

'Because it's a secret message.' Mercury places a finger on his lips. 'Besides she says it is good exercise for me, that I sit too long at my compu.'

'That's true. You do, you swot.'

'Better than being a bimbo with nothing between the ears like you. Anyway I thought you'd be pleased to see me?' He dances round her, elbows and knees sticking out at odd angles, trying to make her laugh.

He succeeds. A huge beam spreads across her moon face. 'You know you're always welcome here,' she says, tipping her face to one side mocking him. 'As long as you don't smudge my nail varnish.'

How well the two of them get on together. When Mercury

came to C55, some twelve years ago, he was only four years old. Kali, the snake woman, appropriated him and, to all intents and purposes, has been his mother ever since. Isis arrived two years later when she was eight and Mercury, six. The only children here, they grew up together, almost like brother and sister, although Kali was never a mother to Isis. The poor girl has had to manage without a female role model.

Physically the two youngsters couldn't be more different. Mercury has no obvious mutations at all. To look at him in repose, sitting at a compu for example, you could almost believe he's a complete human being living in the time before The Great Plague. But when he moves and speaks his jerky movements and high-pitched squeaky voice reveal his mutant status. Mercury is skinny and has always been short for his age, whereas Isis is tall and well built. Her mutations are immediately notable, her moon face and extra arm.

Mercury skips over to me. 'Kali says to tell you that Ra's visit has been confirmed for tomorrow. He intends to interview everyone in turn. She has elected to be interviewed first and suggests that you go last. She wants to check you are happy with this arrangement before distributing the list of interview times to other members of the workforce.'

That is considerate of her. She's chief administrator and isn't obliged to consult me. I am pleased with the arrangement. By the time it's my turn, it will be well into the evening. That gives me plenty of time to prepare.

'Alpha and Omega,' I say.

'Speak English,' says Isis.

'Even you must know what that means,' says Mercury. 'First and last letters of the Greek alphabet: Alpha and Omega. Kali and Odysseus are first and last on the list to be interviewed – positions that reflect their importance. Don't you ever read anything but beauty tips?'

Isis sticks her tongue out at him and giggles. 'Don't be cheeky. I'm not a child any more, you know.'

'Oh yes you are.'

'I assure you I'm not. I'm a woman now.' She looks him straight in the eye. It would be difficult to miss her meaning.

The colour rushes up Mercury's cheeks.

'Well,' I say to break the embarrassment. 'Everything seems to be in order. Fine. Tell Kali I have no problems with the order of interviews.'

Isis stands up and shows me her nails. 'A work of art, would you say, Ody?' She has taken the daring option, each nail a different colour. Fifteen shades of effervescence. 'As good as the Grosz?' she asks.

So she was listening after all.

'Different. An original Isis,' I tell her.

She giggles, slings her red patent bag over her little arm. 'I'll go back to the compu-centre with Mercury. Gotta show the girls my latest effort. What do you bet I've started a trend? Next week they'll all be at it.'

'Copies,' I smile. 'There's only one genuine Isis.'

'See you later.' She waves her multi-coloured claws at me and, forgetting she's a woman, not a child, races off down the corridor with her little friend Mercury.

Chapter Two
Ra,Ra,Ra
(according to Odysseus)

From what we've heard about him, we imagine Ra making a spectacular entrance, his arrival at Compound 55 a veritable piece of theatre. He will storm into the compu-centre, roaring like King Kong, beating his chest and barking out orders, firing employees with ruthless brutality.

This is not what happens. Not a bit of it. He's too clever for that.

By the time we arrive for work on the appointed day, Ra is already ensconced in Man1, the huge managerial office at the end of the steel-plated cylindrical passage that connects it to the compu-centre. No doubt he's been teleported in molecules from Compound 99, the headquarters of Worldwideculture, in the middle of the night and reassembled there, as in Star Trek, that archaic science-fiction series. I understand teleporting is the usual techno system used for travel between compounds as well as for transporting goods. We have AES to thank for these innovations, or rather the scientists who channel these new sources of power to install such devices.

A memo is in place on every auto-put. Kali's work. Ra will interview each member of the workforce in turn to discuss the possibility of continued employment under his leadership. A list of employees and the time of each interview is attached. As anticipated, Kali's name is first and mine last. Alpha and Omega.

I spend the morning in the histo-lab planning my strategy. It shouldn't be difficult to convince Ra of my efficiency. He only has to examine my database and factoid files to ascertain my diligence. What I will have to do is to satisfy him that my research is relevant, indeed crucial, for the healthy future of our cultural lives. I must also make it clear that I, myself, am an indispensable asset to the company, a loyal team player, keen to contribute to the achievements of Worldwideculture.

In view of what I've heard about him, I will endeavour not to be controversial, but accept (nominally at least) his vision of the future, whatever that vision may be, and assure him that I will work alongside him to help achieve his aims.

Once my position is confirmed and my job secure, if I find I do not approve of the future he proposes, I will not be above indulging in a little sabotage myself. I'm not called cunning Odysseus for nothing.

At lunchtime I cruise through the compu-centre past row-upon-row of gleaming blue metallic workstations to see for myself what is going on. A few heads turn to admire my progress as I glide around the perimeter of the room and swing smoothly to a stop like a skater on an ice rink. I survey the scene.

About half the workstations are deserted, telling their own story of jobs lost, careers ruined, possibly lives over. Those still waiting to be called for interview try to look unconcerned, but restless hand movements give them away. Extra nervous colleagues pace up and down, bodies skewed at all angles, arms and legs awry, bumping into desks or into each other. All of them keep tapping their ear-clips to check that their inter-fones are working, just in case Ra changes the order of the interviews. It wouldn't do to miss the summons. Those who've already had their sessions with Ra and passed whatever test he set them, sit at their shiny blue workstations, heads down, focused on their work.

I'm pleased to note that Kali is still with us. Her organisational skills are indispensable to our sectoid. She runs this place with firm efficiency. She raises her huge blue-black head and looks steadily at me. The fierce-looking snakes at her neck and wrists open and close their mouths and shoot out thin, triumphant tongues. Kali uses her pets to keep the workforce compliant, but the truth is they posture more than attack. How perceptive of Ra to keep her on. A good decision.

My eye scans the other successful colleagues, most of them diligent researchers. Not surprisingly Mercury has passed the test. He looks up as I pass, gives a little wave and immerses himself in his work again.

Heracles has survived too. My feelings about his survival are ambivalent. On the one hand it would be a reflection on me as his mentor if Ra had fired him; on the other, I can't help wondering what Heracles has told Ra about me. Has he told him that he considers me "past my sell-by date" and that I should be put out to grass like an old warhorse to make room for a younger humanoid? I can't be sure.

Heracles gives me a nod as I pass, but I have no way of knowing what that nod implies, apart from the fact that his job is safe. It's very quiet in the compu-centre. Only the hum of the auto-puts and the occasional thump or thud as the pacers misjudge the space and bump into a wall or workstation. There seems to be a consensus that it is not politic to discuss what has taken place during the private sessions with Ra. Maybe my colleagues are afraid that their comments could be heard over the intercom-net or seen on the surveillance cameras, afraid that Ra will swing open the door of Man1 and thunder along the cylindrical corridor like a giant troll, to inform them that Compound 55 is not a viable unit, that it is to be shut down. The atmosphere of fear that has built up over the past few weeks continues to prevail. There is no chit-chat, no caffeine breaks, no feedback about the new boss's appearance or behaviour, no tips to the next in line on how to handle the interviews, no farewells to those less fortunate colleagues obliged to make a hasty exit.

A sudden scream. A dishevelled young woman appears through the heavy grey door of Man1. She scuttles along the corridor, helter-skelter, her three legs and multiple arms crashing against the metallic curved walls. All four of her eyes are wide open and tears stream down the cheeks of both her faces. No one looks up as she twists and turns and rushes out of the main door – the door that's normally kept locked but today opens at a single push. I hesitate. I could follow her and attempt to console her, but decide against it. What would be the point? I have no power to reinstate her and she's not worth risking my reputation over. Or my health, exposed as it would be to the atmosphere outside. Ra has recognised that she's an ineffectual worker and acted accordingly. I feel sorry for her, but my confidence in Ra's acuity increases.

Isis receives the call, takes her time, picks up her bag and strolls to Man1, swinging the bag as if she hasn't a care in the world. She doesn't look at me. I tried to prepare her for the interview, told her to take deep breaths before going in, to keep calm and to answer the questions as honestly as she can, but I'm not sure she was listening. She's in there a long time. A good or bad sign? I trust that Ra will not be misled by her glib comments and consider her shallow. I can't bear the thought that he might let her go.

After about twenty minutes she emerges, runs helter-skelter down the metal cylinder swinging her red bag on the short arm across her body. She rolls her eyes until only the whites remain, pushes her way past the other mutants in the compu-centre and barges through the main door. Ra must have fired her. I can't believe it. I rush after her, slipping and sliding, no longer caring what others think about me, or about my health. Outside, the wasteland stretches before me: dry earth, a few shrubs and a couple of leafless trees against a bleak, grey sky. No sign of Isis. She's disappeared. I call her name. No reply. I shiver with cold and fear. I stumble back inside and make my way to the histo-lab.

It must be a mistake, a cruel joke. Isis must have careered out of one door and in another.

She will bounce in any minute now, grin at me, roll her eyes upwards in her moon face and say, 'What's up, Ody? You don't think you can get rid of me as easily as that, do you?'

I sit at my workstation, head in hands, eyes closed, and think about Isis. It's ten years since she was transferred to this compound. Ten years. Apparently her mother died and it was thought better to let Isis start life afresh elsewhere. I have no idea why. Maybe no one from her previous sectoid offered to look after her. I don't know why she was sent to this particular compound, C55. She certainly received a cold welcome here. She arrived looking lost, a somewhat sullen, over-sized girl of eight, not what you'd call a personable child. She rejected any overtures of friendliness, refused to utter a word at first, just kept raising her eyebrows and rolling her eyes. When finally she did open her mouth, she made curt, derogatory remarks. I have to admit that all too often she was downright rude. I suppose she was grieving, missing her mother. No one seemed inclined to take responsibility for her so finally I agreed take her on, intending to educate her and pass on to her my love of things past. I haven't always succeeded in my objectives but I've never given up.

What I have never done is attempt to persuade her to talk about her mother or her life in the other compound. That may have been a mistake, but I've no experience of dealing with children, especially young females, and thought it best for her to get on with her new life without dwelling on past traumas.

As she became used to me, she began to chatter away about all kinds of things, but not her past.

I like to think that, as time has passed, Isis and I have grown comfortable in each other's company. The thought that she is out there in the wilderness alone, that she could die, is an anathema. An unbearable thought. There is a lump in my throat that refuses to go away.

It was different with Mercury. He became the darling of Compound 55 as soon as he arrived. All the female mutants adored him and spoilt him, but he wouldn't allow any of them to touch him, apart from Kali. Most mutants nowadays are infertile so I suppose this little humanoid provided an outlet for surplus maternal feelings, but he screamed when anyone other than Kali tried to lift him up and cuddle him. Sad really. I've often wondered about his past and what had happened to make him so suspicious of females. Although only two years older than him, Isis, big, strong, awkward Isis, tried to pet him too but he was having none of that. Instead, as the only two children in the compound, they became companions. I wouldn't say they played together. No one taught them to play, but they looked up things on the compus together – that sort of thing. And they giggled, bounced on the shapers in the Relaxation Room and chased each other round the furniture. Kali didn't allow such behaviour in the compu-centre but turned a blind eye in the RR. We adults were amused by their antics, treated them indulgently and smiled to see them happy. We knew that being trapped in a compound would give them little scope for pleasure as they grew up and were pleased to see them enjoying life as children while they had the chance.

As they have grown older the relationship between the two young humanoids has changed. Mercury has become more serious, devoted to his compu, intent on learning as much as he can. He continually surprises me with how much he knows. His compu is his teacher and sometimes I think he has assimilated every piece of data it can offer him. When the compu fails him he is not too proud to come and ask me a question and I'm delighted to enlighten him – if I am able to do so.

Isis is less academic. Actually I have to face it, she's not academic at all, but that doesn't mean she's not intelligent. She's more concerned with what I suppose are female things, fashion and domestic matters. I encourage her to find out how human beings dressed in different historical periods but sitting at the compu doing research bores her.

She prefers practical pursuits. She likes to adorn her dormo-cube with cushions and tapestries that she's made herself or to convert swathes of material into attractive covers for her bunku. I often marvel at what she can make out of odd pieces of material, or metal, or glass: a piece of jewellery, a decorative box or a rag doll.

Isis and Mercury tease each other a lot when they are together but it is good-natured ribbing. The bond between them is still there, as strong as ever. If Isis doesn't come back, Mercury will miss her too.

The afternoon drags on. Isis doesn't return. I pray that she's been rescued and transported to another compound, even if that means I'll never see her again. At least she'll be safe. Alive.

It's way into the evening before I am summoned.

I slide smoothly into Man1. Ra is behind the desk, not

a giant but squat short. His huge trunk of a neck seems to grow straight out of the desktop. As rumoured he is three-headed, a rare phenomenon, even for a mutant. The huge central head, rooted on the massive neck, like the bust of an ancient warrior on a marble plinth – Achilles perhaps – is square, the face broad with one unblinking eye in the centre of the forehead. No welcome there. This central head must be the decision-maker. The other two heads look up expectantly at it.

Ra nods at the chair opposite him. A skater on ice, I coast across the floor and slip neatly into the seat. His one eye stares at my one eye. We hold the gaze, summing each other up. I note that his eye is larger than mine, darker, deeper. His black pupil slips to the right as he addresses one of his subsidiary heads. When he speaks his voice is deep, rich, full of authority.

'Ra Two, give me your assessment of Odysseus.'

Ra Two's voice is not as deep as Ra One's but it is measured and calm. 'Odysseus is a diligent employee, thorough and meticulous in all he does. He is passionate about his work and the artefacts in his possession.'

I allow myself a satisfied smile. I couldn't have written this appraisal of my strengths better myself.

Ra's pupil slips to the left, requesting the opinion of the third head.

'Passionate, you think?' says Ra Three. 'I would say fanatical.'

I am shaken, not just by what is said, but also by the high-pitched, strident voice. Looking more closely, I see that the features and hair of this head are definitely female. Hermaphrodites are not unknown among mutants, but rare, very rare. I find myself intrigued, wanting to catch sight of the rest of the body or bodies hidden behind the desk – in the cause of research, naturally.

'Not fanatical,' says Ra Two. 'Odysseus treasures the artefacts he collects, records and archives.'

'Fanatical,' insists Ra Three, 'and secretive. He allows no one else to see the collection apart from him. Only he watches the movies, only he reads the books, only he listens to the music.'

Ra One looks straight ahead, testing my reaction.

Am I to speak now? I wait.

Ra Two speaks on my behalf once more. 'Odysseus is the guardian of the histo-lab, not a librarian who issues library tickets. He is storing them for posterity, for future generations.'

'A waste of space to store obsolete items. No one has the machines to play these DVDs, CDs or videos anymore. Apart from this one humanoid. Anyway, who else would want to play them? All the music, filmograms and paintings can be reproduced electronically on the auto-puts, the sound and picture quality of the originals enhanced.'

'Not enhanced. Distorted. Odysseus believes the originals should be kept intact for the instruction and enjoyment of future generations.'

'He keeps them for his own pleasure. He has a stash of antiques in his private dormo-cube. He wallows in nostalgia. It's not healthy. He should look to the future. Not the past.'

'He believes if we study the past and learn to appreciate it, we will have a firm base on which to build the future.'

'We have all the history, all the art we need on the auto-puts. There is no need for originals.'

Just as I think I will explode with frustration, I realise what is happening. Ra Two and Three are playing good cop, bad cop, as in the old movies, intent on provoking a reaction. I sit back and fold my arms. It's too ridiculous. This is Worldwideculture. How can such a company support the idea that museum pieces are defunct, that original artefacts of all kinds have no place in our culture? It doesn't make sense. They are playing a game and I have no intention of participating.

Ra One stares at me, dares me to speak. I remain silent. I won't lower myself to answer these accusations. Ra is considering both sides of the argument. Whatever he decides is good enough for me. My compliance should ensure my future employment. That is my only objective. At the moment.

Ra One hedges his bets. He informs me that my position is safe – for the time being. He needs to inspect the artefacts I have collected before coming to a definite conclusion. If I have enough items of quality, he may see his way to funding a museum to house them.

A museum. That is a vision beyond my wildest dreams. I move from frustration to elation in one moment. Where would it be built? Underground perhaps with tunnels to other compounds. I note Ra trying to assess my response.

We gaze at each other, eye to eye, and a pact is made: a museum in exchange for my unconditional acquiescence.

'Have you any questions you'd like to ask me?' Ra asks.

'Just one. Can you see a way to allow me to keep my assistant, Isis?'

Ra raises his eyebrow and looks down at Ra Three. 'Isis?'

'The moonfaced female,' she replies. 'You let her go. She showed little interest in history or the company. She was rude to you, called you a ....'

'Yes, all right, no need to remind me.' Ra One glares at me. 'Why do you want to retain her?'

'She's a good sounding board. She presents me with the viewpoint of the youth of today. Young humanoids like her are the future. She stops me from taking myself too seriously and becoming too set in my ways. I am her mentor, but she has things to teach me too.'

Ra's huge face twists into his version of a smile. 'Good answer,' he says. 'Done. She's yours.'

The female head purses her lips, not pleased with the decision, but Ra turns to his auto-put, highlights a couple of commands and touch-initiates them. 'She's on her way. She'll be waiting for you in the histo-lab.'

I envisage Isis being teleported in molecules from the middle of the wasteland back to Compound 55. I thank him politely and start to stand up, but he hasn't finished with me.

His sticks out his chin and narrows his eye. 'One more thing. I give you Isis – you give me Heracles. Would you kindly inform him of the change of plan? I'll send him confirmation by auto-put in, say, an hour's time – but I'd like you to dismiss him first, face to face.'

I'm not happy about that. Heracles will think I am the instigator of his dismissal. I also realise that this could be a test on Ra's part. Does he expect me to obey him without question or will he respect me more if I fight to keep Heracles as I fought for Isis? They are both my assistants. Don't they both deserve my loyalty? I take a deep breath. 'Heracles is young, a bit immature, but he has learnt a great deal since being my assistant. With further training he could be in line to be the new chief chronicler when the time comes to replace me.'

Ra's face doesn't move a muscle. 'Heracles must go. You must dismiss him.'

'What will happen to him? Will you find him a post on another compound or will he be turned out into the wilderness?'

'That is not your concern, Odysseus. You must avoid this tendency to be sentimental. It won't do. I can't have a chief chronicler who's soft in the head.' He stares at me and holds the gaze for several moments. 'My problem is not Heracles, but you, Odysseus. Your first and only loyalty is to me. The question is: are you willing to carry out my instructions unconditionally? Think carefully before you answer. Are you with me, or against me?'

'With you, Ra,' I assure him, but I have the feeling that it will be some time before he will trust me completely. He may even change his mind about renewing my employment. Perhaps it will be me receiving a memo of dismissal.

'Just remember that if you follow my instructions in all things, Odysseus, for the foreseeable future your position as chief chronicler will be secure.'

I find myself reiterating my pledge of loyalty and thanking him profusely for his time. Is he going to stand up and shake my hand? No. He gives me a curt nod. I pull myself up, swing round and glide out into the metallic cylinder.

As I approach the histo-lab, I hear a familiar giggle and know she's back. I can't wait to see her and receive her thanks for interceding on her behalf. She must have been very frightened and cold out in the wilderness and be in need of reassurance.

I peep round the door, thinking to surprise her. The histo-lab is almost dark but I can see well enough to register that they are both there. Isis and Heracles. They are lying on the floor, clothes askew, hair tousled, limbs entangled, like the writhing tentacles of an octopus. Her moon face rests on his chest. Her mooneyes shine up at him. The fingers of her short arm caress his cheek. Her nails gleam like glow-worms. He leans over, thrusts his tongue deep into her mouth and their bodies begin to move in unison.

I close the door quietly, slide along the corridor to the nearest lavat-cube, my stomach heaving. I vomit in the bowl. I don't know why seeing them together like that should disturb me so much. They are both young. Sex is acceptable, even encouraged, between mutant humanoids.

I rinse my mouth, splash water over my triangular face and blink my one eye. For someone who considers himself so intelligent, I have been very obtuse, unaware of what has been going on right under my somewhat bulbous nose. Now I understand. The bickering between Isis and Heracles has been nothing but foreplay: a flirtation. The cutting remarks from Isis about Kali were signs of jealousy. Perhaps Heracles has been playing one off against the other. That would be just like him. From what I've just witnessed, I gather that Isis seems to have won the contest – if contest it has been – and Kali is out of the picture. I'm a bit confused. Not least by my own response to the scene.

I must pull myself together. I have not been looking forward to informing Heracles that his services are no longer needed, but now I rather relish it. I coast smoothly along the corridor. Outside the histo-lab, I cough a few times and blow my nose loudly to let them know I'm back and give them time to make themselves presentable.

I open the door and ask Heracles if I can have a word with him in private.

Tomorrow he will be gone and I will have my surrogate daughter all to myself.

Chapter Three
Sister-wife
(according to Kali)

Hugo is restless. His snake head twists and stretches, he opens his mouth, flicks out his tongue, whistles, looks from side to side with his beady eye, hoping for someone to nip. Ah, here comes someone, but it's Mercury, my little messenger. Hugo won't hurt him.

'Kali, she's here!' Mercury's voice is beginning to break. It fluctuates between a shrill high-pitched shriek and a croak. At the moment it's at its shrillest and Hugo retracts, coils himself snugly round my neck. His brothers and sisters at my four wrists poke out their heads and give Mercury a friendly hiss, his mates as always.

Two weeks have passed since Ra created such a stir by sacking half the workforce. Now he's appointed another member of staff.

And here she comes. She emerges in a flare of light at the end of the silver cylinder and floats towards the compu-centre. I smell trouble. I have a nose for it. She's a mutant humanoid like the rest of us, but she's – well – there's only one word for it – beautiful. Or rather two words: breathtakingly beautiful. I can almost hear the communal gasp as she appears. Damnation.

From the neck down she's the reincarnation of a beauty queen. A curvaceous body and two long shapely legs shine through the luminous pink of her mono. Her mutant status is clear from the two heads poised on elegant necks that emerge from her smooth shoulders. One of the heads is topped by a profusion of gold curls, the other by a sleek blue-black mane that falls down her back like a satin curtain. No need to choose blonde or brunette. Here are both in one neat package. Her cheekbones are set high, as if sculptured, and her cornflower-blue eyes, one for each face, are framed by fluttering black eyelashes. The mutant males flex their muscles. You can almost smell the testosterone. The females stare at her, unable to believe their eyes. Damn and double damn. Trouble ahead, without a doubt.

'Shall I bring her to you?' Mercury is determined to be the first to greet her.

I nod and off he dashes and flits around her. She takes as little notice of him as she would an extinct mutant fly.

'Come and meet Kali, our chief administrator,' I hear him say in his high squeaky voice. 'She will show you to your workstation.'

Oh no, I won't. I won't even speak to her. My sixteen fingers and four thumbs work overtime on my multi-compu. I fill my multi-screens with hieroglyphics no one can understand. Not even me. Gobbledegook. I'm furious. How could Ra send me this creature? Is it some kind of terrible joke? I can smell her too-sweet perfume. I don't look up but continue tapping and clicking.

Mercury is jiggling up and down. 'Kali, this is Sati.'

Sati? What a joke. Kali and Sati, two of the brides of Shiva. Sati, the ideal true and virtuous woman, faithful to her husband even after his death, offering herself to him in the flames of his funeral pyre. Sati, the sanctimonious bitch, a demon in disguise. Well, she will learn that black-earth-mother Kali is a destroyer of demons. Hugo lets out a long hiss. His siblings, Henry and Henrietta, Hugh and Hannah uncurl themselves from my wrists where they lay like bracelets, extend their slippery bodies, open their mouths and whip out their tongues. I may not have the weapons of the original Kali but I do have my precious pets. I continue to stare at the compu-screens. Tap, tap, click, click go my fingers.

'Kali,' Mercury prompts, 'Sati is here. What are your instructions?'

'I'm busy!' I snap and pound the keys. If Ra has to send me a sister-wife why can't it be Jagadgauri, the yellow harvest bride. Or Durga, the war goddess. On a Worldwideculture management course, the three us swore the ancient oath of fealty. Both are my sort of women, slayers of demons, their fierce beauty a far cry from the simpering prettiness of Sati.

'Find her a workstation,' I order Mercury. 'She can start straightaway.'

Little Mercury looks around. Half the workstations are empty since the redundancies. Out of my half-closed third eye, high up on my forehead, I spy grey-faced Merlin hovering by an empty desk hoping Sati will sit next to him. The slimy toad! Jason lounges by the caffeine-dispenser ready to offer her a tab. He puffs out his chest and cracks his fingers. Show off!

Apollo leans back on his compu-shaper and puts on his sunniest smile, determined not to stand up and reveal his three stumpy legs. Males! How easily they are turned on by a pretty face – or, in this case, two.

Isis mocks them by showing the whites of her eyes. For once this moonfaced female and I are in agreement. A rare occurrence indeed.

I make a mental note to have a chat with Isis later and ask her how she's settling in at the compu-centre. Just after Ra's visit she asked to be moved from the histo-lab away from 'that dirty old man'. The reason for her request surprised me. I've known Odysseus for a long time. I realise he's a bit full of himself, likes to show off his knowledge and what he calls his smooth perambulation as he slithers about from place to place, but I can't imagine him making a pass at his assistant. Maybe I'm wrong. Maybe all males are the same. Even an intelligent mutant humanoid such as Odysseus must sometimes think with his dick.

Tedious as it is, I must attend to the newcomer. Mercury has found Sati a workstation near the back, between two females. Good thinking. Leaning over her, are Merlin, Jason and Mercury, all keen to demonstrate their compu-skills – among other things. Apollo smiles and nods from where he sits, not too far way. Sati smiles tentatively back. The others grin. Apollo is no permanent threat. Just wait till he stands up. He's so short his head won't reach her waist.

Time for me to intervene. I spring up, stride, hop and leap across the compu-centre, repeating the sequence that has become my signature movement. Today my strides are longer, my hops bouncier and my leaps higher than ever. I jump over a couple of workstations en route. Rocket power. The three males scuttle off and leave Sati to me.

We stare at each other, summing each other up. She's bold, self-assured. Well, I'll soon show her who's the boss of this sectoid.

'Come, follow me.'

I stride, hop and leap to the edge of the compu-centre. The electronic wall slides open. I look over my shoulder and wait for Sati to catch up.

She walks on her toes, tiny steps, an old-time ballerina on points, yet the effect is remarkably fluid. Her feminine elegance makes my power jumps appear unwieldy. Well, I don't have to hop or leap. A power walk is sufficient.

She gazes wide-eyed at the circular area we have entered. 'It's very high tech,' she says, 'almost an extension of the compu-centre. Not very cosy.'

I see this area everyday but now I see it through her eyes. We call it the RR, the relax room, but she's right, it doesn't look like a comfort zone. It's a huge space and the silver and white décor is not exactly welcoming. The glossy body-shapers, singles, doubles and trebles, face large curved screens that follow the shape of the circular walls. I flick a switch and the screens light up. A kaleidoscope of colour.

'You show films here?' she asks.

I shrug. 'Sometimes.'

I rarely use the RR, preferring to stay at my multi-compu in the evenings. There's always plenty to do and the body-shapers at our desks are designed for comfort to encourage the workforce to work long hours. The only time I come in here is to watch the monthly propaganda programmes, instructive directives from the CEO, intended to motivate our research and creativity for Worldwideculture.

'You have parties in here or is there another space?'

'Parties?'

'You know – a place to dance, eat and drink and mix socially.'

'No other space,' I say. 'And no parties.'

'In C99 we have parties. Such parties you wouldn't believe and there's a disco-cube too and kitchens where we cook together, prepare delicious dishes. Great fun.'

'We don't do fun. In Compound 55 we're dedicated to our work.'

That shut her up, but not for long. 'There must be a kitchen and dining hall.'

'No kitchen. Just a small facility in each dormo-cube to heat up food, a neo-micro-system. We receive a food packoid every day from the storeroom.'

'Where's that?'

'You don't need to know. The packoids are delivered to our dormo-cubes.'

'Sounds dead boring here.' She pauses for a moment. 'Where's the gym?'

'No gym.'

'No sports facilities at all?'

I shake my head. 'None.'

'How do you keep fit?'

'We're fit enough. Come on, let's find you a dormo-cube.'

A section of the wall slides open on the opposite side of the RR and we make our way, she on her toes, me striding out, down another metallic corridor with a series of doors leading to individual cubes. Because of the exodus of half the staff, there are plenty of unused ones. I decide to install her in the one next to mine so that I can keep tabs on her.

She looks around the small space in disbelief. 'Are you serious? This is to be my apartment? It's like a prison cell! I can't live here.'

'You'll get used to it, like the rest of us.'

Most of us have lived here since we were very young. We haven't known any other place. I can't help thinking about the compound Sati has left and the kind of life she led there: communal cooking, parties, discos and sport. In C55 we work hard and have very little free time. We consider it the norm. The idea that some sectoids have more facilities than others I find unsettling. Why has Sati been sent here? Did she do a bit too much socialising in C99? Has she been sent here as a punishment?

She sits on the side of her bunku and sighs. For a moment I feel quite sorry for her. She's undergoing a culture shock.

'You can personalise the room, make it more homely,' I tell her. 'Remember, we work for Worldwideculture. We're encouraged to be creative. For example, you can download and print out your favourite pictures and hang them on the walls.'

She doesn't look too thrilled about that. I don't sit down

beside her, my sympathy doesn't stretch that far, but I do ask her, as kindly as I can, why she has been sent here.

Her answer surprises me.

'Ra has sent me to be the assistant curator of the new museum. I'm to work in the histo-lab with the chief chronicler, a mutant humanoid called Odysseus. Tell me – what's he like?'

Isis stomps up to my workstation and demands an explanation. 'That bitch is going to work with Odysseus? Over my dead body she is!'

She doesn't believe me when I tell her I'm just as surprised as she is by Sati's appointment.

'Really? And you and Ra such buddies. How could you not know?'

Ra and I are far from being buddies. If I give that impression it is simply to consolidate my position as head of C55. 'I assure you I didn't know, but I can see it makes sense. Your decision to leave the histo-lab created a vacancy. Ra has filled it.'

'You knew all right. It was your idea. You did it to pay me back, you vindictive snake.'

An unfortunate choice of words. My precious pets streamline their bodies and lash out at her with needle tongues. She takes a step back.

Pay her back for what? I have no idea what she's talking about, but I am aware that the entire compu-centre is listening to our exchange. Not good for discipline. Pity Ra didn't keep his word and fire her on the day of reckoning. She continues raging and I stand up and try to steer her towards the caffeine dispenser. A couple of tabs might calm her. She shoves me away her arms flailing, bursts into tears and stumbles off through the sliding wall. Colleagues exchange glances. The male mutant humanoids are not happy about

Sati's move to the histo-lab either and are interested in my response. I glower at them. They drop their heads and continue working as I follow Isis into the RR.

She's curled up on one of the body-shapers, sniffing and snuffling. She looks up at me, her round eyes pink at the edges. 'How could Odysseus do that to me?' she sniffs. 'How could he replace me with that bimbo? I only moved to the compu-centre to scare the shit out of him, to teach him a lesson. I never intended to leave the histo-lab permanently.'

I squat down beside her. Maybe I'll find out if Odysseus really did make a pass at her, but she sits up straight and starts to rave at me again, waving her half-pint third arm like a crazy person. 'You must have told Ra, told him I wanted to give up histo-data.'

I shake my head. 'I didn't need to tell him. There's not much Ra doesn't know about us. He must be aware you've been working exclusively in the centre for the last couple of weeks.'

She thinks about that. 'It's like we're always being watched. Frightening.' She looks at her nails that are covered in little crescent moons and stars and waves them in my face. 'Artistic or what?' she asks. 'Ody encouraged my make-up projects, called them ultra-mod art.'

I'm surprised she speaks so naturally about Odysseus, even using his pet name.

'I wouldn't have stayed away forever, but I was that upset. To do what he did was unforgivable.'

No comment. In my experience of power management, people are far more likely to confide in you if you keep quiet. No point forcing the issue. My ruse works, but what she tells me is not what I expect.

'What a bastard, to fire him like that. Out of bloody jealousy. Just because he found us bonking on the histo-lab floor he got rid of him, turned him out to die in the wilderness.'

It takes me a minute to realise what she's talking about. Then it hits me. Heracles. She's talking about Heracles. She thinks Odysseus sacked Heracles because he found them having sex! Heracles and Isis? I can hardly believe it. What would someone as intelligent and – well, let's face it – as hot as Heracles, be doing with this moonfaced girl? Unless of course, he succumbed to her when someone else turned him down. My head is spinning. I shake my head free of the image of the two of them together.

At any rate, the stupid girl has got it wrong. Odysseus didn't sack Heracles out of jealousy, but because Ra told him to.

I explain the situation to Isis. 'Odysseus doesn't have the power to fire anyone. Not even I can do that. Not without Ra's permission. In this case, it was Ra who asked Odysseus to dismiss Heracles.'

Isis opens her eyes wide. 'You're kidding me.'

'The day Ra came to Compound 55, his objective was to reduce the staff by half. Odysseus had two assistants. Ra told him he could only keep one. Odysseus chose you. That's why he fired Heracles.'

'Ody chose me over Heracles?'

'Incredible as it seems, yes. Think about it. Ra sent you off into the wilderness, but whisked you back. Why do you think that was?'

'I never really gave it much thought.'

'Because Odysseus asked Ra to bring you back and he agreed, but in exchange Heracles had to go.'

'Oh Zeus, what have I done? I thought…. I so must go and see Ody before that bitch gets her hands on him.'

'I really don't think that's a good idea.'

'But I so have to apologise. You don't the half of it. I called him all the names under the sun, told him I hated his guts and that if he ever laid a finger on me I'd squeeze his balls to pulp. That's totally bad, isn't it?'

'Totally.' I feel my mouth twitching but know I mustn't laugh.

'You must let me go to him, Kali, before it's too late.'

'It's already too late. Ra has sent Sati as a replacement and there's nothing we can do about it.'

Isis narrows her eyes. 'I know about you and Heracles.'

'What? Nothing to know.'

'You wanted him, but I got him. You can't forgive me for that. You brought that female mutant here to pay me back.'

Unbelievable. Somehow I keep my cool, but can't resist a dig. 'You are misinformed. I didn't want Heracles. He wanted me. When I turned him down, I guess he had to make do with you.'

'Liar! Heracles loved me.'

'Love? What do you know about love?'

'Odysseus showed me all those old movies. "Love Story," "Gone with the Wind," "Romeo and Juliet" and lots more....'

'They're not real, Isis.'

'Don't you think I know that? Nothing's real what we do. Looking at a screen all day, doing research, being creative. What's it all for? We don't have a life. We're mutant slaves. That's what we are. What I shared with Heracles was different. That was real. Where is he now? Wandering about in that foul-smelling wilderness or lying dead in the scrub. What a waste. To tell the truth I don't care if you do turn me out. I've been in half a mind to follow him anyway. I'd have been gone by now if I could have opened that bloody door, but we're locked in. Prisoners – that's what we are. Mutant-slave-prisoners. That's the truth.'

Her eyes are blazing. She rants on, 'You can threaten me with what you like. I don't care. It's dreadful out there, cold and there's a bitter wind, but nothing is worse than being stuck in here with no histo-lab, no Ody and no Heracles.

Nothing left to make my life worth living. Only words and pictures. And you nagging us to meet those fucking targets.'

That's probably the longest speech moonfaced Isis has ever made. Her brain's scrambled, of course, yet a lot of what she says has a kind of logic. Mutant slaves. Prisoners. Her words ring in my ears.

I tell Isis that she must pull herself together. 'I don't know what the future holds for you, Isis, but I will give the matter some thought.'

She rolls her eyes upward. 'Think what you like, say what you like, it makes no difference to me.'

My snakes raise their heads and spit. 'Enough. Return to your workstation. Now.'

She gets to her feet and ambles across the RR in her slapdash way.

I call after her. 'No more tantrums.'

She turns, gives me a mocking look, rolls up her eyeballs, swings round again and strolls through the sliding wall.

Chapter Four
Dilemma
(according to Kali)

I lean back, put my feet up, my whole body sinking into the double shaper. A pleasant sensation. It's a long time since I've taken the opportunity to relax. I spend my entire life working and motivating my team. I think of what Isis said about the monotony of our existence, shut up here. Mutant slaves in a prison. Compound 55 is my past, my present and my future. Every day is the same. There is nothing worth remembering and nothing to look forward to. One thing is certain. It's no good fretting about it, making myself sick with despair. Change will not come from the outside. No chance of that. There is only one person who can bring about change in this sectoid and that is me: Kali, the black-earth-mother, Kali, the all-powerful.

I think about the facilities in C99 that Sati described and begin to consider how we could convert this compound to include similar leisure zones. If we knocked down the walls between those unused dormo-cubes there would be plenty of room for a gym or some sort of exercise area. More space could also be created by cutting down the size of the compu-centre and the RR, both too big for our depleted workforce. I'll hold a competition to redesign the compound and the points earned by the winners will go towards our monthly targets for

Worldwideculture. Nothing like a new project to liven things up. Great. I feel better already.

I close my eyes and visualise the finished conversion. A gym, a dining room and here, in the RR, a disco.

A slow number. Couples dance up close and personal. Heracles approaches, his massive body on his three powerful legs rolls towards me. He asks me to dance. I shake my head. I mustn't dance with him. One thing could lead to another. He is muscular, good looking and clever but I am not willing to put at risk my position as head of this sectoid by indulging in intimacy with a member of my workforce. I must keep control. Power is my aphrodisiac, not a male mutant humanoid, however handsome. My precious pets raise their heads and give my skin a nip, but, as Heracles leans over and takes my hand in his, I feel myself losing ground, falling into an abyss....

'Kali, Kali, wake up!' Someone is shaking me.

I jolt awake. The music and the flashing lights disappear and so does Heracles. I'm back in the original RR. It's Mercury trying to grab my attention.

I close my eyes again and drift back in time. Four-year-old Mercury stands by my bunku and wakes me up. 'Bad dream,' he says, his eyes wide with fear, tears rolling down his cheeks, and I take him in my arms and comfort him and, after a bit, he calms down and curls up to my back and falls into a peaceful sleep.

'Kali, Kali, don't go back to sleep.' His voice is as insistent now as when he was a child..

I sigh and shift my body on the shaper. 'What's the matter? Why can't you leave me alone when I've having a little rest for a change?'

'Kali. Something terrible is happening. You must come quickly.'

His little face is bright red and he doesn't know what to say, how to tell me. 'Come and see for yourself,' he says and grips my hand to pull me up. My snakes make no attempt to stop him. Sometimes I think they're fonder of Mercury than of me.

'OK, OK, keep your hair on. I'm coming.' As I stride across the room, Mercury at my heels, Hugo puffs himself up eager to see what's going on, and his siblings – Hugh and Hannah, Henry and Henrietta – give my wrists a squeeze, their dagger-tongues sliding in and out.

The wall slips open and I step into the compu-centre. I pull up short. What I see is beyond belief.

The entire place is in uproar. Sati sits astride Apollo and gyrates her hips as she bounces up and down, a rider on a bucking bull at a rodeo. A circle of male onlookers shout out the number of Sati's bounces and presumably of Apollo's thrusts: thirty-three, thirty-four, thirty-five.

A group of females stand by the caffeine dispenser comforting Apollo's erstwhile partner, Serena.

I stand transfixed, unable to believe my three eyes. I suspected that Sati would be trouble, but I'd not imagined she would go as far as to organise such a public display, an orgy no less, in the compu-centre. Outrageous.

Mercury gabbles in my ear. I pull him back into the RR to hear what he's saying.

'Kali, she sent a message by intercom-net to males and females alike, with a list of names attached. It said, "You are the chosen ones who will participate in love-sex with me. Attached please find the order of operations." We'd hardly had time to open the attachment before Sati skipped into the compu-centre, swinging her hips, fluttering her eyelashes, a wide smile on each of her faces. She made straight for Jason, number one on her list, pushed him over his desk, began to adjust his trousers and take out his....'

'No need to go on. I've got the picture. What number on the list is Apollo?'

'Number two. You wouldn't believe it, Kali, she just

ASCENSION

pushed Jason away when she'd finished with him, sailed over
to Apollo and....'

'Enough. Are you on the list, Mercury?'

'Yes, but I wouldn't dream of....'

'What number?'

'Second from last.'

'Who is last?'

'You're not going to like this, Kali.' Mercury takes a deep
breath. 'The last name on the list is yours.'

'Fifty!' sing out the chorus as with a hop, a skip and a jump,
I leap into the middle of the compu-centre.

'Stop!' I roar. My precious pets hiss and lash out their
tongues.

Silence, but Sati continues to move up and down.

'Stop this at once!' I say again.

Sati shoots me an insolent look. 'That's a bit mean. Apollo
hasn't reached his climax yet.'

A burst of laughter.

I must keep control, must show them I'm in charge. I
rarely use violence. The posturing of my snakes is usually
enough, but this is anarchy. Something drastic is called
for.

I approach Sati. The snakes thrash about, desperate to
attack. The onlookers step back. I lean over Sati's pretty
neck. Hugo's tongue strikes deep.

'That hurt!' Sati cries, holding her neck as she kicks one
leg high over Apollo's three thighs and climbs off.

'It will hurt even more later,' I have pleasure in informing
her, 'when the poison begins to take effect.'

'I don't believe you,' she says, but the look in her eyes tells
me she's scared all right.

I smile. 'You don't have to believe me. In ten minutes you'll
find out for yourself just how much venom is implanted in

your neck. It will take a few hours to infiltrate the blood stream before you....'

'You wouldn't dare,' she says. 'Ra sent me here. You can't kill me.'

'It's not me who is killing you. It's Hugo. Ra will understand. Accidents happen from time to time. Especially with snakes.'

Both her faces turn ash-white.

'Come,' I say. 'You don't need to die in public.'

I swing round and say in my most authoritative voice. 'Back to work everybody. I don't want to hear another word from any of you.'

She teeters and nearly topples over, but I catch her in my four arms, lift her up and hold her tight. She squirms and squeals but stands no chance. Everyone watches, amazed at my strength as I carry the wriggling Sati along the silver cylinder to Man1.

I plonk her down on a single shaper. 'Now, Sati, we need to have a serious talk.'

Sati pouts. 'I don't understand. What did I do wrong? Those men all wanted me.'

'Dormo-cubes are the place for sex, not the compu-centre.'

'For Zeus's sake, it's so boring here. That tedious old man – he calls himself my mentor and never stops talking. I just had to get away for a while. I thought a bit of communal sex might liven things up a bit.'

'You didn't think about your female colleagues, many of them sex-partners of the males you intended to fuck.'

'Not fuck,' she corrects me. 'That's an ugly word. I only do beautiful things. I make love-sex. I give a little bit of love to all my sex-partners. I've never had any complaints. As for the females, quite a few of them have come on to me too. Some of them are on my list.'

'Well – you won't have time to "make love-sex" to any of them now. Your time is running out.'

'Oh Kali, come on, you can't really mean to let me die. You must have an antidote you can give me.'

'Even if I have, what makes you think I'd give it to you?'

'What if I promise to be a good girl in the future?' Her four eyes look up at me. Does she really think I'm susceptible to her charms?

'A good girl? A good female mutant humanoid, you mean.'

'You know I'm less mutant than most.'

'I know you're very arrogant and sure of yourself, but I am immune to your charms. That reminds me, how dare you put me on your list? What impudence.'

'On the contrary, I thought you'd feel insulted if you were left out.'

What impertinence! At that moment I see a flicker of pain pass over her faces. The poison is beginning to work.

'I think you'd better lie down,' I tell her, directing her to the treble-shaper in the corner of the office. 'The pain is going to get worse.'

'You're not really going to let me die,' she says, as she lurches across the room, but I hear the panic in her voice. She has no idea how far I will go to maintain control of my sectoid. As she sinks into the treble-shaper, her eyes narrow. 'You do realise that I'm Ra's favourite.'

'Are you indeed? No, I didn't know that.'

'If it wasn't for that bitch Athene, I'd still be in C99 now, but- make no mistake – Ra still adores me. I can't imagine what he'd do if anything happened to me.'

I give Sati a contemptuous smile, stride out of Man 1 and lock the door behind me.

Back in the compu-centre, all is quiet. Only the tapping of keyboards breaks the silence.

Serena has calmed down but I note that Hermione, Jason's ex-squeeze, has moved to the workstation next to hers. Adversity has drawn them closer together. A false calm reigns. Another storm is bound to come but, for the moment, I am grateful for the respite.

I'm just about to settle at my multi-compu when I realise that Isis is missing. My first thought is that she has found out how to unlock the outside door and that the silly mutant has gone out into the wilderness, but my second thought is more logical. She has taken advantage of Sati's appalling conduct to slip down to the basement to see Odysseus. I switch on the surveillance camera and the multi-screens pop up. I click on the histo-lab and there she is. The chief chronicler and his former assistant are sitting close together. Her three hands are enclosed in his two. They have clearly resolved their difficulties. This leaves me with a dilemma.

The sensible thing to do would be to reinstate Isis in the histo-lab but what to do with Sati? If she is to remain here, I will have to find a way to prevent her causing further trouble. She will be grateful to me, of course, for not letting her die and, for a while, will conform to my rules, but something more is needed: a project for her to work on. With Sati's experience of C99, she'd be the ideal person to help me transform our redundant areas into recreational ones. The project would not only keep her busy but also keep her close to me. I could keep my extra eye on her and control any future outbreak of unruly behaviour. I shall warn her that she must learn to keep her sexual activities private – confined to the dormo-cubes. If not, Hugo may get frisky again and next time there will be no antidote forthcoming.

I unlock my workstation drawer, take out the antidote and stride down the silver cylinder to bring Sati back into the land of the living.

Chapter Five
Satiated
(according to Kali)

It is a chastened Sati who accompanies me when I organise the workforce to move the abandoned workstations and stack them in an empty office, Man3. Two of the spare desks are put in Man2 so that Sati and I can work together on the designs for the new facilities without distractions. She shows interest in the project and has come up with some good ideas. It is at her suggestion that we are to have a games room for indoor sports such as darts, table tennis and billiards and it is Sati who persuades Ra to increase the budget substantially to buy gym equipment. He did draw the line at an ice rink. A good decision. Imagine some of our clumsy movers on ice. The mind boggles.

Some of the stronger male humanoids have been detailed to knock down the walls of empty dormo-cubes to make an enlarged area for the proposed gym. They seem to enjoy the physical work, a change from sitting all day at compus.

I do spend part of my time in the centre to make sure those not concerned with the renovations keep working as usual, but already there is a better atmosphere. When Sati appears there is a kind of heightened anticipation as if they are all holding their breath, waiting to see what she intends to do next; but Sati doesn't look at anybody. She has stopped flirting. For the time being.

At night I hear movements, whispers and little gasps and sighs in the adjacent cube to mine as Sati indulges in "love-sex." I don't comment or make a fuss. At least she is being discreet.

What does concern me is that many of my colleagues no longer communicate with their previous sex-partners and there are tight lips, expressions of disgust, jealousy and suppressed anger on many faces. Emotions are running high and all too often the quality of work is affected. Documents prepared by one mutant are scrambled or deleted by another. Input to Worldwideculture.inc is deteriorating and it's my job to address the problem. Is Sati the cause of this breakdown of team spirit?

Mercury, as always my source of office news, tells me that everyone is vying for Sati's attention, anxious to be next in her bunku.

I have noticed that both males and females have taken to adding colourful accessories to their basic dark blue monos, a bow or a scarf, a kind of sexual preening.

'They all resent the fact that she sleeps with some mutants more often than others,' Mercury informs me. 'Jason seems to be the favourite and does he know it. He swaggers about a lot, proud of his status as Number 1. The others hate him. Those keen to take part in her love-sex sessions do eventually get a turn. Sati seems insatiable.'

'At least it's behind closed doors. Not in public.'

'Sometimes she takes two or three to her bunku at the same time, especially ex-couples. I know for a fact that Serena and Apollo were there last night. Look at their faces. They can't look each other in the eye today.'

'Are you saying I should do something about it?'

'You could have a word with her but I doubt it will make any difference. She only thinks of herself and, in my opinion, she enjoys being disruptive.'

My little Mercury is very perceptive. My influence. I've taught him to be a good judge of character. I take advantage of the time Sati and I spend together in Man2 to ask, as casually as I can, how she thinks she is getting on with her colleagues.

She gives me an odd look from under those long lashes. 'I'm getting on with them very well indeed, thank you. Giving them the experience of a lifetime actually.'

'You think they are happy?'

'Deliriously happy.'

'It seems to me that some of them look a bit down.'

She shrugs. 'Not my fault. They're so possessive. It's ridiculous. Once they realise that there's plenty of love-sex for everyone they will begin to enjoy it more. Not just with me. Good Zeus no. Even I have my limits.'

She gives me a shrewd look, wondering how much to tell me, how much I already know. 'That's why I often invite several of them at the same time, males and females. To show them that it's fine to have love-sex with different partners, that's there's no need for secrecy. Or jealousy.'

I think about the whispers I hear through the wall of her dormo-cube. Could it be that these conversations are concerned with something more sinister than love-sex?

'I'm not sure your strategy is working, Sati. It's seems to me that every day there is more bad feeling in the compu-centre.'

'Then I must re-think my "strategy" – as you call it.'

'Something has to change because, quite frankly, it's beginning to affect everyone's work.'

'Oh work. That's all you think about.'

'We have to keep on target. When we've finished the renovation of the sectoid there will be plenty of opportunities to relax.'

Sati smiles and keeps her head down over the sketch of the

games room she is designing. I can't help wondering what goes on in her pretty little heads. That she's manipulative and enjoys power as much as I do, I am beginning to understand. The difference is that I'm working for the good of the company, to make a better life for all of us all, while she's working for her own gratification.

One morning we all receive memos from Ra to attend a presentation in the RR. There is nothing unusual in this. These motivational presentations take place on the big screens about twice a month. Just before the allotted time, 11 o'clock, the employees start assembling. Normally they appear in twos to show off new couplings or confirm relationships. This time, there are fewer couples. Instead small groups of the same gender or lone individuals enter through the sliding walls. Jason rolls in on his own but without his usual swagger. Apollo seems to take up a lot of space with his awkward stumpy three-legged gait. A group of ungainly females push their way in. Mercury flits about, guiding his colleagues to their preferred shapers like an old-time cinema usher. There is much hesitation about where to sit, a clumsy jockeying for position, an anxiety about landing up next to the wrong mutant.

I take my place at the back of the room, Sati at my side. We choose to stand. I look around making sure everything is going smoothly. Mercury gives me a nod. Sati leans against the back wall, eyes half closed as if nothing or no one in the world could disturb her. I have a feeling she is biding her time.

Odysseus glides in, his triangular head held high. Following him comes moonfaced Isis with her uncoordinated walk, her little arm swinging in front of her like a fashion accessory. The two of them make their way to the front of the RR and sit together on a double-shaper. I glance at Sati. Her expression does not change.

The presentation begins. Ra's voice reminds us of the purpose of our work: recording the past: planning the future. There's nothing new in his speech, nothing to enlighten us about the nature of that future.

A series of images float by. The Dubai skyline with the Burj Al Arab tower that resembles the sail of a dhow is lit up in ever-changing colours against the night sky. Does this luxurious hotel still exist or is it an emblem of past architectural achievement, already defunct like older antiquities such as the Brandenburg Gate and the Tower of London? We have no way of knowing. Also in Dubai they show us the island in the shape of a palm tree built because everyone wanted an apartment with a waterside view: an example of capitalist greed. It's an unkind image to show us, imprisoned as we are in a building without windows. Another city of elaborate palaces coasts by. Abu Dhabi, Doha, Marrakech? Or are they hotels built in the style of palaces? Again we have little sense of period, no indication of what exists now or what has been lost.

It's the same with the images of artwork that follow. Pictures of the old masters are superimposed with modernist, post-modern and ultra-modern paintings and sculptures. Time and space have been fused. It occurs to me that this mishmash of periods and styles might be deliberate, that we are being bombarded with a hotchpotch of images to blur our vision of what is real and what is not. Or maybe the disorientation is not conscious. Maybe the filmogram-makers themselves are ignorant of the distinction between past, present and future. I wonder what Odysseus makes of these images.

Ra appears on the screen, or at least the top part of him, his tree trunk of a neck supporting his huge central head and the two smaller ones either side, one male, one female. Has anyone seen the rest of his body? The voice from the main head booms out. He gives us praise for the important cultural work we are doing. The names of no individual mutant humanoids are singled out but one or two compounds are credited with particular success. Not ours. Not C55.

I note that Sati's previous location, C99, receives several accolades, maybe proof that enriched leisure facilities do lead to improved creativity. A series of paintings, poems, extracts from fiction follow, snatches of musical compositions and a glimpse of designs for new buildings and machines, all computer generated.

'This is your culture,' Ra tells us, 'your contribution to the long tradition of creative activities already recorded by Worldwideculture.inc. Keep up the good work.'

As suddenly as he appeared, he has gone, the presentation over. My colleagues begin to stand up and shuffle out. They don't get far.

The wall slides open and the dark shape of a huge mutant humanoid with three long muscular legs blocks their way.

A squeal from Isis and she runs, legs and arms askew, towards the figure silhouetted in the entrance of the RR, gives an almighty leap, clasps her arms round his neck and locks her legs round his waist.

'Heracles,' she breathes. 'You've come back to me. Thank God you're alive.'

He attempts to release himself from her embrace. 'No,' he says. 'No. I haven't come back for you. I'm here to take Sati home.'

Isis lets out a huge wail. 'Sati? What have you got to do with Sati?'

He doesn't answer but looks over her shoulder, scanning the RR, pushing Isis away from him.

Isis clings on to Heracles. He tries to prise her hands, arms and legs from their grip on his body. She makes a fist at the end of her short spare arm and pummels his chest. He manages to yank her arms and legs away and give her a push. She trips over and falls on the floor at his feet. Heracles steps over her and strides with his three-legged athlete's roll towards the back of the RR where Sati and I are standing.

Out of my extra eye I see Odysseus go over to Isis and help her up. Good old humanoid. She resists a bit, waving her arms about, but he manages to get her on her feet. She rants at him, tells him to leave her alone and tries to break free, but Odysseus holds her arm firmly and speaks quietly in her ear. She leaves, sobbing, holding on to Odysseus. Really. The girl has no sense of propriety. None at all.

Sati doesn't look at all pleased to see Heracles. 'What the hell are you doing here?' she asks, in a voice loud enough for everyone in the RR to hear. Now Isis has gone the focus is on Heracles and Sati. There are a few exchanged looks, but everyone is quiet, not wanting to miss the next part of the drama.

'I've come to take you home,' he says. He puts his arm round her – or tries to.

She shakes him off. 'I'm not going anywhere. And certainly not with you.'

I realise that I will have to deal with this situation before it gets out of hand, but not in front of the entire workforce. I order the would-be-spectators to go back to their workstations. For an awful moment I think they are going to defy me, but they do go, albeit reluctantly. Jason and Apollo glare at Heracles as they pass, but no words are exchanged, perhaps because my precious pets are hissing in anticipation of further action.

After everyone has dispersed, I tell Heracles to come with me to Man1 for a private chat.

'What about Sati?' asks Heracles.

'She'll be working next door in Man2 drawing up plans to renovate this compound.'

'Is that why you don't want to come with me?' Heracles asks Sati. 'Because you are doing something useful here?'

She shrugs. 'I told you I don't want to go anywhere with you.'

He looks puzzled and moves close to her. 'How can you say that when you know how good we were together.'

She shrugs again. 'Good? Love-sex is always good, who ever I'm with. I've moved on.'

'It was special with us,' insists Heracles. 'You know it was.'

'It may have been special for you,' she says, 'For me it was normal.' She turns her back on him and trips her way down the silver passage to Man2.

I take Heracles by the arm and hustle him down the same corridor, passed Sati's closed door to Man1. I sit behind the huge workstation and motion for Heracles to sit on the shaper facing me.

'What's going on?' I ask him.

'I'm in love with Sati.'

'You and how many others,' I say dryly.

'It was different with Sati and me. We made love and it was like nothing I've ever known before.'

That's one in the eye for Isis, I think. Thank Zeus I didn't sleep with him.

He has the grace to apologise. 'Sorry, Kali, but you know it could never have worked for us. You thought more of your job, of your position in the company, than you did of me.'

I choose to ignore that remark. 'Tell me, how did you survive in the wilderness?'

He looks puzzled. 'I've never been there.'

'You must have been. When you were fired.'

He throws back his head and laughs. 'Come off it, Kali. I wasn't fired. Ra wasn't going to send a brilliant young humanoid like me into the wilderness. He saw my potential and decided to keep me for himself. Teleported me straight to C99.'

'Ah, I see. That's where you met Sati and fell in love.' I can't help the sarcasm.

Heracles leans forward, his eyes aflame. 'You can't imagine what it was like. Electric! Sparks flying between us. Really. I couldn't get enough of her. Or she of me. We spent every night together and, whenever we could manage it, the daytime too.'

'And she was faithful to you? That doesn't sound like Sati.'

'I tell you it was something else. Totally special. Two whole weeks in paradise.'

'Perhaps that's why Ra sent her away. Too much love-sex, not enough work.'

'You would think that. I don't know why she was transferred but I think Athene had something to do with it.'

'Sati mentioned Athene. Who is she?'

'A stuck up bitch who thinks she's better than everyone else. She's beautiful, I'll give her that, but manipulative. Very. She's inveigled her way into Ra's good books.' He leans back again. 'Or perhaps Ra sent Sati away because he fancied her himself and when he saw she was with me couldn't take the competition.'

Just the sort of immature remark Heracles would make.

'I doubt it was personal,' I tell him. 'After all, he's sent you to bring her back.'

'Ah, well, actually,' Heracles grins. 'Ra doesn't know I'm here.'

I frown. 'Ra didn't send you?'

'Good Zeus, no. I teleported myself here. You see, when she'd gone I spent all my free time searching for her – that's how I knew it must be love.'

He leans forward and frowns.

'But it wasn't that easy. Even using the top of the range compus at C99, some data is censored.'

He explains that he had to hack into blocked sites to find the co-ordinates for each compound and to decode the teleport links. 'Not easy – even for me. That's why it's taken so long. Bit of a shock to discover she was here in my old compound, I can tell you. Poor Sati, I thought, she'll be bored out of her two little heads. Look, Kali, you've got to help me. For old time's sake. Help me persuade Sati to come with me. I've got to get back quickly – before Ra realises I've gone.'

I shake my head. For someone who rates himself so highly, he's been pretty stupid. 'Tell me about C99. Is it as fabulous as Sati says it is?'

'It's certainly better equipped than this compound. It's the flagship, you see. The showcase.'

'No, I don't see. The flagship for what?'

'I really don't know. Can I see Sati now?'

'You say you're a good researcher and a good hacker but you don't know much.'

'I've been concentrating on trying to trace Sati. I didn't have time to do much else.'

'Oh, Heracles, what a big disappointment to me you are.'

He has no idea what I'm talking about. With access to high tech auto-puts and his superior compu skills, he had the opportunity to find out if the wilderness is still polluted and, if not, why we mutant humanoids are still living in these compounds and to discover who put us here in the first place. So much research he could have done, but he wasted his time looking for Sati.

'Please, Kali, can I see her now? A few minutes alone with her and I'm sure I could persuade her.'

How naïve he is to trust me. One call by intercom-fone is all it will take and Heracles will be on his way. Not back to C99. Oh no. This time there will be no transfer to the flagship compound. It will be the wilderness for sure this time.

I look him steadily in the eye. 'Wait here a moment.'

As I come out of Man1, I notice that the door to Man2 is wide open and the office empty. With a stride, a hop and a leap I'm down the silver cylinder to the compu-centre. It's empty too.

The wall to the RR slides open at my touch and there they are, my mutant humanoid colleagues in couples on the shapers, making love-sex as if it's the most natural thing in the world to do in a public place.

On a central three-shaper become bunku, the nipples of her pert breasts erect, her arms flung high in the air, a naked Sati rides her willing quarry as if he's a circus horse. A group around her are chanting, counting the thrusts, egging on the protagonists of this sickening scene.

Heracles is right behind me. He takes in the scene and yells at the top of his voice. 'No Sati, no!'

'Yes, yes,' she says and holds herself firm on Damocles, the latest recipient of her power game. Because that's what it is. I see that now. She wants power. Just like me. Just like all of Shiva's wives. Everyone claps and laughs, but the laughter is hysterical. It makes me realise how frustrated these young mutants must be to take part so willingly in this – obscenity. The new recreational facilities must be completed as soon as possible to give them alternative outlets of release.

Sati swings her legs off Damocles and stands up. 'Witness my new strategy, Kali. Better for it all to be in the open. No secrets. No tensions. Everyone can make love-sex freely with whomsoever they wish, whenever they wish. Next!' she says and Merlin creeps towards her.

'Sati, no!' says Heracles.

Sati twists her mouths down at the corners. For a moment she looks quite ugly. 'Oh do give over, Heracles. You'll have to wait your turn. Last to arrive, last to be served.' She gives me a sly grin. 'After Kali.'

Heracles turns to me. 'Kali, what is this? What exactly is going on?'

'I think you can see quite clearly what is happening,' I tell him. 'Sati has seduced my entire workforce and, in her own inimitable way, has taken charge.'

Chapter Six
Mutiny
(according to Kali)

I stride towards Sati. Hugo strikes out with his tongue. Hugh and Henry hiss. Henrietta and Hannah let out a prolonged whistle, but to no avail. My former colleagues form a mutant-humanoid-wall to protect Sati, like footballers defending their goal.

'I must speak to Sati,' I insist. 'I don't want to hurt her. Only talk to her.'

'We don't believe you,' says Jason. 'Look what happened last time. You poisoned her. We can't allow you to do that again.'

'We've had enough of your tyranny,' says Apollo. 'You expect us to work all the time, day and night, with no chance to relax.'

'I'm making changes,' I remind them. 'That's why you've been knocking down walls and getting rid of the old workstations. We're going to have a gym and a games room. You'll have more spare time and plenty of things to do once everything is finished.'

'Sati's plans. Not yours,' snaps Merlin. 'She doesn't need your help to complete the renovations.'

'We don't need you, Kali. Or your snakes,' Jason says. 'You should leave now while you can – you and Heracles. Teleport yourselves somewhere. Anywhere. You're not wanted here.'

For once I'm lost for words. Sati's heads appear over the top of the mutant-humanoid-wall. First one head speaks and then the other, alternate sentences. Formidable.

'All this is your own fault, Kali. You've oppressed your colleagues for long enough,' says Blondie.

'Work, work, work is your answer to everything,' mocks the dark-haired head.

'What kind of life have your colleagues had here? Do you wonder they were ready to rebel?'

'All they needed was the right leader to show them the way. Then I arrived, a gift from Ra.'

'You would never have thought of turning the wasted spaces here into recreational areas if I hadn't told you about C99.'

'These are my ideas. All mine.'

'You have to face it, Kali, it's time for regime change.'

'Time for you to leave. If you don't go of your own accord, we'll throw you out into the wilderness.'

'See how you like that.'

I rush forward, intent on pushing my way through to her, but the wall of her loyal followers – my disloyal workforce – forces me back and pushes me over.

I can't believe what's happening. How can they change their allegiance from me, Kali, the Earth Mother, to Sati, a bitch on heat. I have always been an efficient and fair leader: she is the personification of chaos. I look up and am pleased to see that several of my colleagues look a little sheepish, ashamed to have taken part in my literal downfall.

Heracles helps me to my feet and shouts out, 'Sati, listen to me, you slut. You will pay for this.'

With as much dignity as I can muster, I swing round and stride back down the silver cylinder to Man1, tears streaming down my face. My precious pets shrink into their skins. It's over. I'm finished. She's used her only weapon, her sexuality, to win over my sectoid.

Behind me, I hear a roar of triumph and Sati says, 'Now, where were we. Merlin, you're next I believe,' and the chanting and counting begin again.

I hear Heracles call out, 'Sati, if you come with me now, I'll have a word with Ra and do my best to save you,' and Sati's mocking laughter in reply, echoed by the wild laughter of her fans.

Damn and double damn. She's won. She's taken away the one thing I can't live without. My sectoid. Without my power, my authority, my control, C55 will plunge into chaos.

I pace up and down in Man1. I must come up with a plan to regain control. I stare at the transparent cubicle in the corner of the room. The teleport. That's the way Ra arrived. And Heracles. If they could teleport themselves, I can do the same, but where can I go? Who will welcome me, who will come to my aid, a disgraced sectoid leader? Whatever I do, wherever I go, I will need permission from Ra, but I'm loathe to contact him and admit that my sectoid has been overrun by a sex-crazed bimbo with no respect for me or anyone else.

In rushes Heracles in a tizz and on his heels my loyal messenger, Mercury.

'Do something, Kali,' shouts Heracles. 'You must do something quickly. She's making a mockery of everything. Of me, of you, of this compound. If you don't take charge, Ra will demolish it and eliminate us all.'

I stare at him. 'Ra is capable of doing that?'

'It's not the first time he's destroyed a compound,' Heracles tells us. 'Why, only last week it was the turn of C21. He pressed a button and wham, it was as if it never existed.'

'Ra did that? How do you know?'

'I heard a rumour, hacked in to my compu and checked it out. Gone. Kaput. Not the only compound they've eliminated either. That's what they do when a sectoid stops being productive. They delete it, like an error in a doc-script. Do something, Kali. Stop the destructive bitch from annihilating us all.'

I look at him thoughtfully. A good researcher, who knows how to hack into forbidden sites, could prove a useful ally.

It is Mercury who asks, 'Who do you mean when you say "they"?'

Heracles shakes his head. 'I'm not sure, but believe you me I will find out. Ra is not the real head of Worldwideculture. That much is clear. The previous controller was erased because he was hesitant about firing incompetent staff and refused to demolish compounds. Ra is not afraid of anything. That's why he was appointed.'

'He seems quite reasonable to me – open to suggestions.' He accepted my proposals for Isis and Sati readily enough.

'Take my word for it. He's a manipulator. Gives with one hand and takes away with the other. Believe me, I know him. As well as being CEO of Worldwideculture, he's also head of C99.'

'You don't think we should rely on him to help us?' Mercury asks.

Heracles snorts. 'No. We've got to beat Sati ourselves.'

'You've changed your tune,' I say. 'I thought you were in love with her.'

'She's a slut. I wouldn't touch her now if she begged me to.'

That's Heracles. That's my proud, angry boy. Back on track.

Mercury hovers at my shoulder. 'You can't beat her, Kali. Not alone. What we need are reinforcements.'

'How right you are, Mercury,' I tell him. 'Have all my members of staff defected to Sati? Are there any left loyal to me?'

Mercury frowns. 'There's Odysseus and Isis. I'm sure they will support you.'

An old pedant and a female mutant humanoid with no idea how to control her bodily movements or her emotions? What use are they? Oh well, any supporters are better than none. 'Use the intercom-fone, Mercury, and summon them to Man1.'

Now for the practicalities. I ask Heracles to teach me how to use the teleport.

'You can't leave now, Kali. If you do you will lose everything.'

'I'm not leaving. I need to teleport reinforcements.'

I'm a quick learner and once he shows me how the teleport works I'm in business. He hacks into the compu to find the coordinates I need.

Now I am ready to summon up my sister wives.

Durga materialises first in shower of golden rain. Durga, the beautiful war goddess, armed with gleaming gold shield and sword. Durga, the renowned slayer of demons.

In a mist of silver dust, Jagadgauri surfaces, Jaga, the yellow woman, the harvest bride, who challenges Sati in the beauty stakes and has a deadly aim when throwing a spear or a scythe. They're not real goddesses. Just mutant humanoids the same as all of us, but who will know the difference? Such are the limits of our confined lives that few of us can distinguish between the real and the surreal.

The three of us stand side-by-side, ready for battle: Durga, Jaga and Kali, all warriors, all-powerful. A formidable team. Unbeatable.

Heracles draws in his breath. 'Yes,' he says, 'Oh yes.'

Odysseus and Isis arrive and pull up short at the sight of the three warrior wives of Shiva. Heracles ignores Odysseus but gives Isis a nod. She refuses to look at him. Can't blame her for that. He humiliated her in public. I quickly explain the situation.

The plan is to strike fear into the traitorous workforce

of C55 and silence Sati, the usurper, so that I, Kali the terrible, can take control of my sectoid again and save it from extinction.

Durga, Jaga and I march along the silver cylinder followed by our motley group of loyal colleagues: Heracles on his three muscular legs, little Mercury scampering along behind him, Odysseus gliding along with his ungainly assistant at his side.

The wall slides open and we enter the RR. Sati is making a speech to an attentive audience. She is describing the new recreational opportunities they will enjoy when the rebuilding and refurbishing of the spare areas are completed. It's not a bad motivational speech. I could almost have written it myself.

She looks up, sees us, and motions for her devoted followers to group around her, aware she needs protection. Durga brandishes her golden sword and Jaga raises a scythe, a curved instrument designed for cutting down wheat but deadly if used on mutant humanoids. As for me, a glint of steel catches the light as I raise my dagger. My serpents unwind themselves from my neck and wrists and extend themselves to their full length, mouths open, tongues out. A fearsome spectacle.

To do her justice, Sati doesn't flinch. She has no weapons apart from her sexuality, which she has already used to full effect. And, of course, her bodyguard of mutant humanoids.

'Welcome, my sister wives,' she says smoothly. 'Welcome to Compound 55. Long time no see, Durga. You look as splendid as ever, your breastplate, shield and sword at the ready. No need for any of those accessories here, I assure you. Jaga, just as beautiful as ever, I see, but no need for that deadly-looking weapon in your hand. No corn to cut here. You are both welcome.'

She speaks as if the sectoid belongs to her, but we are here to show her it isn't hers yet and, if I have my way, never will be. My serpents wriggle, ready to attack, but Sati ignores them, ignores me. It's insufferable.

'Attack!' I cry and throw myself forward but, at that very moment, the curved screen is filled with white light and for a moment we are all blinded. Ra's three heads appear on the screen. An intervention. His central head looks stern. It is listening intently to the other two heads, and we are compelled to stop our attack and listen too as they discuss the future of Compound 55, our future.

'Kali is an excellent leader,' says Ra 2, the male head. 'She has made sure that the input from this sectoid has been of a consistently high standard. She always reaches the monthly targets. The mutant humanoids in her charge respect her.'

'Until Sati arrived and showed them what they've been missing,' the female head says. 'Kali is only interested in what the sectoid can produce.'

'Just what we expect from a sectoid leader.'

'There is such a thing as being over-zealous, making your subordinates work all hours with little reward. Kali has no compassion. Such a leader is a dictator. The workforce can only put up with such treatment for a while, then they are bound to rebel.'

'They were quite happy until Sati came along.'

'I doubt that. Sati was only able to win the mutants over to her side because the seeds of discontent were already present.'

'Kali intends to address that problem through the installation of recreational facilities….'

'Which she wouldn't have thought of if Sati hadn't described the facilities available in the flagship compound.'

'True, but Kali was open-minded enough to take the idea on board and initiate the project. She's not a dictator. A dictator wouldn't do that.'

'The point is, Sati doesn't need Kali to complete the project. She's capable of doing that on her own.'

'Possibly, but is she capable of keeping the respect of her colleagues, now she has had love-sex with almost all of them?'

'Why not? She has taught them the importance of open relationships, taught them that secrecy leads to tensions within the group. I have no doubt that Sati will make an admirable leader of this compound.'

My snakes hiss and whistle and extend their slippery bodies even further, but it's only posturing. There is no way we can attack while Ra is deliberating.

'Enough,' says Ra's huge central head. 'I have listened to all your points and am ready to make a decision. I have three options. 1) To reinstate Kali. 2) To leave Sati in charge. 3) To demolish the entire compound and its staff.'

Exchanged looks of terror. Demolish the entire compound? Would he do that?

Ra pauses before delivering his ultimatum.

'I have decided on an interim measure. I cannot reinstate Kali. The regime change has already taken place and not even a powerhouse like Kali can win back the confidence of her workers overnight.'

I open my mouth to protest but Durga shakes her head at me, warning me not to antagonise Ra, and I realise she is right.

Although I am seething with anger inside, I must keep my cool.

Ra continues to speak. 'Sati will remain in charge for the time being and carry on with the plans for the renovations.'

I am ready to explode. How can he make such a decision? He's rewarding her for her appalling behaviour.

Mercury slips to my side and grips my hand. Somehow I manage to contain my anger once more.

'I do have some reservations, however, about Sati's ability to inspire her colleagues to produce the work required to meet the monthly targets,' Ra goes on. 'So I have decided that one of her sister-wives will remain here to work alongside her.'

A pause for dramatic effect. I look at Durga but she looks straight ahead. She's head of C98, in charge of the army of golden warriors. It would be demotion for her to be ordered to support Sati.

'Jagadgauri, you have proved yourself a competent chief administrator in C50 and will, I believe, be able to counter-balance Sati's more outlandish ideas here. C55 will not therefore be eliminated. For the moment. It's up to Sati, Jagadgauri and the entire workforce to prove their worth. You are all on probation. If anything untoward happens to hamper the effectiveness of the new regime, I shall not hesitate to implement drastic measures.'

Ra's one eye appears to penetrate the screen.

'Now for those of you who do not wish to remain here under Sati's jurisdiction.'

He addresses Durga first as the most senior person present. 'You have shown your loyalty to your sister-wife, Kali, and now I suggest you return to C98 where you are proving a well-respected, efficient and fair leader of the sectoid and the army.'

Durga nods, pleased with his decision.

Next he addresses me. 'Kali, I understand that you've lived here for most of your life. You will benefit from a change. I am sending you to Headculturedome to be retrained and afterwards, depending on how well you cope there, we will find you another post to suit your not unremarkable skills. Time for you to move on.'

I am too choked to speak but I have no choice but to accept Ra's decision.

I try to keep calm, but I'm gutted to think of Sati taking my place as leader of this sectoid. Why should her outrageous antics be rewarded in this way? How could Ra come to such a decision?

I feel sick at the thought of what will happen to the compound without me here to control it. Will Jaga be strong enough to curb Sati's excesses? I very much doubt it.

'Mercury will accompany Kali to Headculturedome,' Ra continues. 'He's a clever young humanoid and will benefit from the opportunities offered at our training centre, often known as the university of Worldwideculture.'

Mercury grins and squeezes my hand but I don't return his smile. He is excited about leaving here. He doesn't seem to realise how much I am suffering.

'And now Odysseus.'

Odysseus opens his mouth and shuts it again. I know what he's thinking. He can't bear the thought of deserting his treasures in the histo-lab.

'Don't worry, Odysseus,' Ra says, as if reading the chief chronicler's mind, 'I am moving you to a research centre better equipped than the present histo-lab. You may have wondered why work has not begun here on the proposed museum. That's because there's been a change of plan. The compound that is to be the site of the new museum is Durga's, C98. In fact construction is already well underway. As soon as it is ready you will be considered for promotion to chief curator, a post for which you are well suited. I assume you would like your assistant, Isis, to accompany you?'

Odysseus exchanges a look with Isis. 'Thank you, Ra. I'm grateful for your faith in me and yes I would like....'

Ra cuts him off in mid-sentence. 'As for you Heracles, you are an impetuous young mutant humanoid. You have a good brain, but I cannot allow you to take matters into your own hands as you have done. Much as I'm tempted to get rid of you, I'm going to give you a chance to redeem yourself. You have certain skills that could prove useful to us. Consider yourself on probation. I cannot allow you to return to C99. Not yet, anyway. You have forfeited that privilege. You will go to Headculturedome where, among other things, I hope you will learn to control your temper and your impulses.'

Heracles looks straight ahead and makes no response. He's got off lightly.

'Fellow mutant humanoids, that is all for now. Long live Worldwideculture!'

The screen goes black.

Sati skips off, her arm linked in Jagadgauri's. 'Come, Jaga, I'll show you around,' she says, 'and explain what I'm planning to do.'

She can't resist throwing a smug smile in my direction but, although it makes me sick to think of her in charge of my sectoid, I manage to stare at her fiercely until she is obliged to look away.

So, I'm to go to Headculturedome and Mercury and Heracles are to come with me. I look round the RR and stride through the compu-centre where my previous colleagues are already at work. A couple of mutant heads look up as I pass and give me a rueful smile. I do not react.

I shall be sorry to leave here, the only home I've ever known, but I have no choice. With Mercury trotting along behind me, I leap down the silver cylinder for the last time and give a giant hop for good measure, my power not over yet. My head held high, I make my way to Man1, the teleport and a new life.

Chapter Seven
Mr. Suit
(according to Mercury)

I've never seen a non-mutant humanoid. Not in the flesh. Only in filmograms made before 2020. Until today that is. I suspect the other students here in Headculturedome are as amazed as I am to see him. There he stands on a raised plinth in the conference hall staring down at us. We stare back at him and see a humanoid with two eyes, one nose, one mouth, two arms and two legs. Dressed in a silver-grey suit, neatly pressed trousers, jacket to match and a pristine white shirt and purple tie, he reminds me of Daniel Craig as James Bond or a chat show host. Not a politician. The latter are usually tie-less, shirtsleeves turned up a bit to show that they are of the people and therefore for the people. Though no one is fooled. Think of Cameron or Obama. But this man – let's call him Mr. Suit – makes no pretence of being one of us. No dumbing-down for this smoothie with his sleeked-back hair and chin held high. He's a cut above us and makes sure we know it.

We've been instructed by auto-put to assemble here. A special visitor is to address us. And here he is. His slate-coloured eyes scrutinise each of us in turn as they sweep in a wide arc reminiscent of that long one-camera shot of Gene Kelly dancing in the rain. Maybe his eyes are mini-cameras. Implants. Recording our every expression, noting our body language. Even here in Headculturedome we are not privy to every new technological advance, so I have no idea if it is possible for humanoids to have camera implants in their eyes or not.

I don't know if I'm imagining it, but I sense that as those steely eyes retrace their route, anti-clockwise, they linger a little longer on my face than on the others. The mini-cameras move on and swing back for another look. No doubt about it. Mr Suit is focusing on me, little Mercury.

A shiver runs through my body. A cold sweat breaks out on my forehead. That reaction will no doubt be recorded too. Or at least noted.

What is Mr Suit planning? Who is he? What is his position in the hierarchy of Worldwideculture – above Ra, our three-headed CEO, or beneath him? I look at Kali but her face is a blank.

Since she lost her position as chief administrator of C55 and came here to be retrained, she's been a different person. She has fallen into a kind of depression, unable to come to terms with the change of direction expected of her.

Mr. Suit has stopped his perusal of us and is making a speech. He speaks effortlessly, unlike our jerky efforts at communication. 'Good evening, fellow humanoids,' he says. 'My name is John Smith and I'm delighted to have been invited to Headculturedome to see for myself the incredible progress you are making.'

Fellow humanoids? John Smith? He is a politician after all. He's trying to show us that he is an egalitarian, down-to-earth guy, but I sense something patronising about his attitude as he continues to feed us the same old stuff, the same old Worldwideculture line, talking in clichés, about how we are all pulling together, working side by side to create a better world. Blah, blah, blah.

He is generous with his praise. 'I am very impressed by your diligent and enthusiastic work and I thank you for that from the bottom of my heart.'

Smooth. Definitely a politician. Next thing I know he'll be taking off his jacket and tie and rolling up his sleeves. Lulling us into a false sense of security, that's what he's doing, treating us as equals when we all know that, even among mutant humanoids, some are more equal than others. Orwell knew what he was writing about in *Animal Farm*.

His voice drones on, uttering generalities. More of the same. Blah, blah, blah. I can't help wondering what hidden agenda lurks at the back of Mr Suit's mind or in the minds of the other non-mutant humanoids he represents, for surely he cannot be the only one. At times his voice wavers a little. His hands are never still and there is something in way he leans slightly away from us that suggests he's not completely at ease. Not used to being in the company of mutants is my guess, as wary of us as we are of him. A wonder he doesn't talk to us from behind shatterproof glass for protection, if not from bullets – no guns here – but from breathing the same air as us. We are different from him and, deep down, under that arrogant exterior, he is afraid of that difference.

Once or twice during the speech, I imagine his camera-eye rests on me again, but it doesn't linger, soon moves on. He is summing up now, coming to the end. He thanks us all for our attention, treats us to a self-satisfied smile and strides off without a backward glance as if, having done his duty, he can now get on with more important matters.

A buzz of chatter as he departs as everyone speculates on the reason he is here and where he's from. I sit for a moment and wonder what it could be about me that caught Mr Suit's attention. It comes to me that the reason he gave me a second look could be because, at first sight, I don't look like a mutant humanoid. True, I'm of diminutive stature and have rather large ears, but I only have one head and the requisite number of eyes and limbs. Yes, that's it. He thinks I'm like him, a non-mutant humanoid. He's wrong of course. He hasn't heard me speak, is not aware of my high-pitched voice. Neither has he seen the erratic spurts of speed that constitute my efforts at moving about.

What he doesn't know either – nobody does apart from Kali – is the fact that I have lumps on my shoulder blades that, if not trimmed regularly, sprout feathers. Kali is my feather-trimmer. At least she was. They are badly in need of a trim now. If something isn't done about them soon they will develop into fully-grown wings and I will fly away.

As a child I used to beg Kali not to cut them. 'Please Kali,' I'd say, 'let the feathers grow into big angel wings. I want to fly.'

'Where would you fly to?' she would ask. 'There's nowhere to go.'

I didn't want to go anywhere, I told her. I just wanted to fly round the compu-centre and the RR. For fun. For the sheer joy of it. She laughed at what she called my nonsense and made me lie on my stomach while she clipped those feathers as close to the bone as she dared. She's not interested in clipping them now. And I can't ask anyone else to do it. No one else knows about those feathers. Kali always told me to keep them a secret, although I doubt she cares any longer. She doesn't care much about anything since she's lost control of her sectoid. She certainly doesn't seem interested in me. Ever since we came here Kali has spent most of her time lying on a double body-shaper, metaphorically licking her wounds. Heracles hovers close by. She takes more notice of him than of me but I do try to encourage her to take an interest in working again.

I tell her about the great selection of filmograms available and the pleasure of research with no purpose other than to educate. Her black eyes dull to a smoky, lacklustre grey. She can't see the point of working with no targets to reach.

Making sure her workforce attained the weekly targets was the focus of her existence at C55. But I'm determined not to give up my efforts to revive her.

To tell the truth, I'm worried about Kali. She's changed from the caring mother and dynamic leader I once knew to a sluggish lump of flesh.

My first real memory of Kali is the day I first arrived at C55. I have no recollection of my life before that. If the nightmares I suffered as a child were any indication of the previous time, it is just as well not to remember. For me, life began when Kali took me to her dormo-cube, sat me on the side of her bunku and introduced me to her snakes, one by one. 'So that you need never be afraid of them,' she said. Hugo, the fattest and longest, was coiled round her neck like a thick rope. Kali spoke to him gently and he stuck out his tongue and licked my cheek. Hugh and Henrietta were circled like mottled bracelets on her right wrist and Henry and Hannah on the left. They unwound themselves as she presented them to me, put their heads on one side and hissed a welcome.

On that first day she piled cushions on a shaper and sat me at a compu for the first time. At first I only looked at the pictures, but it wasn't long before I'd taught myself to read. I'd sit there all day, engrossed in my own little world, no trouble to Kali or to anyone else. So I'm told.

It was Kali who named me Mercury even though my budding wings were on my back, not my heels. She used me to deliver the messages she considered inappropriate to send via the public domain of intercom-fone, auto-mail or intercom-net. She named me Mercury, she told me later, not only because I was her little messenger, but also because I suffered from a mercurial temper when crossed. 'Mercury rising!' she would say. 'Just watch it.'

The main cause of my anger was always the same. I didn't want to do anything that took me away from my beloved compu. I remember one particular incident, involving Isis. She was still a child herself, only a couple of years older than me, but much bigger and stronger.

'Come on, Mercury, let's go into the RR and snuggle up on a double-shaper for a bit.'

'Don't want to,' I said, not willing to be parted from the compu.

Isis stroked my hair and wheedled, 'Please Mercury. You can't sit at the auto-put all day. It's not good for you. Come and have a cuddle.'

She ran the fingers of the hand at the end of her little arm through my spiky hair. All the female mutants seemed to like doing that.

'Get off!' I yelled, but she grabbed hold of me under my arms and tried to lever me off the shaper. I held on tight to the edge of the workstation, but she managed to lift me halfway out.

'Leave – me – alone!' I screamed. My legs and arms thrashed about all over the place, my nails scraped her cheek. Still she wouldn't let go. I lowered my head and sank my teeth into the fleshy part of her short arm. She dumped me back down quick enough after that and ran off, limbs all over the place, screeching that I was a vicious little brute. She learnt her lesson though. She didn't approach me again when I was busy at my beloved compu.

Kali kept a close watch on me after that. Her swift warning, 'Mercury rising!' whenever I was in danger of spinning out of control, taught me to control my temper. I rarely lose it now, although there are lots of things in our world that make me angry, so I'm always aware that my anger could return. Funnily enough, Isis and I became good mates. I wonder how she's finding things in C98. I wonder if I'll ever see her again.

Unlike Kali, I love it here at Headculturedome. The dome itself is light and airy, the compus powerful, the screens massive. I've had access to more data in the last three months than in all my years in C55. Here we are positively encouraged to immerse ourselves in history, to watch old filmograms, political, sociological and geographical, to wander in virtual art galleries and museums and to attend concerts, both classical and popular. I've enjoyed concerts by the Berlin Philharmonic, watched with awe conductors such as Herbert von Karajan, Claudio Abbado and Simon Rattle as, their batons waving like wands, they magic incredible sounds from the orchestra. I've become a fan of the Rolling Stones, Cold Play and The Killers, all long gone, but made immortal by filmograms.

I can find few, if any, examples of new performances of any kind after 2020. The world must have fallen apart soon after that.

Here in the dome we make our own schedules, watch what we like, when we like. There are no targets to meet, although we are expected to keep a journal. It's worth the trouble. I read mine from beginning to end each morning to remind myself how much I am learning. How lucky I am to have been selected to spend time here. I just wish Kali shared my enthusiasm, but she takes little notice of me. Heracles, that big three-legged oaf, always fickle in his affections, now fawns on her and she seems to lap up his attentions. He sits beside her and makes what he considers witty remarks. Once or twice he has managed to persuade her to leave the comfort of the body-shaper, sit at a compu next to him and watch comedy programmes. Frothy stuff: Saturday Night Live, Thirty Rock, Two and Half Men, filmogram-series from the early 21st century. It's a start, I suppose. They lift her spirits and, because I care about Kali, I am pleased to see her smile, but I don't trust Heracles. He may be good for Kali in the short term but Kali's happy moods don't last. She soon reverts to her customary inert state and sits, head in hands, unable to concentrate. The learning programmes that I find so riveting, leave her cold.

I look around. Most of the students have drifted back to their compus or gone to the games room to play snooker or darts. On my way back to my workstation I see Kali, lounging in the RR, Heracles at her side as usual.

I skip up to her in my usual manner, determined to make her move off the body-shaper. I stroke Hugo's head. The other snakes look up listlessly. They're sulking because Kali is no longer the feisty mistress she used to be. They've caught her mood.

'Kali, guess what I saw this morning. A docugram. Neil Armstrong taking his first steps on the moon. Listen to this, Kali, there's a virtual programme – you put on a sort of helmet and experience for yourself what it is like to walk with no gravity.'

I lift my knees up high and move my hands in slow motion. 'Imagine it. A simulation of what it's like to walk on the moon. How exhilarating is that?'

I think of her signature movements, her hops, strides and leaps, the incredible way Kali defies gravity. Or used to. Surely she'll be fascinated by the moonwalk.

She waves me away. 'If you find it so exciting, so – exhilarating – go back and play your little compu-games. Stop bothering me.'

She exchanges a look with Heracles. To her I am just an irritating child. But I'm not a child any more.

She sets the snakes on me, all five of them at once hissing and whistling. They don't frighten me, these old mates of mine, but I do feel sad to be treated like this.

I do give up on her, for the moment at least, and continue

on my way, but before I reach my workstation there's a vibration in my ear. The intercom-fone.

It's Mr Suit asking to see me in the guest suite. I glance over at Kali. I'd like to tell her that I've been summoned and ask her opinion on what to expect, but she doesn't look up, her head lifted up towards Heracles. As so often these days, she isn't giving me a thought. So off I dash, keen to find out what Mr Suit wants.

Chapter Eight
Mercury Rising
(according to Mercury)

The guest suite is large, furnished with what I take to be antiques, armchairs and sofas upholstered in fabrics embroidered with designs of flowers and leaves. They are not made for comfort like the spongy body-shapers, but for elegance. The wallpaper is decorated with leaves too, matching the chairs, and there's a large old-fashioned desk and an upright chair with carved legs in dark wood, but no sign of a compu. Through an archway I glimpse a four-poster bed with heavy velvet curtains tied back. I imagine that at night they can be drawn to enclose the bed for privacy or warmth. I'm not sure I'd like that. The style of furniture in this dormo-cube or apartment is, I believe, what they call "retro." I've only seen such things before in a virtual museum or in filmograms. I do my best not to stare. In the corner is a transparent box, its high tech design at odds with the other furnishings. The teleport.

Mr Suit greets me but stops short at shaking my hand. 'Mercury, delighted to have this opportunity to get to know you better.'

He motions for me to sit down on one of the hard armchairs and sits opposite me in an identical one. He leans back, crosses his legs and places the tips of his fingers together to make a tent-shape or perhaps a steeple. It reminds me of the old rhyme,

Here's the church and here's the steeple
Look inside and see the people.

No chance of me leaning back. I've had to hitch myself up to sit on it and my short legs dangle over the edge of the chair like a puppet's.

He turns the church upside down to *see the people* and stretches out his arms. His bones crack.

'How do you think it went?'

I have no idea what he's referring to.

He helps me out. 'My speech. Did it go down well with…' he hesitates, searching for the right word, 'your colleagues?'

What can I say? Should I be polite and congratulate him or be honest and tell him it was crap, the same old-old we are dished out by Ra.

He seems tense, as if my answer to his question is important in some way.

He sees my reluctance to offer an honest opinion and leans forward. There is something passionate about the way he speaks. 'Please, be frank. I'd value your opinion.'

Why he should do that I haven't a clue, but I take a chance. 'You speak well, very fluently, it's a pleasure to listen to your voice….'

'But…' his slate grey eyes do not leave my face.

'You said to be frank.'

He nods encouragingly.

I take a deep breath. 'OK then. Here goes. You said nothing we hadn't heard before. It was company-speak.'

He throws his head back and laughs, a rich full-throated laugh. 'Too right,' he says. 'I didn't write it. It was given to me to read.'

So he's not in charge. Someone is telling him what to do – Ra or someone else?

'Thank you for answering that question truthfully,' he says, his face a bit more relaxed. 'A good start to what I hope will be a fruitful exchange of ideas. Tell me, Mercury, are you happy here?'

That is an easy question to answer. 'Very. I'm proud to have been given the opportunity to learn more about Worldwideculture in such a rich environment.'

He gives an odd little smile. 'Now who is using company-speak?'

I feel the colour rush up my cheeks. 'It may sound like that, but I really mean it. I've learnt so much in the three months since I've been here. I find out one thing and that puts me on track to dig deeper and learn more.'

He nods. 'A perfect student.' There is the little smile at the corner of his mouth again. 'You don't need to convince me of your dedication, Mercury. Your progress – everyone's progress – is monitored. We are very pleased with your aptitude for study.' He leans forward again. 'But what I really want to know is – are you *happy* here?'

I don't know what he's getting at. How could I not be happy with all these powerful, big-screened compus where I can surf the net, watch a wide variety of filmograms or take part in a series of fascinating virtual trips?

I start to explain this to him, but he waves his hand to stop me.

'I mean socially? How do you get on with your colleagues? Have you any special friends?'

I think of Kali and her seeming rejection of me. As for the other students, I like them well enough and they seem to tolerate me, but I've never been one to have close friends, apart from Isis. There is a games room with darts, billiards and table tennis, but I rarely go in it. In Compound 55 we had no leisure facilities. That's all changing now of course. Sati's innovations will provide a gym and a social centre but, even if I were still there, I can't imagine joining in such activities.

'I suppose I'm a bit of a loner. A nerd,' I tell Mr Suit.

He raises his eyebrows. 'Where did you learn that word?'

'Same place I learn all my words. Online or from watching filmograms. What I mean is, I don't socialise much. I prefer to sit at my workstation.'

'Why do you think that is?'

'It's what I'm used to. At C55.'

'Ah yes, in the days of Kali's regime.'

He talks about it as if it is something in the distant past, something defunct, which I suppose it is.

'Tell me about Kali,' he says.

At last something or rather someone I can really talk about. 'Kali is – was – a wonderful leader. Everyone respected her. She always reached her targets.'

'I heard it was a reign of terror.'

I stare him. 'Then you heard wrong. Kali cared for her workforce, always aware of any problems that individuals might have and she did her best to solve them.'

'She didn't threaten them with her snakes?'

I pause. 'Only when absolutely necessary.'

'She poisoned Sati, tried to kill her.'

'No. It was necessary for everyone's sake to sedate Sati for a while. That's all. If she'd wanted to kill her she could have done, but she didn't. Kali is a balanced, thoughtful humanoid, dedicated to the welfare of her workforce and to the company.'

'You use the past tense. Do you think she's still loyal to the company now?'

'Of course. It's in Kali's nature to be loyal.'

'She's rather neglected you lately I understand.'

'We don't spend so much time together as before but that doesn't mean....'

'You are very loyal to her. You obviously admire her a lot.'

'Indeed I do.'

'The thing is, Mercury, your ex-boss doesn't appear to be as enamoured with the learning process here as you are.'

'Are you surprised? Kali was chief administrator at C55, a position of authority. Now that authority has been taken away. She must feel…'

'Resentful?'

'She resents the fact that her sectoid is being run by Sati, yes. Who wouldn't? She has to live with the knowledge that she has been replaced by a woman who is no better than a prostitute – except she gives her body away freely to anybody who wants it.'

Watch it! Mercury rising! I mustn't let this humanoid make me lose my temper.

Mr Suit's lips twitch. A ghost of a smile. 'I take it you are not a fan of Sati?'

'I most certainly am not. She has behaved appallingly. I can't believe that she's now in charge of C55.'

'With Jaga, who will surely tone down any wild ideas that Sati might have.' He runs his hand down the knife pleat of his trousers. 'You disagree with Ra's decision to put the sectoid into their hands?'

I look him straight in the eye. 'Kali worked hard to make it work efficiently. Now it's in the hands of a slut and a farmer.'

He doesn't disguise his smile this time, but gives an approving laugh. He leans forward and the intense look returns. 'You feel passionately about this.'

'I do.'

'It was a legitimate regime change, Mercury. Ra had already sacked half the workforce and those who were left were forced to work all hours with no let-up.'

'Kali was determined to show Ra that his faith in her was not misplaced.'

'She pushed the workers too hard. Oppressed people are

bound to rebel sometime. They were ripe for it. When Sati arrived they were ready for a change of leader.'

I don't believe that's a true assessment of the situation, but I keep quiet. I've been outspoken enough. I don't want to antagonise this man. I still don't know who he is or what he wants.

Mr. Suit makes his fingers into a church steeple again, clearly thinking about what to say next, or how to say it. 'What I am interested in is Kali's attitude now. Of course, any deposed leader would feel – what shall I say – ill-used. It's a natural reaction, but she's been treated very fairly. Been given another chance to polish her leadership skills. But she's resistant to the retraining programme we've set up for her. In fact she's never once logged on to it in the three months she's been here. Why is that, do you suppose?'

'You'd better ask Kali the answer to that, not me.'

Mr Suit sits back. 'What a loyal person you are, Mercury. I like that. I like that very much indeed.'

Is that what all these questions are about? A test of my loyalty? It suddenly occurs to me that he's called me in here to persuade me to spy on Kali, that "they" don't trust her. My mercurial spirit leaps up. I don't care who this humanoid is, how high up he is in the hierarchy of Worldwideculture. I will not betray Kali. I wriggle somewhat awkwardly to the edge of the solidly upholstered chair, slide myself off it and place my feet firmly on the leaf-patterned carpet. I draw myself up to my full height and make an announcement. 'I must inform you, Sir, that, though at times I have been a messenger, I have never been, nor ever will be, a spy. I am a proud mutant humanoid who will never betray my fellow mutants. If you think I would be willing to spy on Kali or on any of my colleagues for that matter, you have chosen the wrong mutant humanoid.'

Mr Suit opens his eyes wide and begins to clap his hands

very slowly. He is grinning broadly from ear to ear. I do seem to have passed some sort of test.

'You have misunderstood my intentions,' he says, his voice as smooth as the sheen on the velvet curtains on the four-poster. 'I have no intention of asking you to spy on your colleagues. In fact, I am here to ask you to come back with me to Planet Oasis.'

'Planet Oasis? Where's that?' I've never heard of such a place.

'To be accurate, Oasis – as it's generally known – is not a planet but a man-made satellite. It floats in space, way above Earth. That's where I live.'

I must look as gob-smacked as I feel. He seeks to reassure me. 'It's a good place, Mercury. You'll like it. It has lots of computers with no censors to block access. Imagine – unlimited knowledge at your finger tips.'

I can't take it in. 'You live on a satellite? In the sky?'

'That's right. That's my world. I live there with others like me. It was constructed along with quite a few other satellites soon after Earth burnt out.'

'So – it was built to protect humanoids like you from pollution.'

'How quick you are, Mercury. Mercurial indeed. Yes, it was built for complete human beings – completes.'

It's the first time I've heard that term, "completes", and I don't like it much. 'While we mutant humanoids were left to rot in the wilderness.'

'Left on Earth, but not to rot. We built the compounds to keep you safe.'

'And to keep us away from you – in case we should infect you.' I take a peek at his face to see if I have gone too far but he answers reasonably enough.

'There was fear of contagion at first, yes.'

'We had no say in the matter. We were herded into the compounds and locked in like prisoners.'

'It wasn't quite like that, Mercury. What we did was for your own good. We couldn't let you wander about on contaminated ground. You wouldn't have survived.'

I think about what he has told me. 'If Oasis is only for humanoids without mutations why do you want to take me there?'

'I'm impressed with your thirst for knowledge and dedication. Sometime in the future you could become some sort of liaison officer between Oasis and the compounds, between completes and mutant humanoids. To help us understand each other better.'

'A kind of ambassador for my fellow mutant humanoids?'

'You could call it that, although…. Mercury, you would be ideal for such a post. Your love of learning for its own sake, your intelligence, your insights – you have so much to contribute to both cultures.'

I stare at him. How does he know so much about me? He's offering me a job, a real job, on a satellite that floats above the Earth. In the sky. What young man brought up on sci-fi and action filmograms wouldn't be tempted by what he is offering?

'You will love Oasis. You can't imagine what treasures we have there. A museum full of artefacts from every period and place and state-of-the-art technology to die for. Oasis could have been made for someone like you.'

But it wasn't made for me. It was made for "them." I shake my head. 'I don't want to leave. I'm fine here.'

'You'll be leaving Headculturedome soon anyway – this is only an interim place to study or retrain. If you don't come with me you'll will be sent to another mutant humanoid compound which, I assure you, will be nothing compared to Oasis.'

He's certainly persuasive. I think about what he has said about compus with no censors. Unlimited access to the world wide web. It's very tempting. 'If I do come, I will have to leave Kali?'

'If you stay here you and Kali will be separated soon anyway and sent to different compounds.'

Pause for thought. 'I'd like to discuss this – proposition – with her.'

'Impossible.'

'Why? I've told you she's reliable and completely loyal to the company.'

'No, I can't allow it. No one must know. I take your word for it that Kali is trustworthy, but what about her companion, Heracles? Is he?'

I think of the way Heracles hacks into computers and how he broke the teleport codes to bring Durga and Jaga to C55 to help Kali fight Sati. Heracles, the hacker and code-breaker. No, I can't swear to him being trustworthy. Neither can I be sure that Kali would not confide in Heracles.

'If you decide to come with me, Mercury, we leave tonight.'

'That's impossible.'

'Why? You don't need to take anything with you. You'll have everything you need on Oasis.'

He leans forward and his intense gaze returns, compelling me to listen to him.

'Mercury, you've admitted you have no close friends here and what you like best is the virtual reality of the compu-systems. Let me tell you something. Once you switch on our unlimited access machines you'll wonder how you could ever have thought Headculturedome so special.'

He's right. I have no close friends. I don't want to leave Kali without saying goodbye, but I have to face the fact that she has already left me and, as Mr Suit points out, I shall soon be moved to another compound without her. The halcyon days of childhood, C55 and Headculturedome are over. The uncensored, open access compus high up in the sky beckon.

Yet I hesitate. There is something he isn't telling me. Why is he so keen to take me to Oasis, a satellite intended for uncontaminated humanoids – completes? Because I can help both cultures to understand each other better? I don't buy it. There must be another reason.

My thoughts turn to other possibilities. Am I to be some sort of humanoid guinea pig? Do they want to dissect my brain to find out how a mutant humanoid thinks? Will I end up a ghastly experiment in a laboratory?

'You say that if I go with you I can never come back?'

'I assure you that you won't want to come back.'

'I don't understand. You say the compounds were built for mutant humanoids and the satellites for – there are other satellites?'

'Yes, there are others. On Oasis the predominant language is English, on others….' He spreads his hands in a gesture that speaks for itself.

'Different satellites for different nationalities, but all built for – non-mutant humanoids.'

'For completes, yes.'

I take a deep breath. 'I have to ask you – why do you want to take me there? I'm not a complete. I'm a mutant humanoid.'

He sighs. His shoulders hunch, his hands are trembling. He stands up and begins to pace about the room, his whole body tense. He paces a little longer, comes back to his chair, perches on the arm and crosses his legs facing me, his hands clasped.

'I know you're a mutant humanoid, Mercury.' He lowers his voice to a whisper. 'You have feathers on your shoulder blades that, if not kept trimmed, could develop into fully-fledged wings.'

My mouth drops open. 'No one knows that. Only Kali and me.'

'I know.' He looks me straight in the eye. 'I've seen them.'

'How? When? I don't understand.'

'In a maternity hospital, just after you were born. I saw those little outcrops on your back and the tiny white feathers trying to push their way through. I picked you up, wrapped you in the nearest thing I could find, a pillowcase, frantic to hide you, but the midwife snatched you away from me, her eyes wide with horror as she realised you had mutations. Everyone was terrified of contagion in those days. She held you at arm's length as if she couldn't bear to look at you or touch you and rushed out of the room. You were screaming at the top of your voice. I've never forgotten that scream. I've heard it every night in my dreams for sixteen years.'

Tears are streaming down his cheeks. I can't believe it. Mr. Suit is crying.

'There was nothing I could do. No one was allowed to keep a mutant baby. That was the law.' He swallows, trying to control his emotion.

I watch him, amazed, trying to make sense of what he's telling me. 'You say you saw me just after I was born? Where was this hospital? What were you doing there? Are you a doctor?'

He looks confused by my multiple questions. 'It was a hospital on Oasis and no I'm not a doctor. I was there for the birth of my son.'

I stare at him. He can't possibly mean what I think he means.

He sees my disbelief and adds, so that there can be no mistake, 'Mercury, I am your father.'

Impossible. Mr Suit, my father? How many more stories is he prepared to make up in order to persuade me to go with him? I shake my head. 'I don't believe you.'

'Why would I lie about something as important as that?'

'To persuade me to go with you. I don't know why you want me to do that, but you're obviously prepared to do or say anything to convince me.'

Mr. Suit looks pretty upset. The smooth lines of his face have crumpled. He leans forward and takes my hands in his.

'You are making things very difficult for me, Mercury.'

On the contrary, he is making things very difficult for me.

'I've been searching for you for years and when I saw you online, sitting at that auto-put in Headculturedome, I was almost sure it was you. I did a bit of research into your background. The timescale was right and everything fell into place. I came here today to make sure it really was you and to take you home with me.'

I'm feeling a little weird, not sure what to think. Part of me still thinks he's telling me a sob story to get me to go with him but his distress at my failure to believe him strikes me as remarkably genuine.

Suddenly he lets go of my hands, stands up, rips off his jacket and tie and pulls his shirt over his head.

Taking his clothes off is anything but fatherly. I take a quick look behind me at the door of the guest suite. How easy would it be to escape?

'Look at this,' he says and swings round to show me his back. There are no bumps or feathers, but there are faint scars on his shoulder blades, evidence that surgery has taken place – that something or some things have been removed. Is it possible? I screw up my eyes.

He swings back to face me. 'This is top secret,' he says, like one of those undercover cops in *Bourne* or *The Undefeated*. 'You mustn't tell a soul. You do understand what this means?'

I nod dumbly, not knowing what to say, what to think.

He spells it out for me. 'I too was born with protrusions on my shoulders and feathers that persisted in poking themselves through. Take a closer look.' He turns his back towards me again and nods at me over his shoulder. 'Go on, you can touch it. Check it out for yourself.'

I don't want to touch him, but if this is proof that he's who he says he is, I have little choice. I run my fingers over his back, over and around the scars. Under the skin I can feel the stumps of what could be the base of emerging wings. It is possible. It really is possible.

This is my father, I think to myself. He's telling me the truth. He *is* my father. I try to swallow but there is a lump in my throat that makes this impossible.

'My parents were lucky. They were rich and influential,' he tells me. 'They managed to arrange for me to have my abnormalities removed in secret. That was forty years ago.'

'But that means you are a mutant humanoid.'

'Correction. Was. I was a mutant humanoid. Now I'm a complete.' He's putting his shirt on again and doing up the buttons. 'What my parents did for me, I intend to do for you, my son. I'm going to make you into a complete.'

I am so shocked I can hardly take in what he says next.

'Tonight, provided you agree, we will go to the hospital satellite, Hos-sat. A hospital in the sky. There have been great advances in surgery since I was a baby. With improved neo-laser treatment there will be no scars left on your back to tell the tale.'

It takes me a moment to realise what it is he expects of me. I feel as if I'm going to be sick and look around for the bathroom. He's still talking, explaining why this is necessary. 'I can't take you to Oasis as a mutant humanoid. You must see that. You wouldn't be allowed in. At Hos-sat you'll be in excellent hands. Top surgeons with all the latest equipment. Not only will they operate on you to erase your bumps and feathers but they'll also be able to adjust your vocal chords and the way you move. You'll be a new person. A complete.'

He looks pleased about that, but I can't help thinking that if I undergo the surgery it will change me into someone I am not. I wouldn't be a complete but a mutant humanoid in disguise. A living lie. I try to explain to him how I feel. 'It doesn't feel right. I don't want to lose my identity.'

'You're bound to feel uncertain at first. I've sprung it on you. It's a shock. Too much to take in. Give it time. You'll receive counselling and, if you decide you don't want the operation, I will teleport you back here. No problem. But I'm sure you'll get used to the idea. You won't lose your identity. You'll still be little Mercury although – ' he stops mid-sentence as something occurs to him, 'actually, we will have to change your name. Completes don't have the names of gods or other mythical characters.'

'What's your name?' I ask him. 'I don't suppose it's really John Smith.'

'No, that was the first name that popped into my head.'

Not very original, but it's not the moment to be provocative. 'What's your real name?'

'Alexander Court,' he tells me.

'Alexander is a mythical name too,' I point out. 'A hero's name anyway. Do all human beings have two names – like in the filmograms? Like James Bond?'

'Generally speaking, yes. Some have more. The first name is the given name and the last is the surname passed on from father to child.'

'What is my given name?'

He pauses for a moment and says, 'Michael. I've always thought of you as Michael.'

'So – I am to be Michael Court.'

'So you are.' He can't help smiling, and it's a warm smile, full of sunlight. Or so it seems to me. That is the moment he knows that I believe him and that I've made my decision.

'Michael was an archangel with huge wings.'

'So he was,' he says. 'So he was.'

We smile at each other, Alexander Court and Michael Court, and a bargain is struck. We both know I will do whatever it takes to go to Oasis with my father. Even if does involve surgery and a change of identity. The one thing I have lacked in my life is a father and I have no intention of losing him now.

Chapter Nine
Golden warriors and the Olds
(according to Isis)

We're teleported to Compound 98, Odysseus and me. Real creepy feeling when your body breaks up into what Ody calls molecules and then knits together again. Totally weird. We find ourselves in a massive space, a sort of Roman arena. Not in the open air, of course, but under a dome of shining glass. Gold letters over an arch inform us we're in The Great Hall. We're standing round the edge with lots of other mutant humanoids. They seem to be waiting for something or someone. I roll my eyes. What now?

Trumpets sound. The central area is flooded with golden light. Enter Durga, the demon-slayer, standing upright in a golden chariot pulled by golden calves. Her helmet, a bull's head with massive horns, her breastplate, sword and spear gleam bright gold. Im*pres*sive or what? The chariot sweeps round the hall in a huge circle. We scuttle out of her way, our backs to the wall. She wheels round and takes up a position at the end of The Great Hall. Are her weapons fashion accessories or is she is preparing for battle? An attack on another sectoid, perhaps? Compound 55 would be cool. Teach that slut Sati a lesson.

More trumpets, and in march a troop of warriors with animal-shaped helmets – wolves, lions, tigers, hyenas, the lot.… Their gold armour and weapons glitter. The warriors come to a halt on either side of Durga's chariot. If only I could be one of them, my helmet in the form of a wild cat, my little arm swinging, the glint of a dagger peeping out of my extra hand. Imagine, me, Isis, standing in my own chariot whizzing round, a sword or perhaps two whooshing through the air, daring anyone to come too near. How cool would that be?

Music now. Mystical. Enter more humanoids, their mutations disguised by long blue gowns – though they can't hide their multiple heads, eyes and ears. Mouths wide open, they're singing at the top of their voices. They arrange themselves on a high platform behind the warriors.

An ancient humanoid appears, a two-headed crinkly-crumbly with an off-white sheet slung over one shoulder.

Durga raises her sword. The singing stops. She begins to speak. Her voice is deep and raw and reaches everyone in The Great Hall though it is to the little old humanoid she speaks.

'Thank you, Brahmin, for the music rendered by your choir. An inspiring start to the day.' She inclines her head and the crinkly mutant bows, his heads almost touching the ground. I swear that one of them is loose. Will it snap off and roll along the floor? That would be a laugh. No such luck. He's even older than Odysseus and Ody must be at least fifty.

Durga speaks again. 'I would like to welcome two new members to my sectoid. Odysseus is to work alongside Brahmin in the histo-lab and Isis will be their assistant.'

I feel Odysseus bristle beside me. He's not happy about having to share the histo-lab with someone else. And what about me? What a joke to have to be an assistant to these two decrepit olds. Imagine. They'll be arguing about some long forgotten histo-detail that no one in their right mind cares a fig about and I'll be piggy in the middle. Bor*ing*. Fat chance of riding to battle in a golden chariot at Durga's side. I'll be stuck in the histo-lab, another useless relic gathering dust.

'I'll now ask the Brahmin to lead us in prayer,' announces Durga.

Oh my Zeus, he's not only choirmaster and histo-noid but priest as well. What's with all this religious stuff? We didn't pray at C55. We just got on with our work. Still, I suppose if you're going into battle, a prayer or two won't hurt.

After the prayers, another couple of hymns, more toots on the trumpet and Durga rides off followed by the army and the choir.

Brahmin approaches us, a purple-veined hand outstretched. 'So, we meet at last. I've followed your excellent work with interest, Odysseus.'

'I'm afraid you have the advantage. I know nothing of your work.' Ody's answer is quiet but deadly.

'Ah – not such a brilliant researcher as I was led to believe,' says Brahmin with a malicious smile.

'Not my field, I'm afraid,' says Odysseus. 'I don't believe in all that religious bunkum.'

Brahmin puts his heads on one side and gives Odysseus a look full of pity. 'Your loss, my friend,' he says. 'Your loss.'

I know Odysseus is irritated by Brahmin's remarks, but he's far too clever to show it. 'Come on then, show me the histo-lab,' and he glides off smoothly in his accustomed manner, leaving poor old Brahmin limping along behind him. Odysseus slows down a little, slides to a stop, whizzes round and smiles. 'I'll wait for you, shall I?'

Round one to cunning Odysseus, but I suspect that he and Brahmin will prove pretty evenly matched in the clashes of opinion that are bound to follow.

I have no choice but to go with them. We pass through

various other halls or arenas where young mutant humanoids are practising warfare of all kinds: one-to-one combat, the throwing of spears and the shooting of arrows. There is even a rifle range.

One young warrior is removing his lion helmet. He shakes out long blonde curls. His deep blue eyes stare at the sight of us as we pass, me trotting along after the two olds. The warrior treats me to a wink from the third eye in the middle of his forehead. I feel my heart skip. He's hot.

All morning, while Odysseus and Brahmin examine the artefacts and play their verbal games, I think about the young warrior. I can't wait to see him again. It's not long before I have a chance to do exactly that, but first Brahmin shows us the empty underground chamber, a huge scooped-out cave, which is to be the museum. Odysseus screws up his eyes, taking in the layout and making up his mind where the best place for each group of artworks and artefacts should be.

'The Old Masters here, I think, as we enter, leading in chronological order to later works.'

Brahmin disagrees. 'We should have an eclectic mix. The work should be arranged according to themes – religious or secular, symbolic or naturalistic, regardless of period.'

'I never heard of anything so ridiculous,' says Ody. 'In any case, I am to be the curator of the museum, not you, so it will be my decision.'

'Not so fast, young upstart. Who says you are to be curator?'

'Ra informed me himself.'

'Which of his heads told you that?'

'The central one, naturally.'

'When was this?'

'Several weeks ago.'

'Since then the other heads have clearly changed his mind. Durga notified me last night that I am in line to be the curator.'

'We'll soon see about that,' says Ody in a huff. 'I'll go and see her straight away to put her right.'

'You can't just go and see her. Durga is the head of this sectoid. You need an appointment.'

'Fine, so I'll make an appointment. Where do I go to do that? Who is in charge of her engagements?'

Brahmin grins through his rotten, black teeth. 'I am.' He sniggers, pleased with himself. He really is a revolting specimen. 'Tell you what, Odysseus, we'll go and see her together and sort out this – misunderstanding.'

Ody grunts. He's lost this round. I'd like to be a fly on the wall when they have their meeting with Durga.

I raise innocent eyes to theirs. 'Can I come too?'

They both turn on me and snap in unison. 'No you cannot.'

Here, in C98, we don't work such long hours as in 55. We stop for breaks several times a day and have the entire evening free. As I'm keen to avoid spending my spare time with my aged mentors, as soon as the trumpet heralds the end of the first session, I dash out of the histo-lab, my young limbs flying this way and that, and follow others into the dino-cube. I collect my food packoid from a counter at the side and squat down in a corner to open it. In C55 our food packoids were delivered to our dormo-cubes so I am used to eating alone. It's different here. Everyone seems to sit in pairs or groups, talking as they eat. I catch sight of the curly-haired warrior but he's busy chatting to his colleagues. I stuff my nutri-ration into my mouth and down it as quickly as I can. I've only just finished when he strolls over and gives a little bow. How formal is that?

'Osiris,' he says.

I open my eyes wide. 'No way,' I say. 'I'm Isis.'

'I know,' he says. 'That's why I said I'm Osiris.'

He's teasing me. Flirting with me.

'So – you'd like to be my brother, would you?' I raise big eyes to his.

'If being your brother means having the same relationship with you that Osiris and Isis shared, I wouldn't mind,' he grins.

I feel the colour rush up my cheeks. It's a long time since I've sparred with another male mutant humanoid like this. Not since the bantering bouts between me and Heracles – and look what that led to. Nothing but heartache. But this warrior is something else. He's soooo hot....

We meet again at the next break. He brings me a drink. 'Try this. It's Soma,' he jokes. 'The nectar of the Gods. Sweet, intoxicating. It will take you out of yourself. '

'I'd better not drink it then,' I say. 'I like to be in control.'

'So do I,' he says.

I take a sip of the drink. It's thick and sweet: liquid honey.

'What's your real name?' I ask.

'I'm known here as Dionysus,' He leans over and whispers in my ear, 'but to you I'll always be Osiris.'

'I hope that doesn't mean that your brother, Set, is going to kill you.' I'm showing off a bit, proving that I know my mythology. Mind you, we all know the origin of our names and the stories that accompany them.

He's amused. 'What if he does? I know you'll magic me alive again.'

'You think I'm going to pick up all the joints of rotten meat that were once your body parts and reassemble them?'

'Why not?' He puts his face close to mine and whispers, 'Apart from the one piece missing.'

I blush, well aware of the piece he's talking about. His words turn me on. I can't help it. My knees are totally wobbly. It won't take long for me to give in and let him have his way with me. What then? Will I just be one more notch on his sword?

I decide to change the subject. 'What's with all this warrior business anyway? Is Durga preparing for a real battle? Or is it – like – just a game?'

'It's no game. I can promise you that, but what she actually has in mind I can't say.'

'Why not? Because you don't know?'

'Because it's top secret.'

'Bull*shit*. You don't know what she's up to.'

'As a matter of fact I do, but if I tell you – I'll have to kill you.'

'Oh well then, you'd better keep it to yourself. I'm not ready to die yet.'

He laughs. 'You know, Isis, Durga won't mind if you don't spend all your time in the histo-lab. She'd like you to see what we do here – how we reach our targets. It'll make you more of a team player, which is what she really wants all of us to be. It's a bit different here from the other sectoids. I'd be pleased to show you what we do.'

I don't need any further urging. We sit together at a workstation and he introduces me to a series of online computer games. First he tells me there are lots of different types and tries to teach me the jargon. I hear his voice as if in a dream. MMORPG – massively multi-play online role-playing game, MMORTS …. real-time strategy, MMOFPS ….first person shooter, MMOSG … online social games….

'There are browser games too involving the use of graphics and technologies such as Flash and Java.'

I can see he's dead keen on these games and I really do try to take in what he's saying, but he's sitting so close to me, his thigh against mine, that I can feel his body heat and find it difficult to concentrate.

'You have to learn *leetspeak*,' he says. '*Leet* is short for elite and it's a form of symbolic writing used in computers. Are you following me?'

I nod. To the ends of the Earth, I think. You lead, I'll follow.

'What kind of game do you fancy? Doom? That's a death-match, first-person shooter game arena-style play. Or would you prefer a sci-fi based game?'

'You choose,' I say.

He goes into Halo, a sci-fi game with Master Chief John 117, a cybernetically enhanced super-soldier, and his AI companion, Corfana, and they "frag" and "respawn" and "telefrag" and "translocate" until I totally lose the plot.

I try to look as if I'm as excited by the action as he is and I am excited, but not by the game. His attention is focused on the computer, mine on him. He's soooo hot….

The skills needed to win these games are based on the strategies for warfare, he informs me. The different levels a player reaches award him points, which go towards the targets for the sectoid. He's right. It is different here. Very different from C55.

That evening we sit on a double-shaper in the RR, his arm slung loosely round my shoulders. 'Online computer games teach us how to use our initiative in battle. They also sharpen our senses and train us to react quickly and accurately. Vital skills for a warrior.'

I haven't got the right mindset for these war games. Osiris has. He's totally smart, totally savvy and I love the way he talks, just like Hugh Grant – upper class, precise. I raise my mooneyes up to his. He suggests that tomorrow I come to see him practise his fencing skills. I can't wait.

The next morning in the histo-lab I apply gold varnish to my fifteen nails and spray my face gold.

'How fantastic is that?' I give Ody a twirl.

He beams and tells Brahmin, 'Isis is an artist in her own right.'

Brahmin raises a weary eyebrow. He mutters something about women and war paint. I don't care. My body art is not designed to impress him.

Odysseus has found a chest full of clothes and material and calls me over to pick out a robe to go with my make-up. We discover a swathe of embossed gold silk, which he drapes over one of my shoulders and attempts to hold in place with a huge gold brooch he finds in a box full of ancient jewellery. The silky material keeps slipping and his hand shakes as he fumbles to fasten it. His trembling fingers rest a moment too long on the skin of my shoulder. He always tells me I'm the daughter he never had, but maybe I was right after all when I believed he'd sacked Heracles because he fancied me himself. That would be like incest, wouldn't it? You never know what's going on in the minds of old men. Or in their pants.

'There. Let's look at you.' He stands back and gazes at my transformation, his hand still shaky.

The two old men circle me, adjusting a fold here, adding another pin there. God, is this what it's come to? Being dressed by two olds? As long as they don't *un*dress me – that would be gross.

Osiris does not disappoint with his reaction. 'You look lovely,' he says, and holds me at arm's length to study me. 'A true daughter of Durga, my golden princess.'

The way he talks is a bit old-fashioned. He sounds as if he's been to one of those posh private schools I've seen in filmo-series but, like me, he hasn't been to school. The compounds don't do schools. I like the way he speaks, especially the way he says "my golden princess." Makes me feel special.

He invites me to sit on a gold-framed chair that, in my eyes at least, resembles a throne. I spread out my golden robe, ready to watch him practise fencing. How fab is this? To sit here, decked out like a princess, looking at the sleek body of this young humanoid stretched out revealing the shape of the muscles in his legs, one bent forward, one back at a right angle. His left arm is bent at the elbow and points at the roof. His right holds the foil and lunges forward to attack his enemy, another young warrior. A few thrusts and the tip of the foil lands on the other's chest.

'A hit, a veritable hit,' Osiris cries. 'Seems you're dead, man. Be a good sport and lie down.' Off he strides, well chuffed.

His opponent laughs, turns to me and introduces himself. 'I'm Indra the Destroyer,' he says, 'and I'm about to get my revenge on Dionysus. Watch this.'

I glare at him, my eyeballs two white pebbles.

Osiris takes up his stance again. The two warriors parry and feint for a while – I think those are the right terms. Indra takes the attacking position. Osiris, in defence, shunts backwards. Indra's foil catches the light and 'Gotcha!' Indra shouts, and looks at me for approval. He's too cocky for my liking. I look down at my nails as if this play-fight means nothing to me.

Osiris plays dead for a moment, springs up and assumes the fencing posture again, rear leg bent to balance himself, left arm bent upwards at right angles, his sword arm and right leg focused on Indra, determined to make the next hit, which he manages with no problem at all. All these hits count towards their personal targets. Both warriors are very competitive and, as far as I can make out, well matched. Osiris has three eyes, Indra four, two on each of his heads. I tense every muscle in my body, willing Osiris to win.

A tinge of fear. Is Durga training these young men for a real battle, to use real weapons, to kill and be killed? If there is a war, will Osiris leave here, never to return? I tell myself I'm being melodramatic, but the fear is real enough. I shiver and decide it's time to go back to the histo-lab before I make a fool of myself and start blubbing.

Chapter Ten
A prayer for Osiris
(according to Isis)

Durga sends an inter-com message saying Odysseus and Brahmin should work together, not bicker about who is in charge. They should use their talents and sharpen their intellects to work as a team and plan for the future success of the museum. Neither of them is pleased by this compromise. Brahmin grumbles about sharing his power with this "new broom" and Ody complains that Ra has gone back on his word. Neither is able to change the situation and they still engage in heated disputes as to how the artefacts should be displayed or what cataloguing system to use. Odysseus cheers up a bit when another message from Durga arrives, telling them that some new additions will soon arrive to increase the stock of the museum.

'No details at the moment,' says her inter-com-mail, 'but some long-lost assets are in the process of being retrieved and they will embellish our museum in ways beyond your imagination.'

Odysseus is thrilled by the thought of getting his hands on more useless old objects and hums as he works. Excruciatingly gross. Both men speculate as to what these assets could be and where they are coming from. They manage to disagree about that too. They go on and on, arguing, day after day. Honestly. As if anyone cares. It's so boring I want to scream. I let them get on with it and escape whenever I can to see Osiris.

We have begun to tell each other our life stories, Osiris and I. Not much to tell in my case. I know I wasn't born in Compound 55 but I've spent most of my life there. Boring. Much better here in C98.

'I lived in another compound first,' I tell Osiris. 'Can't remember which one. They transferred me to C55 when my mother died. Don't remember much about her either. I guess I tried to forget her.'

Osiris sits next to me on a double shaper, his arm slung loosely along the back, almost touching my shoulder. 'You must remember your mother.'

I screw up my face in an effort to recall what she looked like. 'Not really. Sometimes in a dream I see her. And smell her. I know it sounds funny but she always smelt – warm.' I shake my head. 'It's all a long time ago. I try not to think about that time.'

His hand brushes my shoulder. 'Must have been terrible to lose your mother. Painful.'

I don't move an inch, waiting for his hand to touch my shoulder again.

He thinks for a moment and then says, 'They might have injected you with a serum to make you forget.'

That has never occurred to me. 'Who are "they"?'

'The ones who put us in the compounds.'

I frown. I don't want to show my ignorance so I don't ask him what he means.

The story Osiris tells me about himself is rather different. His mother came to C98 when she was pregnant and he was born here.

'Our mothers must have been some of the last females to give birth,' Isis says.

'You're right. As far as I know, no more children have been born since that time. Certainly not in this sectoid.'

'Nor in ours, C55. There was only ever me and Mercury. A pity there were no more babies. When I see kids on the auto-put, I always think they look so cute. They have their own little personalities and the little ones are so cuddly. I saw this family on the auto-put once, sick of the plague. Terrible it was. I'm not sure if it was real or a drama series. There was a tiny baby who wouldn't stop crying. I wanted to hold him, comfort him. He died the day he was born. I couldn't believe it. I wept buckets. If he'd been mine I'd have made sure he didn't die.'

'Perhaps you couldn't have prevented it.'

'I'd have tried harder than she did. His mother didn't seem to care. She kept flinching every time he cried, put him down on the ground instead of rocking him.'

'You'd be a good mother. I can see that.' Osiris looks away, embarrassed.

What am I doing sharing my crazy dreams about having a baby with this handsome young warrior? It'll put him off me for sure. I must pull myself together. I decide to change the subject. 'Will I meet your mother?'

'Not very likely, I'm afraid. She was sent to another compound when I started my training. To be a warrior you have to be absolutely dedicated. A mother is considered a distraction.'

'What a dreadful thing to do. To separate you.' I think about what he's said. 'Are you dedicated? To being a warrior?'

'Absolutely.'

He's totally dedicated to being a warrior and, in the future, war might turn out to be more than a game. 'If I had a son I'd hate to be parted from him. I bet your mother thinks about you every single day.'

'I think about her too and wonder if I will ever see her again.'

'Can't you ask someone about her? Durga, perhaps? '

'I have asked Durga, but she's quite a – well she's the kind of leader who rarely gives you a straight answer. She likes us to work things out for ourselves.'

I think of how Durga refuses to tell the two olds which of them is to be the curator. Maybe she thinks she can get the best out of both of them while they're in competition with each other. It's her battle strategy – like in the compu war games.

'I think about the past a lot,' Osiris says. 'Don't you ever wonder what life was like in the time before, when there were towns and cities, and how exactly we came to be living like this?'

'Not really. No.'

He's quite a deep person is Osiris, thinks about all kinds of things. Not like me. I've always taken things as they come. I live from day to day, not giving much thought to anything; but being with him is making me see things in a different light. For years Ody has tried to teach me the importance of the past but I've never seen what it has to do with my life. With Osiris it's different. I'm beginning to be interested in how we came to be shut up in these compounds. He asks all kinds of questions about the future too. For starters – is the wilderness still contaminated and when will we be able to explore the outside world?

'I was out there for hours the day Ra came to C55,' I tell him, 'but it didn't seem to affect me at all.'

His eyes light up. 'You've actually been outside? I'd love to do that. To have the chance to explore. Tell me, what's it like? Still a desert or were plants beginning to push their way through? Anything green at all, any signs of re-generation?'

I screw up my face in an effort to remember. He's so keen to know that I wish I'd taken more notice when I was out there. I've tried to forget that time. I rake through my mind but can't come up with much. 'It, well, it seemed to go on forever – the great expanse of land, I mean, and it was cold, real cold. The wind whipped round me, almost knocked me over. That's what I remember the most. The wind. Green stuff? There were a few shrubs, yes, and there was a tree, but I don't remember any leaves on it. I was lucky. Quite quickly I found a little cave place and squatted down in it, out of that biting wind, kept my head down and hugged my knees. I just sat there and waited to see what would happen, if anyone would come and rescue me – Ody or Heracles. I was there for ages. All I knew was that I didn't want to walk about in that freezing wind. Before that I'd always thought of our compound as a sort of a prison, but when I was whisked back, I was glad to find myself inside again, I can tell you. At least it was warm.'

'You poor darling.' Osiris grasps my shoulder and doesn't take his hand away again. 'You must have been terrified.' He frowns, thinking about it.

'Ody says each compound is like an oasis in the desert.'

'That's one way of looking at it, I suppose. Here we have plenty of food and water. It's a safe haven, like an oasis.'

I know he's trying to cheer me up but I sense he's a bit disappointed that I don't remember many details about the wilderness. He continues talking about it. 'They've started doing experiments to check if it's safe for us to go outside again. When it is, we could make a new world – new buildings, new towns, new everything….' There is a light in his eye that tells me he won't be content until he has been out there exploring, but I hope it won't be too soon. It's lovely sitting here close to him. He's my safe haven, my oasis.

'Do you think we're barren because of everything that happened to the Earth or do you think we've been given another – what did you call it – serum?'

I look up at him to show him I believe him to be much more knowledgeable than me.

He considers this. 'They could have sterilised us I suppose, determined not to allow more mutant humanoids to be born, but I don't think so – otherwise there wouldn't have been any more children at all. They'd be no second or third generation mutants. We wouldn't be here. No, it's the contamination from The Great Plague that did it.'

'So there really was a plague?'

Osiris grins at me. 'Yes, Isis, there really was a plague. Not everything on the auto-put is a soap opera. You could find out about these things for yourself.'

'Oh, I know I don't study enough. Too busy helping Ody.'

'The plague is what turned us into mutants, or at least the children who were born to the contaminated people, our ancestors. That's when they decided to build the compounds, to keep us separate from them.'

Again that "they" and "them." When I was in C55, I remember thinking it was like a prison and that we were slaves, but it's the first time I've considered that some creatures different from us could have shut us up in these compounds. If I'd thought about it at all, I would have believed it was Ra or the sectoid leaders, in our case Kali, who locked us in. The idea of outsiders controlling us is frightening. Who are they? Aliens like in horror filmograms? I shiver.

Osiris puts his other arm round me and gives me a hug. He's eye candy for sure, but kind and thoughtful too.

A few nights later, when Osiris follows me to my dormo-cube hoping to share my bunku, I do not resist. How can I? He's everything I could wish for in a male mutant humanoid. He's so savvy, so smart and he's made me think about life in a way I've never done before. Oh come off it, Isis, I tell myself. Stop this bullshit. It's not his mind you've fallen for but his muscular body, his golden curls and those three deep blue eyes. He's sooo hot. And hot means sexy as I am about to find out....

I have never been so happy. Osiris and I have become a couple. We've exchanged our single dormo-cubes for a double with a large bunku and I've taken to decorating the cube with pictures and ornaments that I nick from the chests and cupboards in the histo-lab.

There are so many artefacts here – far more than in C55 – and Ody is in his element sorting through them and cataloguing them. He gets quite excited about what he calls the genuine items he finds. The promised extra pieces Durga promised have not yet turned up but there are enough here already for all three of us to sort through.

I label each one, give it a number and list it on the compu. A glorified dogsbody, that's me. The point is, it is not difficult for me to pinch a few bits before I list them – not Ody's specials – but things that appeal to me, shiny objects that glitter in the light and look good in our cube.

Today I find a length of glossy cloth to drape over the bunku. Everything I choose is colour-coded: gold and red my favourite combination. Our cube looks like a mini Aladin's cave, full of shimmering goodies. I hide my treasures under my robe to transport them and so far nothing has been missed. Osiris calls me a little homemaker and smiles indulgently at my efforts. It's great to wake up every day to find him at my side. I help him into his warrior gear and watch him prepare for the daily parade, content to be a warrior's love-mate rather than a warrior myself. I no longer feel like a slave or a prisoner. Nor do I have any desire to leave this compound. My life is perfect as it is.

But change is on its way. Rumours abound. An atmosphere of excitement and fear is in the air. The warriors are called for extra duties. Hours are spent on machines in the gym to make sure their bodies are in tip-top condition. Osiris spends more time training than he does with me. I am no longer permitted to watch him. He starts early in the morning and exercises all day and all evening. No caffeine breaks. Nutri-rations and water are provided in the gym.

He comes back late at night, tired but full of enthusiasm, his conversation peppered with words and phrases such as chin up bar, leg press, power cage, iron rings, bench work, sit ups, barbells, dumb bells, slant bar, cable machines and weight stack. He tries to explain what each machine does. The leg press, for example, has a vertical sled. You lie down and have to push the weight away using your legs. It increases the size and strength of your quadriceps, hamstrings, gluteous maximus (whatever that may be) and calves.

Sounds like torture to me. Horrendous. There are exercises for everything: machines to increase bone density, would you believe, others to strengthen muscles, tendons and ligaments.

The warriors trot around doing circuit training to help their metabolism and cardiac function. Makes me feel exhausted to think about it, but my lover's passion for fitness and soldiering never falters.

He sleeps well at night but doesn't always make love to me. Saves his energy for these daytime activities. But he's still here. That's one good thing, but I'm terrified that soon he'll be on his way to fight a real life battle.

I spend more time in the histo-lab on the compu logging the artefacts but my heart's not in it.

I google the gym equipment Osiris has told me about to find pictures of these cruel machines which only make me more depressed.

I click on war, battles and armies and terrify myself even more.

Odysseus doesn't know what is going to happen. His nose is stuck in the past as usual without a clue that something frightful is about to take place. Brahmin nods knowingly and says, 'You just wait and see. Durga will tell us when she's ready.'

She does. We are assembled in The Great Hall as usual. There is Durga in her chariot, flanked by her warriors. Osiris is third on her right in the front row in his lion's head helmet, the most spectacular of them all. The choir sings on a raised platform behind her. Brahmin leads everyone in prayers. Time for Durga's motivation speech, but there is something in the way she begins that warns us that she is about to tell us something special.

'Members of Compound 98,' she says, 'the time has come for the games to stop and the real fighting to begin. After the parade I shall select the warriors I need for the first attack.'

Oh my Zeus. My heartbeat is so loud everyone must surely hear it. I just know Osiris will be selected. How could she not choose him? I've been expecting it, of course, but not this soon. I'm tempted to run out of The Great Hall, find a lavat-cube and throw up, but no one ever leaves the parade until the end when Durga dismisses us. I cross my three arms, hold my stomach tight and try to stop the pain. Some hope. Durga is still speaking.

Here's the totally amazing thing. She says our army is not going to attack another mutant humanoid compound, but some sort of installation in the sky peopled by non-mutant humanoids. Not aliens. Not Martians. She calls them completes. Wow! I had no idea such beings existed. I thought we mutants were all that was left of the human race. Seems I was wrong.

According to Durga, these completes are the ones who

locked us up in compounds on Earth while they escaped to live a life of luxury on planets in the sky, taking most of Earth's remaining resources with them. That's how they've been able to develop technologies beyond our wildest imaginings. They also raided the museums and art galleries and stole most of Earth's treasures.

'It's my intention to recover them,' she claims.

I see Ody's eyes light up. So that's where the promised artefacts are to come from, he thinks.

I don't give a shit if they bring these crappy old things back or not. All I want is for Osiris to come home to me in one piece. I don't want his body parts scattered over some planet in the sky.

'We too shall have the chance to live on an uncontaminated planet,' Durga promises. 'We too will enjoy the better way of life these completes have created for themselves. They have treated us like second-class citizens long enough. We go into battle with right on our side and we will win. The result – a better life for us all.'

A stirring speech. A big cheer goes up, but I only pretend to join in. Osiris is a dedicated warrior. He is going to leave me to go to war. There is no doubt about that.

'Now,' Durga says, 'let us bow our heads and pray for the success of our mission and the safe return of our warriors.'

In spite of Odysseus's belief that religion is a humanoid invention designed to control the workforce, I can't help thinking that, when Osiris marches off to war, a few of Brahmin's prayers can't do any harm. They may even help to keep him safe. I find myself bowing my head. My prayer, the first of my life, pleads with the Gods – whoever they may be – to keep Osiris safe.

I don't care if the mission is successful or not. I don't want my life to change. All I want is for my Osiris to come home to me, safe and sound.

Chapter Eleven
Mercury Reformed
(according to Mercury/Michael)

Journal Entry

We arrive at Hos-sat. A huge dome in the sky. A smell of antiseptic. Pure. Clean. A memory of the stuff Kali insisted on putting on my grazed knee as a child. It stung, biting into the open wound like a jab from Hugo's tongue. Same smell here. Strong, unremitting, invading every space. A cover-up for other less agreeable smells, I shouldn't wonder. And less agreeable activities. A touch of apprehension. My old worry about being some sort of experiment returns. I imagine my body on a slab, opened up, dissected.

Mr Suit, or rather Mr Alexander Court, my father, is clearly well respected here. A person of some importance. He strides down the stainless steel corridors with me in his wake. As he passes the reception areas for each department, I hear a chorus of 'Good morning, Mr Court.' 'All ready for you, Mr Court.' 'This way, Mr Court.' We enter a white-walled room where a group of hospital staff awaits us. I am introduced as "Patient X – the special patient we've discussed." The group is introduced to me as "the A-team, the most skilled team in Hos-sat." Men in suits – doctors or surgeons – thin, efficient-looking nurses in blue and white uniforms, orderlies dressed like me in blue monos and two women in severe black trouser suits, one very tall and broad, the other short and plump – the therapists: all of them completes, as far as I can tell.

'You have all been briefed on the procedures.'

'Yes indeed, Mr Court.'

My father runs those sharp eyes of his around the group, rests them on each person in turn. 'I hardly need remind you that you have been entrusted with a very special task, one that involves top security. No word of what is being carried out here must go beyond the people in this room and I must be kept up to date at each stage of the proceedings.'

'Yes, Mr. Court.'

'Of course, Mr Court.'

'We fully understand, Mr Court.'

James Bond couldn't be embarking on a more secret mission than I am. Or one more fraught with danger. Now I know what it means when they say your blood runs cold. It's me that's being talked about, little Mercury, the messenger, Patient X, a mutant humanoid soon to be transformed into a complete.

Journal Entry

In the end I refuse the offer of therapy. No point. I made my decision to become a complete the moment I realised Mr. Suit was my father.

The first operation is over. When I come round from the anaesthetic, he is sitting at the side of my bunku. My eyes flicker shut and open again.

He grins at me, tells me I look like a chrysalis, wrapped up as I am in bandages.

'Soon,' he says, 'you will emerge as a butterfly.'

I raise an eyebrow. 'A caterpillar grows wings. I'm supposed to have had mine removed.'

He pulls a face. It was a joke apparently. Irony. He's nervous. I can see that.

I try to put him at his ease, although surely it's his job to make me feel relaxed. 'Has it gone well, the operation?' I ask. 'I didn't feel a thing.'

'State-of-the-art technology here you know. Just wait until those bandages come off and you'll be a different person.'

He seems to think I should be pleased about that. I summon up a smile to make him believe that I am.

Journal Entry
My father is here again. He asks me if I have any questions. Lots. I usually try to answer my own questions through research, but without access to an auto-put that is impossible. I start to barrage with him questions. When I am going to meet my biological mother? Who else knows about me? Has he found out where that doctor in the white coat took me when I was a baby? Where was I before C55? Kali told me she'd found me "crying in the wilderness." How did I get there? How did Earth become a wilderness? Was there really a plague that killed everything off? Why did some people become mutations and not others? Did he think it right to shut us up in compounds?

He doesn't answer all my questions, but he does tell me about my mother. I can see by the look on his face that it's not good news. There's a catch in his throat as he says, 'Michael, I'm sorry I have to tell you. Your mother died giving birth to you.'

It's a shock in one way but I'm not really upset. I can't grieve for someone I've never known. Kali is my mother. Always has been and always will be. 'That must have been awful for you – losing both of us at the same time.'

'Michael, I....' He says my name as if he's trying to stamp it on my memory so that I'll get used to it. 'I let people think it was Melanie, my wife, your mother, who had the mutant gene, whereas, as you know, it was me. I can't tell you how guilty I feel about that.'

'You had to protect yourself. It was logical.'

'Logic doesn't always help absolve your conscience.'

He finds it difficult to speak for a moment so I change the subject. I ask another question. Or rather two. 'What happened to me? Where did they take me?'

'At the time I had no idea. I was told to forget about you, to tell others that you had died in childbirth, but I was determined to find you, Michael. I failed miserably. No matter who I asked or how many websites I searched I couldn't find you. Years later when I became a member of the Symposium – that's what we call our government – I managed to access certain secret files. Babies born with irregularities – in other words, mutations – were sent to be looked after in institutions on Earth.' He pauses. 'Compounds specifically designed to accommodate such children. As far as I can make out they were run by trained personnel. When the children were old enough, more permanent placements were found for them.'

'In other compounds?'

'Yes. Procreation between mutants was at an all-time low and there were always females willing to bring up these children as their own.'

'Like Kali.'

'Yes, like Kali.'

'Kali told me she'd found me crying in the wilderness. Do you think I escaped from the baby compound?'

'Very unlikely. And why would Kali go outside to an area she knew was contaminated? No, I think that's a story she made up, Michael, to show you how much she wanted you.'

'Do you think most of the mutant humanoids without parents came from the satellites originally – as babies?'

'It does seem that completes are more fertile than

mutant humanoids. Generally our babies are born without mutations but there must still be a residue of contamination in our bodies so sometimes a mutant baby is born – like you and I.'

'So people on the satellites who have mutant babies don't want to keep them?'

'Most of them would like to. I wanted to keep you. You must believe that, Michael. But it wasn't allowed. Mutant babies were removed straight after birth. It was the law.'

'A law made to segregate the "normal" from the "mutated."' I hear the bitterness in my voice and feel my anger growing but try to keep cool.

'That was clearly the plan. But Michael, you mustn't think I approve of this. I was horrified when I found out what had been going on. Horrified and disgusted. Now that I hold an important position in the Symposium I intend to work to get those laws repealed.'

'What is your important position?'

'I'm the Minister for Culture.'

'Anything to do with Worldwideculture?'

'Not really. Well, yes, in a way. Look, Michael, no more questions for now. It's important you get some rest. You've had a major op, you know.'

I don't feel tired, but Father doesn't want to answer any more awkward questions. His face is drained of colour.

Journal Entry

My father brings me a present. A portable compu.

'Wow! Thanks,' I say, as I fire it up.

'You're going to have a lot of time on your hands while you're recovering,' he says. 'I thought you'd like something to keep you amused.'

'Great. Has it got – you know, what you said – unlimited access?'

'It is uncensored, yes.' His eyes twinkle with amusement. 'It can probably provide you with most of the answers to that long list of questions. But I must warn you, Michael, you may find some of the answers a little disturbing.'

My fingers are already busy and I've found one programme about the apocalypse that looks interesting. I can hardly wait for him to leave so that I can start checking it out.

He has more to say. 'Michael, I do hope you're not lonely here. I know you haven't got many people to talk to and I'm afraid I can't visit every day.'

I don't know what he means by lonely. I've always been alone and now I've got this compu I'll have plenty to keep me occupied.

Journal Entry

Guess what I find out today, dear Journal? Here's a clue.

'This is the way the world ends,

This is the way the world ends

Not with a bang but a whimper.'

I discover various theories about how and when the Earth became one huge polluted mess. There are personal histories, opinions from environmentalists and politicians and theories from academics. I'm hungry for facts but there are so many different versions.

Here's one version. From 2015 onwards everything started going downhill. A plague infected plants, animals and humanoids. It spread quickly, contaminating everything it touched. An evangelist preacher declared it was God's vengeance on the arrogance of the human race, like Icarus flying too close to the sun. That's one explanation.

Like all history, there is more than one version of the truth. I click on to another page and another and another.

I can smell antiseptic again. It drifts into my room through the air conditioning unit as if determined to banish any stray germs that might seep in from the outside world.

Why did the Earth die? Because we didn't take enough care. That's why. We used up the resources. We ignored poverty. With a series of antennae we increased the number of electrodes in the atmosphere. Radiation fever. All because we had to have mobile phones, microwaves, electronic devices of all kinds.

And then there were the wars. War upon war. Chemical warfare, gas, nuclear bombs, nuclear fall-out. No wonder the atmosphere was infected. No wonder people became sick. I read article upon article, rant upon rant about this.

It started earlier than you might think, this carelessness. The first mutant humanoids were glimpsed in 2030. Yes, that early, and it was from that time that public creativity began to die. No more filmograms were made. TV transmissions stopped. No books were written – or if they were, not published or distributed. No artists, no musicians, composers or architects …. Or almost none. It was if, in the face of such depression, humanoids lost heart. Someone – I haven't yet discovered who it was – someone began initiatives to address that problem. To encourage us to re-energise, to be creative. Worldwideculture perhaps, although I have found no mention of that company.

The privileged – those with money or power or both – escaped, sped away in their rockets to pollution-free satellites in the sky, taking many of Earth's assets with them. If you did a lot of networking you might just have been lucky enough to join them. It depended if you knew the right people or slept in the right bed. Those with no money, no power or influence were abandoned in the wilderness to become contaminated by the toxic waste. They became mutants. Or the children of the contaminated became mutants. One or the other. That is not quite clear. The timescale is not clear either. Giant domes, the compounds, were built to house the mutant humanoid survivors and keep them separate. That much is clear and borne out by my own experience.

I read with amusement and not a little anger that computers were set up "*even* in the compounds" so that "*even* the mutants could feel they were contributing to the creative regeneration." I object to that "*even*". It shows what they think of us. All these articles, written by uncontaminated human beings, are so patronising.

Still, I don't suppose they ever expected a mutant humanoid to read this stuff. That's why our compus on Earth are censored. It is gradually becoming clear to me that it is not in the interest of the privileged classes to permit the underclass – yes, the underclass, because that's what we have become, us mutants – to access every single site on the world wide web. We cannot be trusted. If we know too much, we may stop being pliant workaholics and rebel.

I find myself getting hotter and hotter. What a cheek. These people think they are so superior to us. Do I really want to turn into one of them? Is it too late to change my mind?

A nurse bustles in, takes one look at my flushed face and insists I close down the compu for today and get some sleep.

Journal Entry

I've had no pain from the operation. None at all. Wrapped up in bandages I feel more like an Egyptian mummy than a chrysalis. I am not exactly dead, but ready to be born again and today's the day....

The nurse unwinds the bandages and folds them neatly round her arm. The doctor examines my bare back. He nods, satisfied. No pain but lots of itching. I try to look over my shoulder without success. When the doctor has gone I tell the nurse I want to look at my back in a mirror. There were not many mirrors in the compounds (why should ugly mutants want to look at themselves?) but I've seen them here in the bathrooms. The nurse does not recommend it but I insist and, in the end, she is quite helpful. I stand in front of one mirror and she holds another up behind me, adjusting it so that I can see the result of the op. My shoulder blades look a little inflamed and swollen, but she assures me the swelling with go down and that the redness will fade in a day or so. There are no feathers poking through.

Back to my compu. I'm fascinated by the plethora of stories about the end of the world and the efforts to rebuild it. So much opinion is bandied about it is difficult to distinguish fact from fiction. The scientists blame the politicians. The politicians are determined to blame each other. The journalists wrangle among themselves about which of the reports are the most accurate. All the participants in the ongoing debate are so competitive, so determined to prove their opponents wrong that no conclusions are reached. Anyone with an ounce of sense can see that, if they all worked together as we did in C55 under Kali's guidance, they would achieve far more than through this incessant bickering.

Today I find several articles about Planet Oasis. It seems to be regarded as some kind of utopia.

'A vibrant community of utopian living' was one comment. Another suggests that Oasis is the flagship of the new empire. Now where have I heard that expression before?

Journal Entry

A visit from my father. He asks to look at my back and seems pleased with what he sees. The surgeon comes in and has a look too. I'm not used to being looked at and it feels a little odd, especially as they talk over the top of my head, about me but not to me.

'Another couple of weeks and he'll be ready for the next op, Mr Court,' the surgeon says.

'Whenever you think he's ready,' my father replies. 'No hurry. The main thing is to do a good job.'

'Yes, Mr Court.'

I am to have two more operations, one on my vocal chords to adjust the pitch of my voice and the other on the lower part of my spine to release the tendons that make my bodily movements jerky. When the operations are completed it will be time for physiotherapy and speech therapy.

The first op has gone so well and there's been no pain so I'm not afraid; but I still worry in case something goes wrong and I'll be stuck in a body that is neither mutant nor complete and that I won't fit in anywhere. I must trust my surgeon my father says. He will not make such a mistake. The surgeon is quite elderly. It crosses my mind that he could be the same surgeon who operated on my father some forty years ago. That may account for Father's unreserved trust in his discretion. How old would that make the surgeon now? Over 70? Is age a problem as far as surgery is concerned? How shaky are his hands?

My biggest worry is the same as before, that without my mutations I will lose my identity. I tell myself that I have embarked on this course and there is no going back.

Chapter Twelve
Torture
(according to Mercury/Michael)

Journal Entry

I haven't made a journal entry for weeks, possibly months. I haven't felt like it. The other two operations went well enough but now the pain begins. Physiotherapy. It's torture. There's no other word for it.

Janey, the physiotherapist, is a sadist. She's tall, broad-shouldered and very strong. She pulls and pushes the bones and muscles in my legs, determined to straighten them, and makes me walk in a straight line, up and down the same bit of floor for six hours on the trot. Not that she allows me to trot. Oh no. Nor to dash, dart or flit. I must slow down and take long strides like a man, she says, and she plays that song by the Four Seasons, 'Walk like a Man!' until I could kill that Frankie Valli with his high pitched voice – if he weren't already dead years ago.

'Walk like a man,' he sings.

'Walk like a man', bellows Janey. 'Come on, Michael, you know you can do it.'

I don't know. I don't know that I can do it. It hurts to keep my legs straight instead of splaying out at the sides as I move and I'm so accustomed to doing my little dashes it doesn't seem natural to stride out. I'm so tired and it hurts so much, I wish I'd never agreed to these stupid changes.

I wish I could go back to a compound right this minute. Any compound. Preferably the one where Kali is. I want to curl up in Kali's bunku as I did when a child. I know it's impossible but it doesn't stop me dreaming.

'You must persevere,' says Janey and, although I curse her and wish she would go away and never come back, I know she is right.

It was the operations I dreaded, but they were no problem. I felt no pain from them. It is now with the physiotherapy that I feel like giving up. I curl up in my bed at night and wish the night would last forever so that I don't have to wake up and undergo the agony all over again.

When Moira, the speech therapist starts on me as well, it's all too much. At least when there was only Janey I had some free time in the afternoon to surf the net on my porto-compu. Now I have no time at all. It's either Janey, the wall, making me walk the line or plump little Moira forcing me to produce deeper and deeper sounds. My throat is raw meat. I beg to stop. She sprays my throat with some sort of oily liquid that makes me retch and tells me to continue. Hours pass and I beg her to give me something to suck. She laughs. 'Oh we can do better than that,' she says and makes me drink some disgusting green greasy stuff, which she assures me will do the trick.

What with the physical effort and the voice exercises, I'm half dead. The muscles in my legs ache. My throat is sore. My only pleasure is sleep.

My father hasn't been to see me for ages. I wish he'd come. I want to complain about the treatment I'm getting.

At last he is here. Janey and Moira are all smiles. They talk to my father over the top of my head and tell him what a brave boy I've been.

'He works hard and never complains even though the exercises must be a strain,' says Janey.

'He's got a bit of a sore throat, but he never gives up,' says Moira.

'He's making good progress,' says Janey. 'I'm really proud of him.' Yes, she pats me on the head.

'His voice is down half an octave now and we've almost ironed out all those squeaky bits. Just a little longer and he'll be normal,' Moira says, putting her arm round my shoulders and giving me a quick squeeze.

'How much longer do you think?' my father asks.

'About five or six weeks at the most,' says Janey.

'I agree – no more than six weeks,' says Moira.

Five or six weeks? No way. I'll be dead long before then.

My father has no such fears. He nods and looks pleased. 'Keep up the good work,' he tells them.

Journal Entry

During my father's visit today, he seems inclined to talk to me about his life, the life I will soon be sharing.

He speaks to me as if I am a child who may not understand everything he tells me. I put up with this. I'm getting used to the patronising way completes talk and write about mutant humanoids.

'Michael, you'll find life very different on Oasis. I want to prepare you a little for those changes.'

'OK,' I say, longing to get back on line. I've found a fantastic virtual battle between mutant humanoids and completes. I'm determined to make the mutants win, but suspect the game is rigged. I'm having a few less hours with Janey and Moira. They're reducing the torture little by little. 'Weaning me off it,' they call it. It gives me more time online.

My father sits forward, legs apart, his hands on his knees, wondering where to start. 'For one thing, Michael, we don't live and work in the same building as you did in the compounds. Each family has its own home.'

I nod. 'An apartment like in the filmograms.'

'Nobody lives in apartment blocks any more. They were proved non-beneficial to health, both mental and physical. Living high up in the air as we do means there is plenty of space for families to create the size and type of home they would like. All our homes are different. We believe in individuality.'

He is speaking slowly, thinking about what he wants to tell me and what he should leave out. 'You mean you live in a house?' I say to help him out.

'Exactly. A house, but on Oasis we don't call them houses. We call them homes. We like to personalise them. We live in Home-Court-Jameson.'

I frown. 'I understand Court but – Jameson?'

He adjusts the knot of his tie, does up a button on his jacket and undoes it again, clears his throat and takes a deep breath. 'I have another family now, Michael. Stella Jameson became a widow five years ago. We've been together for three years. She has two children. Stuart is ten and Bella's six. My stepchildren.'

A bit of a shock to hear that. 'You all live together in Home-Court-Jameson? '

'Of course. We are all one family. You are to live with us too.'

'I've never met any children. What are they like?'

My father grins. 'Little brats! But adorable brats.'

I must look confused because he says, 'Stuart loves games of all kinds. He's crazy about football.'

'And compu games?'

'Not so much. I have a job to get him to sit at a computer. He hates studying. You'll be a good influence on him with your love of learning. As for Bella, well, she can be pretty opinionated for a six-year-old but she's a little darling. When she looks up at me with her big blue eyes, she knows I will do anything she asks.' His face lights up, becomes softer and more animated when he speaks of the children. 'Anyway, you'll meet them soon enough and make up your own mind about them.'

I'm trying to process what he's telling me. 'What's Stella Jameson like?'

'Stella? Oh she's well named. A real star. Beautiful, intelligent and a very good cook! You'll just adore her.'

'I look forward to meeting her,' I say politely.

'She's dying to meet you. She knows how much it means to me to have found my son after all this time.'

He talks a little more about Home-Court-Jameson. I hear the odd word – ultra modern, huge windows, light, airy, comfortable body-shapers, but the description floats over me. I'm still thinking about the bombshell he's just dropped, the ready-made family unit that is to be part of my life.

'Will I have my own dormo-cube and bunku?' I ask.

'You will have your own large airy room with a window that looks out on to the garden. Forget those hard old bunkus. You'll have a comfortable bed. Better than these hos-beds, I can tell you. Let's call the room your study-bedroom.'

'This big room – it will be just for me?'

'Just for you. We can put your name on the door if you like.'

I point to the porto-compu that I'm clutching. 'Is this mine to keep? Can I take it with me and use it in my study-bedroom?'

'You can use it anywhere. Your own room will be fitted out with a proper workstation and giant screen.'

'Really?'

'Really.'

I try to imagine it. A huge screen, my own workstation and a comfortable bed. I imagine waking up in the morning or even in the middle of the night and using a remote to switch on the compu. Fantastic.

One further thing my father impresses on me before he leaves. My past life as a mutant humanoid must be kept secret. Stella knows. He had to tell her, but not the children. They wouldn't understand. No one else must know. Best that he and I never talk about it, even in private. Best for me to forget my past completely. He has invented a new past for me. I have come from another satellite, Paradise Isle. He makes up a convoluted story about how I used to live with my maternal grandparents there but now they've died so he's decided to bring me home.

'Not much of a story,' I tell him.

His mouth twitches with amusement, not offended by my criticism. 'Perhaps we'll think up a better story between us,' he says. 'The main thing is to remember that you have never been to Planet Earth and have never been a mutant humanoid. You were born and brought up on Paradise Isle and now you've come to live with your father on Oasis. That's all anyone needs to know.'

Again I feel a twinge of conscience. Another lie I must learn to live with in addition to the lie that is my body, my voice and the way I walk.

Journal Entry

The torture is over. More or less. Janey puts her arm round me and gives me a big smacker on my cheek. Ugh....

'This doesn't mean you can sit at your beloved compu all day. You must do at least an hour of the exercises I've taught you first thing in the morning and you must also walk for a quarter of an hour or so for every hour – to keep your muscles from seizing up and to keep fit. Everyone has to keep fit. Promise me you'll do this?'

I promise. I'm so pleased to have finished the physiotherapy I'd promise her anything.

'You must keep it up or you could have a relapse and have

to return to me for more – ' she pauses then adds with a wicked grin 'torture.'

Moira says more or less the same and gives me a hug. She holds me against the soft pillows of her breasts for far too long. I squirm until she lets me go.

She laughs, turns serious and tells me that I must continue practising breathing from the diaphragm and humming to keep my voice forward and I must practise projecting the vowel sounds to deepen the tone.

Half an hour every morning is her prescription. If I'm careful and produce the sounds correctly and breathe correctly I won't get sore throats. Just in case, she gives me a bottle of spray and a special jar of the green greasy stuff. I think I might leave the latter behind, accidentally on purpose.

The A-team stand in a row, the surgeon, the nurses, the orderlies and my two torturers, Janey and Moira.

I am to take off my shirt and display my scar-less back. The exclamations of wonder are praise for the surgeon, not for me.

I have to demonstrate my improved motor skills by striding up and down and round in a circle.

'Walk like a man,' mouths Janey.

I stride along as I've been taught, but at one point I stick out my foot at an angle and perform a quick little dart. That will pay her back for all she's put me through.

Janey is mortified. Her hands fly up to cover her face.

'Just kidding,' I say and continue walking with the big, measured steps she has taught me. Janey does her best to take the teasing well and laughs.

Finally I make a little speech to show off my new voice. I thank all the staff for their expert work.

'Don't forget to breathe,' whispers Moira.

I have a fit of coughing. She's not taken in by my play-acting and shakes her head slowly from side to side.

I take a deep breath. 'You've all been fantastic,' I say, in my toned-own voice. 'Even my torturers, Janey and Moira, have done a pretty good job, I think you'll agree.'

Everyone laughs and applauds. Father beams, his warm smile stretching wider than ever before. I smile back. I am ready to go to Planet Oasis to begin the next stage of my adventure

Chapter Thirteen
Heracles Unlimited
(according to Heracles)

'Heracles,' calls a booming voice, ' I didn't expect to see you back here.'

Thor, as tall and broad as I am, strides across the dino-cube and clasps me in his arms as if we have been mates for life.

'I didn't expect to be back here either,' I tell him, patting him on the back.

It's true. Being placed in Compound 99 is usually a reward for good service. I can't imagine why Ra should reward me, considering the way I messed things up last time. Besotted with that bitch, Sati, I spent every moment I was here either with her or, once she'd left, trying to find her. Waste of bloody time. Though I did learn a lot about hacking and code-breaking, useful skills for someone as ambitious as I am. No doubt about my luck being back. Life is easier here in this sectoid with all its facilities from sports halls to disco-cube, not to mention the state-of-the art technology.

'Let's have a snack and a chat,' says Thor, marching me up to the food counter. Eating is a social activity here and the food much tastier than in C55 or Headculturedome. We take a plate of synthetic ham and reconstituted noodles and find ourselves a table. 'Tell me all. What's been happening, man? Did you find Sati?'

'Don't talk to me about that bitch.'

'I tried to warn you, but you wouldn't listen. Led by your prick as usual. Not the sort of female to get involved with.' He throws back his huge head and laughs, his two mouths, one above the other, wide open. I wonder, not for the first time, which one he uses to kiss the female mutant humanoids. Both I suppose. Double whammy.

I don't need his advice, but he's right. I've already decided that love them and leave them will be my motto from now on. Here in C99 there are plenty of hot mutant females. I catch sight of a few, chatting together at a table not far from ours: a two-headed blonde, a brunette with three boobs and a redhead with a huge mouth. Hmmm. Any one of them would do for a start. I haven't had sex for months. Tonight I'll go the disco-cube and see what's on offer.

'See that one with the three big knockers,' says Thor. 'She's a real goer. I had her last night. I'm thinking of putting a thoroughly recommended memo on auto-mail.'

'Are you allowed to do that?'

'Course not. There's quite a strong feminist faction here. Thing is most of the women in C99 are intelligent with minds of their own or they wouldn't be here – so we have to be a bit careful. Most of them aren't looking for a serious relationship. That's a good thing for us, eh?' He winks at me, finishes his snack and pushes the plate away. 'That Sati's done all right for herself, becoming head of C55.'

I don't want to talk to Thor about Sati. The image is always with me of her orgy with smug Jason, short-arsed Apollo and creepy Merlin. Ugh. Sati's method of getting power was to seduce the workforce. Zeus! Makes me want to puke. I don't intend her to get away with it. I'm going to launch an attack. Not a half-hearted one like last time. What were we thinking? That Sati would be intimidated by the sight of her three sister-wives in battledress and give up without a fight? Crazy. What I need now is a viable plan, followed by specific action. I tried to talk about it to Kali in Headculturedome but she was so down in the dumps she couldn't think straight. Since we've been split up I've had no contact with her. I'm not supposed to know where she is, but I do. There's not much I don't know about what goes on in the compounds. When I'm ready, I'll get in touch with her again but at the moment I'm keeping a low profile. I don't want to attract attention to myself, just in case Ra changes his mind and chucks me out.

'You've heard the latest, I suppose?' Thor continues. He doesn't wait for an answer. 'Sati and Jaga have had an almighty row. Sati wants to turn the basement into a luxurious living space for herself. A kind of Arabian palace. I'm talking about the area originally designated for the museum, where you could have been the curator.'

I'm hardly listening. My ambitions have grown considerably since then. Being curator of a museum, wherever it is sited, is not one of them.

'I haven't really being following events at C55,' I tell him. 'I've had enough of that place and of Sati.'

'You should tap in to the sectoid-mag to keep you up to date. It's a laugh if nothing else. It won't be long before Sati finds she's out of her depth. Jaga is stronger than we thought. Ra knew what he was doing when he made her joint chief.'

The mention of Ra reminds me that I have an appointment with him this afternoon. I push my half-finished meal aside, make my excuses to Thor and agree to meet him later to go sharking at the disco-cube.

Once back at my workstation in the compu-centre I think about Ra. As well as being CEO of Worldwideculture, Ra is also head of this compound. It's Ra who has given me a second chance. What I don't know is why. Has he recognised my extraordinary skills and intelligence and brought me here to assist him?

Or has he decided to keep me close to him because he doesn't trust me? If so, he's right. He must know I'm a hacker and a code-breaker and therefore a subversive. He may think it better to keep me in range of his huge central eye.

Ra knows I'm ambitious but he doesn't know the extent of that ambition. Nobody does. It makes my head spin to think of it. I intend to unseat him and replace him as leader of Worldwideculture. Imagine it – me, Heracles, the supreme leader of all the sectoids. *When* that happens – I won't say *if*, I must think positive – *when* that happens I won't pussyfoot around making stupid speeches like Ra. I'll be a man of action. For a start I'll have Sati assassinated – burnt as a witch – and give Kali back control of C55. I'll eliminate a few unproductive compounds and create new ones. After that I intend to explore the wilderness. It can't still be polluted after all these years. I'll employ researchers to find out. If it's pollution-free, I'll commission new buildings, new cities. Why not? All the best architects are here in C99. I'll build palaces in different parts of the Earth and kit them out with beautiful female mutants. I'll build a high tower and call it the Heracles Tower as a reminder of my virility and the Heracles mausoleum will house my remains when I die. Oh yes, I'm ambitious all right. Very. With confidence and careful planning I can make these things happen.

Today I am to see Ra about a new project. He's bound to want to exploit me, to take advantage of my superior intelligence, but I won't give him all my ideas, just enough to make him dependent on me. I intend to out-manipulate the manipulator.

He sits behind his desk, his great trunk of a neck supporting his three heads, the giant eye in the central forehead focused on me as I amble in and sprawl in the shaper opposite him.

'I have great plans for you,' he informs me.

And I've got great plans for you, I think. *Whiz bang you're dead, man.*

'We have had our differences in the past, Heracles. There were times when I despaired of you.' He moves his eyes to the right.

Head Two begins to speak. 'You have to learn not to be led by your emotions, not to lose your temper at the least provocation and….' what passes for a smile crosses its ugly mug, 'not to fall in love so easily.'

Before I have time to consider a reply, Head Three butts in. Her voice is full of sadness. 'You have not always been loyal to us, Heracles. If you are to work with us that will have to change.'

I open my mouth to assure her that I am a changed mutant humanoid, but Head Two is speaking again. 'Your loyalty to Kali has been noted. Now you must transfer that loyalty to us.'

Head Three says, 'We have been disappointed by some of your seditious activities – your hacking of compus and code-breaking of the teleports.'

'On the other hand,' says Head Two, smirking, 'we admire the way you were able to use those skills to do everything in your power to achieve your objective. What we would like you to do is to employ those skills again but this time to use them – not for selfish purposes – but for the benefit of Worldwideculture.'

The central head takes over the lecture. 'You will work directly for me, report directly to me and your one and only loyalty will be to me. How do you feel about that?'

I'm gob-smacked. Everything is going better than I expected. 'What exactly do you want me to do?'

'Your first task is to check out the efficiency of Durga's army.'

Fantastic. A chance to go and see the golden warriors I've heard so much about. What an opportunity.

'Of course,' says Ra's central head, 'I could go to C98 myself, but I would only see what Durga intends me to see. She would put on a special show for me to demonstrate how great she is and how spectacular her army is, but I'll be none the wiser.'

'Whereas if I go,' I suggest, 'I stand more chance of finding out what's going on by chatting casually to members of the workforce and to individual warriors.'

'No,' says the central head. 'No, no, no,' say the three heads one after the other. 'That is not the plan.'

Head One leans forward and focuses his huge dark eye on me. 'What I want you to do, Heracles, is to hack into Durga's secret files and discover exactly what she is proposing to do and how likely it is that – if carried out – her plan will succeed.'

He informs me that I am to have an office to myself with a compu that has almost unlimited access to the documents and accounts of the other sectoids.

'Almost unlimited access,' he says, 'but not quite. There are always some files that are kept secret. Even from me. They are stored deep in the system but I'm sure you can find them, Heracles.'

I'm sure I can. 'Thank you, Sir. I assure you that your faith in me will be justified.'

'I hope so,' he says dryly. 'I know Durga is plotting something. It is up to you to discover exactly what.'

A private office fitted out with a giant console and multi-screens which show, at a flick of a switch, what is going on in all the sectoids. Great. The whole world revealed to me without me having to move a muscle. The compu and auto-put is a complex organism but it won't take me long to get used to its idiosyncrasies. I set up a device that shows me when Ra is online observing me. It gives me a little leeway to do a bit of extra-curriculum research of my own. When I'm ready. To begin with I don't intend to give him cause to think that I am doing anything but work for him. I am to send him a report of my findings at the end of every day.

Having this big private workspace turns out to have other advantages. It's as if my credit rating in the popularity stakes have gone up several notches.

Thor is dead impressed. 'Heh, man, you must have done something right to be given this,' he says, walking round the console, admiring the compu and multi-screens.

I warn him not to touch anything. 'This is a very sensitive machine. No one is permitted to touch it but me.'

He's a bit miffed when I click off the images and refuse to let him look at what is going on in the other sectoids.

The respect that my promotion generates in C99 is very gratifying. Mutant humanoids I've never met before nod and smile at me. I nod graciously back and note their faces and names. Thor is of help in identifying them. Later when I need supporters for my schemes I'll remember them. As for the females, overnight my chances to pull have increased a hundredfold. I no longer have to take what I can get. I can be really picky. I choose only the hottest. It's like being presented with a box of assorted chocolates all with delicious centres and having to decide which one to sample first. When I start to swing my hips, cavorting to George Michael or Robbie Williams, I am immediately surrounded by a flock of female mutant humanoids. I grin at them all but scrutinize them carefully. By the time a slow number begins, I have already decided which to choose to dance with up close and personal and, by the end of the evening, well….

Thor sulks a bit. 'It's not you they're interested in but your power. They think your connection to Ra will keep them safe. They look on you as an insurance policy. They're just using you, man.'

I grin and shrug. Why should I care? I'm using them too and having a hell of a time. Powerful humanoids have always found it easy to procure the females they want. Nothing wrong with that. Thor is just jealous. It's not just quantity, it's quality that counts and he can't compete with me in that department.

One particular female seems determined not to succumb to my charms. I see her in the disco-cube most nights. She rarely dances but when she does take to the floor she moves with a rare grace.

Athene. I remember her from the last time I was here. Ra favoured her, I seem to remember. She's quite something to look at. Apart from the extra eye in the centre of her forehead she doesn't appear to have any other visible mutations. She has high cheekbones and is beautiful in a classical way, like a statue of a Greek goddess made of white alabaster or marble.

She isn't exactly antagonistic towards me. Just indifferent. Her coolness may not be deliberate. It's just that I rarely have to ask any female to dance. They either cluster round me in a group, leaving it up to me to make my choice of partner, or slide up to me, showing their intent by the lift of an eyebrow or a hand on my arm.

Athene does neither of these things. In the daytime, when I see her in the dino-cube, she's always immersed in conversation with other colleagues and doesn't even look up when I pass.

Thor says I'm only interested in her because she shows no interest in me. There may be some truth in that. I've quickly become accustomed to being the centre of attention. To be ignored by this one female is disconcerting, to say the least.

'Get over her,' says Thor. 'There's plenty more females to choose from, lots of them more attractive than her.'

That's his opinion, not mine. Athene's cool beauty haunts me and her lack of interest in me does increase my desire. I look her up on the staff list on auto-put to find out more about her but draw a blank. She exists but doesn't appear to have a specific occupation. That could mean that her position is classified. I consider hacking into the hidden data but hesitate. It's early days yet to delve into business that has nothing to do with the task in hand. I don't want to do anything to make Ra suspicious. There is no doubt that he monitors everything I do.

'Don't even go there,' says Thor, when he sees I'm still looking at her. 'They say that she and Ra are an item.'

I don't believe it. How can she be in a sexual relationship with a mutant humanoid with no body, only a tree trunk of a neck and three heads? No one has ever seen Ra other than behind a desk. Apart from her, perhaps. The thought makes my skin crawl. The only parts of C99 I can't bring up on screen are Ra's office, his dormo-cube and any other private areas he may occupy. Maybe Athene has personal knowledge of these places. My interest in her takes on a different focus.

In the dino-cube she is sitting alone for once. I amble over as casually as possible. She doesn't look up, though my shadow falls over her plate.

'Hi, I'm Heracles,' I begin.

She does look up then, her forehead creased in a puzzled frown. She has no idea why I should be addressing her. 'I know who you are,' she says.

'I wondered if – when you have a spare moment – we could have a little chat?'

She looks amused. 'Why? What have we got to chat about?'

'I'd really like to get to know you. At your convenience, of course.'

Just in case she hasn't heard of my promotion, I add, 'You could come to my workspace, the office next to Ra's.'

She twists her mouth into a wry smile. 'I know where you work. I should do. It was my office and my job before it was yours.'

I feel my mouth drop open.

'Oh, you didn't know,' she says. 'I thought you wanted to meet me to pick my brains, but if you didn't know you were my replacement, I don't understand what we have to talk about. Unless – oh I see – it's a chat up line. You expect me to be one of your tarts.'

She gives short laugh and stands up. 'Dream on. It's not going to happen.'

She walks away with smooth assurance. I've never seen any mutant humanoid move so effortlessly. Odysseus thinks he's the smoothest mover ever, but he's a joke. He has to concentrate hard to glide even the shortest distance, chin sticking out like a clown, but the way Athene moves is the stuff of dreams.

She's gone. I've blown it. There's nothing more I can do. Thor looks at me from the other side of the dino-cube, puts his thumb up and then down in a questioning gesture. He expects me to tell him what happened, but I don't want to talk to him. I stomp off to my office, which somehow doesn't seem so special now.

I sit in front of the compu but don't feel like working. So this was Athene's office. She was Ra's assistant before me. No wonder she hasn't joined in the general adulation. Ra got rid of her because he needed my special skills but I'm sure that if I make a balls-up of this project, I'll find myself expendable too. Next time it would be the wilderness for me for sure, but Athene has been demoted and is still here. Perhaps because she is Ra's mistress. The thought disgusts me. I don't want to believe it but it comes to me that I've never seen her dance with any males in the disco-cube. She only takes to the floor with one or two females who dance individually, as is the custom. It fits. As Ra's partner she would have to be discreet.

That night I decide not to go to the disco-cube. Thor raises an eyebrow. He thinks I must be ill. I tell him I have work to do. I haven't told him about my conversation with Athene. Better not. I don't trust him to keep his two big mouths shut.

A bit of research for Ra. He wants me to find Durga's secret files. First I flick on the screen to see what's going on in C98.

The warriors are practising their skills: fencing, archery, shooting. A familiar figure is draped over a shaper watching them. Isis. I zoom in and enlarge the image. She's all dressed up in some sort of gold robe. She's a nice enough female but none too bright. If I can persuade Ra to let me visit C98 I should be able to chat her up and pump her for some inside knowledge. I sigh. Fat chance. Ra hasn't employed me for my negotiating powers, but for my computer skills. I'd better try to hack in to Durga's personal files and see what I can find out. It takes some time but at last I think I have it – an untitled file with a five star marker, hidden in the trash. I hesitate. Ra told me that if I find something unusual to pass it over to him immediately, unopened, but I'm tempted to open it. If I give it to Ra and it doesn't contain any relevant data, he'll think me an incompetent fool. I open it up.

I don't understand what I'm reading at first but a series of words stand out: planets, satellites, fresh air, above the polluted atmosphere. I scroll down. Durga appears to be planning an attack, not on an earthbound compound but on one of these satellites floating in space. As far as I can make out she's building a huge teleport, big enough to house an army. Her army. Who lives on these satellites? Who is she intending to fight? I scroll down further and there is a list of what I assume to be the names of various satellites: Italiana, Russiana, Arabiana, Frenchinia, Germania. Each satellite appears to contain humanoids of the same nationality or at least those who speak the same language. Which ones are for English speakers? I search for one called Americana or Britannia without success, but there are some that could indicate that English speakers live there. One of them catches my eye – Paradise Island – and another – Planet Oasis.

I scroll down again and discover accounts about the "completes", elite, uncontaminated humanoids with no mutations, like the man in the suit who came to Headculturedome. They escaped from Earth to start life afresh on the satellites.

No wonder Durga wants to attack them and make them suffer as we have suffered. Pay them back for leaving us to rot in the wilderness while they fled to live in the clean, unpolluted air above the clouds.

A knock on the door. Damn. Just as it's getting interesting that bloody Thor has turned up. I've already told him that I'm not going sharking this evening. What the hell does he want? I ignore the knock and continue my research, but the knocking becomes persistent. I minimise the page and go the door, ready to tell him exactly what I think of him.

It's not Thor standing in the doorway, but Athene. She's wearing a long silver robe and looks more desirable than ever.

'I'm sorry to disturb you,' she says, 'but I really need to talk to you.'

I feel my jaw dropping open again. She must think me a moron. 'Of course. Come in,' I say, and indicate the shaper in front of my workstation. She hesitates. I realise it must seem odd to her to sit there. She's accustomed to sitting at the compu in what is now my place. She doesn't sit, just stands and looks at me.

'I didn't know whom to turn to,' she says. 'He doesn't trust anyone really but I thought he must trust you as he's given you this job and this – this workspace. I can trust you, can't I?'

'Of course you can,' I assure her. Her manner is completely different from the last time we spoke. She seems afraid. No, not exactly afraid, but unsure if she's doing the right thing in confiding in me. She seems vulnerable – a description I never thought would apply to her.

Athene looks down at her long, elegant fingers. They're trembling. She clasps her hands to control them, looks up at me and says, 'I was very rude to you this morning and I regret that. I hope you'll accept my apology.'

'Of course,' I say again. Why am I so inarticulate in her company? I feel like a clumsy, uncoordinated lout. 'How can I help?'

'I'm not sure you can.' She hesitates, makes up her mind and blurts out, 'It's Ra. He's had a heart attack. I need to get him to Hos-sat as soon as possible.'

She must be able to see from my face that I have no idea what Hos-sat is. Then it clicks. Hospital satellite. So Ra – and it seems Athene – know about the satellites.

'It's a specialist hospital,' she explains. 'The best there is. You wouldn't know about it yet, I suppose, as you've only just started here, but if I could use this compu for a moment I could get permission to take him there.' I don't feel happy about her using the compu, but I don't have much choice. Ra's had a heart attack and his previous assistant and perhaps lover wants to get him to Hos-sat as soon as possible. She must be desperate to come to me for help. There must be some advantage to me in this, I think rather ungraciously, as I nod my consent to her use of my special auto-put.

Her fingers fly over the keys as she accesses various codes and sends auto-mails and messages. I note several of the codes include the name Stella and wonder about its significance.

'That should do it,' she says. 'They'll be expecting him. Now, all I have to do is get him in the teleport.'

'Can I help?' I ask.

'That won't be necessary. He's in his wheelie. I'm used to pushing it.'

So Ra is in a wheelchair. That's why we've never seen him away from his desk.

Before she leaves, she gives me a shrewd look. 'I see you've found out about the satellites and Durga's mad plan to invade Oasis.' She smiles. 'You know, it's not enough to minimise the file when someone comes in. Especially someone as astute as me.'

I feel myself blush.

'Thanks for the tip,' I say dryly.

'I can see Ra was right about you. You're quick and thorough. A bit too full of yourself, but I think you're going to be useful to us.'

You're going to be useful to me, I think, as I close the door behind her. She told me something I hadn't yet worked out – though no doubt I would have done soon enough – that the satellite Durga intends to attack is called Oasis.

I sit at my desk and think about what has just happened. Ra and Athene already know about Durga's plan. Why then did he give me this task? The answer is simple. To test my ability and my loyalty. Without another thought I close the unnamed file and send it directly to Ra. He may have had a heart attack but when he recovers he will read my report and realise that, not only am I an expert hacker, but also a trustworthy assistant controller.

I fold my arms, sit back on my desk-shaper and give a

self-satisfied smile. Ra's enforced absence will give me the opportunity I need to carry out a bit of research of my own.

If I can find out how exactly the portals work that allow me to view what is going on here on Earth, I might be able to uncover the mechanism for the portals to permit me to view Oasis too.

Looking at the other compounds is an interesting activity in itself. I click on C55 and witness a fight between Jaga and Sati. They have resorted to a wrestling match and are rolling entwined on the floor intent on scratching each other's eyes out. If – *when* – I become CEO they won't last long. I take pleasure at the moment in deleting them from the screen. Zap. They've gone. In C37 I find Kali. She is sitting at a compu working as part of a team, no longer a chief administrator. I send her a message on auto-mail and invite her into my chat-cube. She's pleased to see me and to hear about the scuffle between her two sister-wives in C55.

'If they're not careful, Ra will decide to eliminate the entire compound,' I tell her.

She frowns, not liking that idea at all. 'Destroying all my good work,' she says. 'Terrible. Better for you to ask Ra to reinstate me.'

'I don't think he'd take much notice of me,' I tell her with a grin. 'I'm the bad boy, remember.'

I don't tell her Ra is not here. In fact I don't tell Kali anything. She knows I'm in C99 but she doesn't know about my promotion.

She starts to moan about Mercury. 'After all I've done for that young humanoid, he hasn't even sent me an auto-mail. He left Headculturedome without a word of goodbye. Talk about ungrateful. I don't even know which compound he's been sent to.'

I have access to all the compounds and I haven't caught sight of him either. I determine to investigate further, for

Kali's sake, although sometimes I wonder why I bother with her. All she does is whinge and whine.

She's still talking. 'Wouldn't surprise me if he's been kidnapped.'

'What makes you think that?'

'I don't know. Seems strange to me he disappeared the day that creepy non-mutant in the grey suit came and that I've not heard a peep out of him since.'

'Why would anyone want to kidnap the little messenger?'

'Why not? He's very bright, you know, and good-looking.' She frowns. 'You don't think that non-mutant fancied him, do you? I do hope he's not a paedophile.' Her snakes shoot out their tongues like sleek swords.

'Paedophile? Mercury's not a child any more. He can look after himself. Trouble with you, Kali, you let your imagination run away with you.'

'But if he's all right, he should keep in touch.'

'Tell you what, I'll try to find out where he is and get back to you.'

I search all the compounds in turn. No Mercury to be found. Perhaps Kali is right and the kid has been kidnapped by the man in the suit and is living on one of the satellites. If so, he could prove a useful contact for me. I could do with a little messenger.

Chapter Fourteen
Oasis Downloaded
(according to Michael)

Journal Entry

This is my first entry as Michael, newly formed and newly arrived on Planet Oasis.

Father decides to give me a quick tour of Oasis, an overview he calls it, before taking me to Home-Court-Jameson.

First Impression: a marvel: Oasis really does float in the air, open to the sky. The buildings have roofs of course, but we are outside, walking outside, my father and I, in the fresh air. Unpolluted, clear, fresh air. I take a deep breath and open my eyes wide.

An ever-moving, ever-changing sky lies above and around us. A bright expanse of blue pierced with blazing beams of sunlight. Feathery clouds fragment into shades of white, grey and black. A cloud bursts and a shower of clear water splatters down. I lift up my chin, open my mouth and drink. Transparent, clean, sparkling water. It splashes over my face and hair and runs down my cheeks. I could stand here forever under this refreshing cascade, but Father takes my arm and bustles me into the cover of a doorway. The temper of the rain is about to change. Here it comes, belting down in wide, shiny, metallic sheets. Liquid glass. Fabulous. I stick out my arm but the vertical water cuts into my skin, knife-sharp. I whip it back under the portal again and we stay there waiting for the deluge to stop. After ten minutes or so it does. The sky fades to a lucid blue and the clouds blow away in tiny slivers of smudged white in an ever-shifting pattern. Incredible.

Second impression: A cityscape. Aluminium and glass towers; central squares with life-size statues of completes; green spaces awash with emerald grass peppered with luminous flowers; a scooped-out pit full of sparkling water. The difference between this city and others that I've seen in filmograms is that everything is spotless. No dirt, no grime. No traffic. I wonder if the absence of cars and buses is due to lack of resources or a conscious decision not to pollute the satellite. The latter, I like to think. A new world correcting the mistakes made by the old.

Father is my guide. He points out the municipal buildings: a library full of e-books for the general public to borrow; a sports centre with playing fields and swimming pools with sliding roofs because of the frequent rain; office blocks with large windows eyeing the outside; a medical centre and hospital (not as big or specialised as Hos-sat but useful for less serious cases – maybe the one where I was born); the Symposium, the ultra-modern, gleaming steel parliament building where Father is based; another green space, the university campus with separate structures for the different faculties; a school with playgrounds and more sports fields; a modern church with a steeple; and most amazing of all, a shopping mall with displays of everything imaginable from clothes to electrical goods to food.

I don't understand everything I see but I ask very few questions. I intend to find the answers for myself on line in my study-bedroom at Home-Court-Jameson where we are to go next. My father is looking forward to introducing me to the rest of the family. I'm a little nervous.

Journal Entry

A residential area. All the homes unique: some with turrets like fairy tale castles, others rectangular, mansions some three or four levels high, others circular with curved walls, all set in their own outside space. I am struck again by how green and refreshing everything looks.

We turn a bend and there in front of us is an ultra-modern one-storey building that gleams in the sunlight. Steel, glass and sun. What a combination. 'The Court-Jameson home,' says Father. 'Your home.'

It's surrounded by bright green lawn. Smooth as velvet. A profusion of metallic pots full of brightly coloured flowers decorate the edges of the lawn.

'Stella has a knack for gardening,' Father tells me. 'A real eye for colour.'

Inside the home are more flowers, plants, wall hangings and furnishings in translucent colours. I'm dazzled by everything I see. Including Stella, who's tall and elegant with sleek blond hair that cups her face. Her love of colour extends to her flowing dress in turquoise and purple.

She puts her hands lightly on my shoulders and kisses me twice, once on each cheek. A surprise. I'm not sure what to think about that.

'I'm so pleased to meet you at last, Michael.' Her voice is silky-soft. 'I've prepared a meal. I hope you'll like it. Tomorrow you can help me choose what to cook.'

'I'll eat whatever you give me. I'm used to that.'

'I thought we'd have lunch on the terrace,' she says. 'It looks as if the rain will hold off for a bit and even if it doesn't we can slide the roof over.'

She leads me to an outside space at the back of the home where a table has been laid for the three of us. I can't quite believe it. Not only are we going to eat together, but outside: the biggest change yet.

'Meals are social occasions here,' Father explains. He knows about the food packoids given to us in the compounds to heat up and eat alone in our dormo-cubes. 'When at home, we like to eat as a family. The children are at school now but we like to make quite a thing of the evening meal to chat and catch up with what's been happening during the day.'

'When can I see my study-bedroom?'

Stella and Father laugh and exchange an amused look.

'After lunch,' says Stella.

The food is not like anything I've eaten before, but I eat it quickly. I see Father and Stella exchange another look. Apparently it's not the done thing to stuff food down your throat as quickly as possible. I'm expected to chat in between mouthfuls. I will also have to learn to use cutlery instead of my fingers. Father tells me all this very politely but it is clear that I have a lot to learn to fit in at Home-Court-Jameson.

My room is just as special as Father described it, with big windows looking out on to that lush emerald lawn. The big screen takes up half a wall. I can't wait to sit at the compu and that's exactly what I do for the rest of the afternoon until Father puts his head round the door and tells me the children are home and the family evening meal about to be served. I say I am not hungry and would rather stay on the auto-put but apparently that is not permitted.

The children don't seem too curious about me. Perhaps they've been told to be on their best behaviour, not to stare and or pester me with questions. That suits me fine.

I expect they have their own little lives to think about. I'm not used to these little creatures. I was always the youngest at C55. They sit at the table and use a knife and fork to eat. Stella tells them there's no rush. I hardly eat a thing. I hope Stella doesn't think I don't like her food. That's not it at all. I don't mind what I eat. My concern is my lack of dexterity with a knife and fork.

After supper, Stuart asks me if I want to play football in the garden. I tell him I don't know how to do that.

'I'll teach you,' he says.

I look at Father and he nods. I follow Stuart on to the lawn. He runs some distance away and kicks the ball to me. I stick my foot out but the ball whizzes past it. After several more attempts, Stuart runs to get the ball and gives it me. 'Here, you kick it to me,' he says.

I try. I really do, but my foot seems unable to make contact with the ball. Or when it does it only slides a few inches away. Pathetic. Father is watching. He must be wondering if the physiotherapy was completely successful.

After a bit I give up. 'Sorry. Football is not really my thing,' I say, hoping to escape to my compu.

Stuart opens his eyes wide. 'Didn't you ever play football with other kids?'

'There were no other children to play with. Only one girl.' I think of Isis and wonder how she is.

'What about at school?'

Father comes to the rescue. 'Michael has been ill for most of his childhood,' he says. 'He's spent a lot of time in Hos-sat and has had several major operations. It's left his legs weak.'

Father lies easily I think, although not everything he says is a lie. I have had several ops.

'What a bummer,' Stuart says. 'I'd just kill myself if I couldn't play football.'

I'd like to go back to my study-bedroom but Father says we're going to watch a film together in what he calls the sitting room, a room with a big screen and lots of body-shapers. It's a bit like the RR but smaller and cosier.

'We like to spend the evenings together relaxing as a family,' Father says.

'I want to sit next to Michael,' says Bella.

'He doesn't want to sit next to a girl,' says Stuart.

'Yes he does.'

'Doesn't.'

Father sorts them out. I am to sit in the middle with Bella and Stuart on either side of me. We watch an animated film from the first part of the twentieth first century called *Shrek*. In some ways the characters remind me of my colleagues, the mutant humanoids, and I feel a little sad that I shan't be seeing them again.

After the film, Stella says it's time for Bella to go to bed, but she says, 'Oh Mummy, I just have to show Michael my doll's house first.'

Stuart says, 'He won't want to see your stupid doll's house.'

'He didn't want to play football but you made him. Anyway you do want to see it, don't you, Michael?' and she raises her big blue eyes up to mine and puts her head on one side, willing me to say 'Yes' which I do. She takes my hand and leads me to her special room full of toys, including the doll's house.

She squats down and pats the floor for me to sit down beside her. She points out all the rooms in the house, the furniture and the miniature people who live there. 'That's Olivia and that's her husband, Malcolm, and these are their children. Aren't they just perfect?'

She chatters to the miniature family as if they are real and moves them about from room to room. I have no idea if I'm supposed to join in with her make-believe or not. It doesn't matter. Bella keeps up a steady stream of chatter, enough for both of us.

Stella arrives. 'That's enough, young lady. Time for bed now. School tomorrow, remember. Say goodnight to Michael.'

I'm not at all sure I like all this happy family business.

Journal Entry

I don't have much time to write in my journal. My days are taken up with a kind of initiation course. Stella is my tutor and she's very strict. She restricts the time I spend on the compu. It's not necessary for me to live vicariously now I'm on Oasis, she says. I'm not sure what she means by that. I understand the words all right. It's the concept I don't quite get. I think she means that I must learn to become an integral member of the family and the community and not spend so much time studying. I need a few social skills, she tells me, and then I'll be well away.

We spend time in the kitchen. She teaches me how to use cutlery – fork in the left hand knife in the right – and makes me practise cutting up meat and vegetables and placing the food carefully on the fork so I don't spill anything. I must never put the knife in my mouth. I'm not very good at it. I've always considered myself a quick learner and my fingers fly deftly over a keyboard without any trouble but give me a knife and fork or even a spoon and I'm as clumsy as with a football. I can hear Janey's voice saying, 'It's all a matter of co-ordination, Michael. You can do it. You know you can.'

While in the kitchen, Stella shows me the contents of her cupboards. The selection of food and drink and crockery and glasses for every occasion blows my mind. She takes a spoon and introduces me to different tastes, looking at me carefully to judge my reaction. She doesn't understand that I don't care what I eat.

The next stage of my initiation takes place in the shopping mall. Massive shop windows full of goods of every kind make Stella's cupboards look empty. She wants to buy me clothes and suggests I choose them. I look at the other young people in the mall but still have little idea. I've only ever worn monos supplied by Worldwideculture. They come in packoids like the food. It's never occurred to me to take an interest in fashion. In the end, Stella chooses for me: jeans, T-shirts, socks, trainers and underpants. The latter are garments I've never worn before, but she assures me they're necessary. In the food hall, I am amazed all over again by the variety of choice, but Stella seems to have no trouble picking out what she wants. It will be some time before I will be knowledgeable enough to know what these items taste like and when it's appropriate to eat them. She pays for everything with a plastic card. They'll be teleported to our home later today.

The mall is crowded and the noise of people chattering reverberates round the high dome. Enthusiastic browsers are enjoying what Stella calls window-shopping. I wonder if I will ever enjoy it.

We take a walk in the park and this is the best part of the day for me. I am out in the fresh air again, looking up at the never-ending sky and the moving clouds and the lanky trees, grassy slopes and flowers in every conceivable shade of red.

Back home, I hope to go on my compu but no, Stella sits me down at the table on the terrace with pen and paper and teaches me some useful changes of vocabulary. I must no longer say compu but computer, not bunku but bed and not dormo-cube but bedroom. I know most of the words already, but it is important that I remember to use them. Between us we make quite a long list. She tests me and I am pleased to say that I am word perfect. No problem with my brain. Only with my motor skills.

'It's your turn to ask me questions,' Stella says. 'The internet is great for facts but there may be more personal things you need to know that only another complete can answer.'

I am so surprised by that phrase "another complete" that I can't think of a thing to ask her.

'Make a list,' she suggests. 'Add things as you think of them. That's the best thing to do. When you're ready you can ask me or Alexander – your father.'

'Can I record the list on my compu – er – computer?' I ask.

The corners of her eyes twinkle with amusement. She knows it's an excuse to escape. 'Go on then. Off you go.'

Off I dash to my beloved computer at last.

Journal Entry

I start going out on my own. I like going to the park. I'm beginning to read the signs in the sky. When the clouds turn to dark grey, almost black, a storm is about to break. Once I was caught out. The water sluiced down on to me, soaked my clothes, beat and cut into my skin, leaving bruises and abrasions. Not pleasant. That's how I learnt to run for shelter.

There are lots of little pavilions in the park, built for that purpose. Now, as soon as I see those dark clouds, I make a dash for one of them. Once under cover, I watch the storm. Rain beats down, branches thrash around, lightning sizzles and thunder roars. Awesome. Spectacular. I stay there until the rain slows down to a drizzle and the rumbles of thunder diminish. Then comes the best part. The aftermath.

The air cools, a pale sun comes out and a scent of freshly washed leaves, grass and dank earth fills the air. Who would ever have guessed that moisture could smell so sweet?

Journal Entry

A distressing incident in the park today.

Some boys about Stuart's age are playing about with a football. Someone kicks it straight at me. It lands on my head and I topple over, legs and arms splayed out at all angles.

'Come on. Kick it back,' shouts a scraggy ginger-haired boy. I scramble to my feet and find the kids staring at me, waiting for me to retrieve the ball and kick it back. I pick it up, put it on the ground in front of me and attempt to kick it. It doesn't move an inch. A second attempt is not much of an improvement. I lean over, take the ball in both hands, lift my arms over my head and attempt a throw. The ball lands at my feet. Pathetic.

The boys burst out laughing and start to jeer, waving their arms in the air.

'Mutant!' Ginger yells. He runs towards me, scoops up the ball and makes as if to throw it at me. I cringe and duck. He grabs the front of my T-shirt and pulls me upright, his face level with mine, nose to nose. 'Can't even kick a ball, you mutant!' he hisses. The others stroll over and form a circle around me, chanting, 'Mutant, mutant, mutant!'

At that moment a cloud bursts and off they all run to the nearest shelter. I stand rooted to the spot in a state of shock. If I don't move, the rain will batter me. It's beating down more strongly every second. I can't go to the nearest pavilion because the boys are in it. I make a quick dash for one further away. I'm completely soaked by the time I reach it.

For once I have no interest in watching the storm. I'm mortified. I can't believe what they called me. They know. In spite of all the operations and therapy, they know I'm a mutant humanoid. Their words ring in my ears all the way home and return to haunt me when I try to sleep at night.

Journal Entry
Several days pass before I venture into the park again. I look round cautiously. Not a boy in sight, but somehow they've spoilt the place for me and I don't stay there long.

Journal Entry
I borrow Stuart's football and practise kicking it in the garden. It takes time but I'm getting the hang of it. One mighty kick and the ball flies up in the air and bounces off

the window. Didn't break. The windows must be made of some special kind of glass. Of course it may not be glass at all, but some kind of new material made on the satellite. I make a mental note to look it up on the web. I need a bit more ball control before I can ask Stuart to give me another chance.

Journal Entry

My list of questions grows. I can find most answers to my questions online, but I have a personal question for Stella.

'I know you look after all of us but do you have a job as well?'

'I do indeed,' she says, 'but unlike your father I work from home.' She hesitates. 'I'm not sure if you're ready for this, Michael, but I'll have to take the risk. Come, I'll show you. I think it's time you found out exactly what I do and who I am.'

I follow her through a labyrinth of colourful rooms and passages until we reach her workspace. The walls are full of pictures and all the surfaces are covered with artefacts. 'Is this your work?' I ask her. 'Is this how you reach your targets for Worldwideculture?'

She looks puzzled and shakes her head. 'We don't have targets here on Oasis. Targets are only for….' The colour rushes up her cheeks. She means the targets are only for mutant humanoids.

The saver-screen is multi-coloured, a work of art in itself. Across it in huge italic lettering is written *Worldwideculture. inc. Private site. Stella Jameson*. It takes me a minute or two to realise what this implies.

Stella smiles. 'Yes, Michael, this office is the headquarters of my company. I am the owner and managing director of Worldwideculture.inc.'

Chapter Fifteen
Stella revealed
(according to Michael)

Journal Entry

'The company has been in my family for years ever since – well – ever since our lives changed forever. Sit down a minute, Michael. I want to show you something.'

Stella clicks on an icon and a series of dome-shaped buildings come up on the screen, a hundred or so of them – the compounds on Earth seen from the outside. The camera skims over mile after mile of desert, the occasional dried-up shrub the only sign that anything once grew there. There are no other buildings, only the domes.

'Planet Earth,' Stella says and sighs. 'Aren't you glad you don't live there any more, Michael?'

'Are these live pictures? I ask because surely the plague ended at least a hundred years ago if not longer. Surely there should be signs of regeneration by now. Plants, leaves on the trees, bits of greenery, that sort of thing….'

'Sorry to disappoint you, Michael. This is a current view of Earth. You are looking at a dead planet. No plants, no animals, no birds. If you'd stayed on Earth you would never have been able to go outside.' She puckers her pretty forehead. 'You do think you're lucky to be here, Michael?'

'Of course. I'm very grateful for everything you and Father are doing for me.' I'm aware I'm being ultra-polite, not completely sincere. I sense that she's not being completely truthful about the present state of Earth. It doesn't make sense that the land hasn't started to revive itself. I can't help wondering if the governments on the satellites are doing something to stop it thriving again: spraying it with the modern equivalent of Agent Orange/dioxin perhaps, to make sure the mutant humanoids stay in the compounds.

I change the subject. 'So, Worldwideculture is your company. Does that mean you are above Ra?'

'In theory, yes, but I rarely interfere with his decisions.'

'You could, though, if you wanted to,' I insist. I am wondering if Stella could use her influence to get Kali reinstated as chief administrator of Compound 55.

'Ra doesn't need help from me.' Stella runs her fingers over the icons that denote the names of the compounds. 'I just keep an eye on what is going on and make sure everything runs smoothly.'

One click from Stella and I see inside a dome, a compu-centre full of mutant humanoids sitting at workstations. Not a compound I know. After a moment or two, she switches to another compound. Some humanoids are playing billiards, others dancing, others chatting. Stella is like Big Brother, or rather Big Sister, watching the mutant humanoids in the compounds, but they have no idea she is watching them. No idea that such a person as Stella exists. I shiver. My mind works overtime. Perhaps I can bring up this screen on my own auto-put and search each compound until I find Kali to see if she's got over her depression. Father told me I have unlimited access online but this is clearly a private site. I'd need a special code to log on to it.

'You say you inherited Worldwideculture. Who created it?'

'A woman called Rebecca Harfield, one of my ancestors.'

'Why did she do that?'

'For the same reason I continue to oversee it. To do

something to help improve the quality of life of those who were left on Earth.'

'The mutant humanoids,' I prompt her. I notice she tries to avoid the m-word.

'Rebecca and others like her believed that those confined to the compounds should live as full a life as possible. The satellites supply the compounds with the basic necessities – food and clothes – but Rebecca believed that being creative would enrich their lives. If it hadn't been for Rebecca there wouldn't have been any computers in the compounds. That was quite a controversial idea at the time. She fought for that. Think how barren life in the compounds would be without them.'

I have to agree with that. Life without compus doesn't bear thinking about. This Rebecca Harfield must have been quite a special person.

But something is worrying me. Everything Stella is saying sounds philanthropic but the fact of the matter is that the completes plundered the Earth, stole its resources and treasures and locked up the mutants in compounds. I feel uneasy about their motives. And about Stella's.

Journal Entry

Stella and I are in her study again. A bit of an argument today. My fault. I'm in one of my provocative moods.

Unlimited access to the auto-put has made me see things from a different perspective and I don't always like what I find. I think of the changed person I have become, but am aware that I have not completely changed. I'm not yet a complete, not yet a fully-fledged citizen of Oasis, mentally nor emotionally. I'm still half-mutant and when I'm talking to Stella it's the mutant half that comes to the fore.

'So, your company, Worldwideculture.inc, is only for mutant humanoids?'

'That's right.'

'Tell me, what is the point of the weekly targets?'

'Everyone is competitive, whether humanoids or completes. It's human nature. Competing with other sectoids and striving to reach monthly targets encourages creativity.'

Mercury rising! I try to keep calm but say, 'So, these targets are not important?'

'Not in themselves. No.'

'But you have tricked us into believing that they really matter.'

'Not tricked, Michael.' Her face tightens.

'I'm sorry, Stella, but where does this emphasis on creativity lead? To churning out the same old speeches of congratulation to the sectoids with the best target figures. Apart from the figures on the spread sheets, where is the evidence of this creativity?'

Stella begins to open files of work on the screen: pictures, architectural designs, poems, stories and pieces of music. 'They're all here, Michael. Look.'

'Great, but I've never seen these before. We weren't encouraged to look at each other's work. We were told that our time was better spent creating the next piece of crap to meet the targets.'

'Not all of it was crap.'

'You know as well as I do that when anyone can put whatever they like online, the web becomes cluttered with rubbish.'

'Look at these pictures from Compound 99. Is that rubbish?'

'Ah C99, the flagship. The sectoid that has everything.'

'You can't call that rubbish,' Stella insists.

'Perhaps not, but has it occurred to you that the work produced there is superior because the artists, musicians or architects live in a better environment than in the other compounds?'

Stella bites her lip. 'So – what are you saying?'

'In C55 we had nothing to stimulate us apart from things seen on the computers. It's difficult to be creative in a vacuum. We didn't care about the success of other compounds because we'd been taught that they were our competitors. It's not creativity that's important in the sectoids but the number of items produced to meet those damn targets.'

Stella looks down at her hands. Her pretty face is troubled. 'Maybe your leader didn't have the imagination to….'

I feel myself flaring up again. 'Kali was our leader and my mother. Please don't criticise her.'

Stella is shocked into silence. We stare at each other. She reaches out a hand as if to placate me, but withdraws it quickly.

'The trouble is, Stella, not everyone is creative. I'm not. Not in the least. I was a child when I came to C55. Kali didn't expect me to reach targets. She made me sit at the workstation all day – that's true – but I was allowed to surf the net, look at whatever I wanted. I'm grateful to her for that. I studied all day and often all evening too, but nothing inspired me to be creative. Sorry, Stella, but I think you need to change the focus of your company. Inspire people to learn about the past and study science and mathematics as well as the humanities and the arts.'

'I'll give it some thought,' she says with a strained little smile.

It must have been a gruelling afternoon for her and it certainly has been for me, one that's made me even more aware of my dual personality. I've seen from a distance all that is wrong with life in the compounds and I'm beginning to suspect that attitudes on Oasis towards mutant humanoids are not as benevolent as I've thought or hoped. I take a deep breath, stand up and tell her I need to leave now. I have to go outside into the fresh air and walk a mile or two to clear my head.

'Just a minute,' Stella says and clicks on another icon with those graceful fingers of hers. 'There's one more thing I'd like to show you.'

The interior of Headculturedome comes up with its students sitting at their workstations. 'Look, Michael. This is where your father found you. You were sitting just there at your workstation. He recognised you immediately.'

'How did he know it was me? He hadn't seen me since I was a baby.'

Stella smiles. 'I don't know if you are aware of this, Michael, but you are the spitting image of your father. When he pointed you out I was as sure as he was that you were his son.'

'But he's tall and I'm short.'

'Your face, Michael. I'm talking about your features, your eyes, the shape of your head, the set of your mouth, the way your hair grows back off your forehead. All those things convinced us it was you.'

I stare at her. It hasn't occurred to me that I look like my father. I don't know what my face looks like. There is a mirror in my study-bedroom but, because I've never been in the habit of looking at myself, I don't look in it. The only mirror I remember using was in Hos-sat to see the result of the op on my back.

'Alexander went to Headculturedome – to make sure it really was you.'

I think of the camera eye resting on my face.

Headculturedome is still up on the screen. I screw up my eyes to see if I recognise anyone there. I don't.

One more question. 'Is Kali still there – at the dome?'

Stella hesitates. 'No. She's moved on.'

'Where to?'

A pause. 'Michael, it's better not to think about Kali. Your home is here now. With us. We are your family and I'd like you to think of me as your mother.' Her lovely face surrounded by that sleek cap of blonde hair is tipped up towards mine so hopefully I can't disappoint her. I've been so horrid to her this afternoon. My bad mood that sprung from those cries of "mutant" in the park I've taken out on her. This beautiful woman wants to be my mother. She's welcomed me into her home and made a real effort to educate me in the ways of Oasis. I put my arms round her and give her a hug. True, not a very elegant hug. She's sitting at the computer and I'm standing behind her and it's an awkward position for both of us, but it is a hug. Her mouth puckers a bit as if she's going to cry. I leave her before we both start bawling.

I rush off to my room to pick up my coat. Just before I leave for my walk, I look in the mirror. Father's cool grey eyes stare back at me.

Journal Entry

A question for my father.

'What about the job you promised me? When am I to start? What will it actually involve?'

He surprises me by saying he thinks I should attend Oasis university for a few years first. 'Give some thought to the subjects you would like to study.'

'Psychology, history and politics,' I say straightaway.

He raises his eyebrows. 'You seem very sure of that.'

'Psychology is necessary for the job of liaison officer. History and politics will give me a secure background to negotiate between Earth and the satellites.'

He frowns. 'You wouldn't rather choose a creative subject – such as art, music or literature?'

I think of the scam that is Worldwideculture and shake my head. 'No thanks.'

Journal Entry

Stuart comes home from school with a black eye.

'What happened to you, darling?' asks Stella.

'Some kid said my brother was a mutant so I had to punch his face in. He punched me back but I won. His face looks like a squashed tomato.'

I bet it was that ginger-haired kid.

Stella screws up her eyes. 'Still, you shouldn't have hit him in the face.'

'Why not? No one is going to call my brother a mutant and get away with it.'

I'm secretly chuffed. My little brother is sticking up for me.

'Fancy a game of football after tea?' I try to sound casual.

'Thought you said you couldn't play,' he says.

'I've been practising.'

He grins. 'You're on,' and he slaps his hand on mine. 'High fives.'

Reminds me of Isis. I wonder how she is, if she's happy in her new compound.

For a moment I feel quite lonely, but kicking a ball around with Stuart will cheer me up.

Journal Entry

Something terrible happens. An auto-mail arrives from Heracles.

'Hi Mercury, Kali is so worried about you. Please reply to this message a soon as possible and let us know that you're all right.'

I'd like to reply to let Kali know I'm fine and to find out how she is but I can't. Father has impressed on me that no one must know where I am. It's not at all sure that Heracles knows. He's a good hacker, but there must be a limit to his skills. He may have sent a similar message to lots of auto-mail addresses, but if I reply he will know for sure. I change my access code and put a block on his.

I try to open the portal of Worldwideculture.inc. I'd like to find Kali and Isis. Make sure they are both all right. No success. Stella has blocked my access.

Chapter Sixteen
Revelation
(according to Odysseus)

At last I've managed to appease Brahmin. I've given him a gallery of his own to display the religious icons. I pride myself that it's the sign of good leader to appreciate the skills and preferences of his assistant and allocate him appropriate tasks. Delegate. That's the answer. I'm not the official curator as yet but if I act as if I've already been appointed it will demonstrate my leadership expertise. Brahmin is quite happy in his own little world arranging and rearranging the ornate silver and gold statuettes and emblems while I am equally content concentrating on mounting the pictures in the grand gallery. All is peaceful in the histo-lab and museum. No more heated altercations. Cunning Odysseus has created order out of chaos.

I'm immersed in selecting and hanging the paintings of the Great Masters from the Renaissance period. Amongst our most prize possessions are several genuine Correggios including the *Madonna della Cesta* (1525) from the National Gallery in London. We also have several copies of Correggio paintings from the cupola of the cathedral of Parma: details from the *Assumption of the Virgin, Saints Jerome and Mathew* and my particular favourite, *Madonna and child with Saint Jerome and Mary Magdalen*. Brahmin and I have had several altercations about whether to include the copies or not but

I insist that they should be hung with the genuine works, as long as we make it clear it that they are copies. Better to show them, I tell him, than tuck them away in a drawer where no one will see them.

Isis raises an eyebrow. 'No one ever sees them anyway, Ody, so what's the difference?'

'They will, Isis. Just you wait. They will.'

Isis thinks we are taking too long organizing the artefacts and that the museum will never open; but I want to be certain that every item is displayed and labelled perfectly before the grand opening when humanoids from all the compounds are to be teleported to C98 to see them. This event has not yet been confirmed by Durga but I'm convinced she'll agree. It will bring great prestige to her sectoid.

I don't hold out too much hope for her pillaging of the museum on some supposed satellite, but if extra artefacts do arrive I shall not refuse them on moral grounds. After all, most art treasures have been acquired during wars. The sacking of Constantinople, for example. Without that ruthless theft we would not have any of the riches of the Renaissance.

At the end of each day, Brahmin and I peruse each other's work. I try to go into his galleria first to remind him who's in charge. I glide round like an ice-skater, stopping every now and then to scrutinise each addition and on I coast to assess its effect in relation to the others. It's a practised performance: an affirmation of my power. Occasionally I make a suggestion, a small adjustment. Nothing too controversial. It's not worth the aggravation. For one thing I couldn't care less how he displays these boring old relics. No one will be interested in visiting this dark galleria, tucked away as it is along a back corridor. For another, I am intent on keeping the peace. Arguments interrupt the flow of my own musings, which could affect the artistic decisions I have to make about more prestigious artefacts.

A few weeks have passed since Durga's dramatic statement of intent, but both Durga and the golden warriors are still with us. Each morning at the Grand Parade they strut their stuff, marching round the great hall. Tension is in the air as if something is about to happen, but I doubt it will. In my experience, we mutant humanoids rarely leave our own compound unless transferred to another and the premise that there are satellites in the sky inhabited by uncontaminated completes seems a little far-fetched. Being a historian I've never been attracted by futuristic fables, too like fairy tales for me to take seriously, but I suppose they are popular with less erudite readers. Escapism from the daily grind. I banish Durga's proclamation to the back of my mind and continue with more tangible matters.

Isis rushes up to me arms and legs all over the place, her face flushed. I am at the top of a small stepladder engaged in hanging a rather special painting. Isis clutches me and nearly knocks me off in her agitation.

'Ody, guess what? They're going tomorrow. Osiris with them.'

Isis and Osiris. What is she talking about? I don't know anyone called Osiris. She must be more befuddled than I thought.

'You know who I mean. Dionysis.'

'God of wine and debauchery,' I say.

'Oh don't be so thick, Ody. You must know him, the blond one with curly hair. I call him Osiris because I'm Isis.'

She's right I have been thick. Obtuse. 'I gather your feelings for this young man are not exactly sisterly,' I say somewhat primly.

'You guess right.'

I know Isis doesn't spend as much time in the histo-lab or museum as she should but she tells me that she's doing other useful work reaching targets on the compus in the centre and of course I have no idea how she spends her evenings. Or nights. I've always treated her with indulgence, allowing her the freedom to do what she wants, but I hadn't realised that there was a young man on the scene. Perhaps I didn't want to know. The incident with Heracles at C55 affected me deeply and now I'm going to suffer again because she's fallen for a handsome young warrior. He will no doubt be just as careless of her affections.

'Ody, they've built a big teleport, big enough for a lot of warriors to be transported at the same time and he's to be one of the advance party, the first ten.'

I climb down the one or two steps. She clearly needs support. 'Are you sure about this, Isis?'

'Positive. The notice is all over the intercom-net. His name is at the top of the list. Get this, they're not even allowed to say goodbye to anyone. They're being kept together until early tomorrow morning until they leave. It's totally unfair. Ody, I might never see him again.'

She almost throws herself into my arms and sobs. My arms slip around her and I hold her close. What am I to Isis? Substitute father, mentor, reliable old friend? My whole body is trembling. Ten warriors in archaic golden uniforms are to be teleported to a man-made planet? Sounds implausible to me. I assure her that everything is going to be fine and that her Osiris will come back safe and sound.

She raises her mooneyes to mine. 'Not to let us say goodbye, Ody! That's so cruel. They say it's to keep them focussed on the battle to come. That they mustn't be distracted.'

She's still in my arms, her warm, soft body against mine.

'That's quite usual, you know, to separate soldiers from wives or loved ones before battle. Why, in Roman times….'

She's not listening. I'm just her boring old Ody embarking on one of his interminable stories.

All too soon she pulls away and wipes her tears with the back of her tiny hand. That's when she catches sight of the painting I'm in the process of hanging. 'I like that one,' she says.

'Raphael painted it circa 1512,' I tell her, 'Julius the Second gave it to San Sisto, in Piacenza. That's why it's known as *The Sistine Madonna* .'

She pulls away from me and steps back to examine the painting.

'Look at her dress and hooded cloak. I could make myself something like that.'

Since the golden robe she made the day after we arrived, she's made herself several different outfits. To make herself look attractive for the young humanoid, I shouldn't wonder.

A little later she finds the material she's looking for and I hear her humming as she cuts and sews. I think how resilient she is, getting on with what I consider her creative work in spite of her emotional state. Or perhaps because of it. Don't we all throw ourselves into something new in order to forget something distressing? There was a time when I too immersed myself in work for a similar reason. I sigh, climb up the stepladder again and shift *The Sistine Madonna* a little to the left.

As if to confirm that the action has begun, a somewhat depleted battalion of warriors attend the next day's parade. Ten less, I assume. Durga is still with us, but she announces that these daily parades are to be suspended until further notice because of the war. I don't think she wants us to know exactly how many warriors have left or indeed when she herself leaves. She doesn't want to risk anarchy while she's away.

'When we return triumphant,' she proclaims, 'there will be a grand parade to beat all grand parades and celebrations for everyone, including a banquet and fireworks.'

She looks just splendid standing in her winged chariot and it occurs to me that it could be capable of taking off and propelling itself upward into the Heavens of its own accord. Absurd. Just as absurd as referring to the sky as the Heavens. More practically, I find myself wondering if the chariot will fit snugly into the newly constructed oversize teleport. Does one huge chariot take up the same space as ten warriors?

I have no answer to that. I'm no mathematician. I can't help wondering if the whole enterprise is a glorified spoof, a moon landing in the Arizona desert. Durga could be inventing these fantasies as a method of motivating her workforce. What a cynical old mutant humanoid I am.

One look at the face of Isis and I have no doubt that she believes every word. She's worried about her lover and can't wait for news. During the day she checks the auto-mails every few minutes. She has finished her gown. It has an ice blue under-dress that is half-covered by a silver-hooded voluminous cloak. As she moves, the cloak swishes along the floor, majestic, if not Madonna-like. She is too restless to have that serene Madonna-look.

Days pass and still no news of Dionsysis/Osiris, nor indeed of any other members of the advance party.

'No news is good news,' I tell Isis, but she rolls the pupils of her eyes upwards until only the glacial whites show. She paces up and down, walks in and out of the histo-lab, visits other parts of the sectoid and returns with snippets of news.

'They can't send auto-mails or use the intercom-net or intercom-fones. Too dangerous. There's a message from Durga, saying that those of us left behind must keep our spirits up and keep calm. Ha! Easy for her to say.'

'"Keep the home fires burning,"' I sing softly.

'What you on about?' asks Isis. 'Are you losing it, Ody?'

I just smile. No point explaining the reference. She's not in the mood.

The next day she prances in, with a different sort of news. 'That Indra – you know, that two-headed Rastafarian – had the cheek to make a pass at me last night. Suggested he could share my double bunku now that Osiris has gone. "In your dreams," I told him. What a moron.'

'Sounds as if you know how to stand up for yourself,' I say. 'I don't suppose he'll bother you again.'

'I'm not so sure about that. I can't go anywhere without him following me. Wouldn't be surprised if he's not lurking outside the histo-lab right now waiting for me to come out.'

I take a look to make sure, but there's no one there. I conclude Isis is so worried about her Osiris that she's a bit paranoid.

All the same, that evening, I make it my business to coast smoothly and unobtrusively through the RR. There is the usual profusion of young humanoids lounging about on the shapers; but Isis isn't one of them. I hang around for a bit, but feel very out of place. I can't join in with their chitchat. I don't understand a word they're saying. Martians chattering couldn't be more alien to me than these youngsters.

I decide to take a look in the compu-centre. Isis isn't the sort to work overtime but she could be checking to see if there is any news of the warriors. I'm right. Her silver-hooded head is bent over a compu in the far corner. I'm just about to glide over to her but, before I have a chance, a young warrior barges past me. He's tall, dark-skinned and athletic. He's off-duty so not wearing helmets and I note that he wears his long black hair in tight little plaits, Rastafarian style. Indra. I turn away and conceal myself in a dark corner obliquely opposite them and hover just in case Isis should need my assistance. Cunning Odysseus has become an eavesdropper.

'Isis,' Indra breathes in her ear. 'I have something important to tell you. The advance party have all arrived safely.'

Isis looks up at him. 'How do you know? I can't find anything.'

'We warriors have special compus with special access codes.'

'Really?'

'Really.'

'OK – tell me the latest.'

'Not much more to say. Just a memogram to say they've arrived on Planet Oasis.'

'A pre-written memogram is automatically released on arrival at any destination. You know that. Doesn't mean a thing. They could be anywhere.'

'They're arrived safely on Planet Oasis. Trust me.'

'Trust you? You must be joking. I'd as soon trust a snake.'

'You don't mean that. I've seen the way you look at me.' Indra leans over and lays his arm loosely across her shoulders.

She reacts immediately and whacks his arm. 'You can cut that out. Get out of here. I don't want any more of your stupid messages.'

'But Isis, I can keep you up to date each day with what is happening.'

She ignores him and continues her search on the compu.

'You won't have any luck on that old thing.' He hesitates for a moment and then says, 'I could probably sneak you in to the warrior compu-centre with its multi-screens and you could see for yourself what is happening.'

She leaps to her feet. 'OK, let's go.'

'I said probably. I have to arrange it. Tomorrow would be better.'

'You're all mouth and trousers.' She sits down again and goes on with her search, but I can see from the tension in her back that she is tempted by the offer. Something in her desperate attempts to find Osiris takes me back to a time when I was enamoured of a certain young female humanoid. She was transferred to another compound and I spent hours on the auto-put frantic to find her.

'The lieutenant's a good mate of mine, and of Dionysis.

I'm sure he will allow you to see what's happening. Just give me till tomorrow to fix it.'

'If you can "sneak me in", as you so charmingly put it, what do you expect in return?' she asks without looking at him, still tapping furiously on the keyboard.

'Nothing. I swear. I just want you be happy.'

She gives a little laugh. 'Oh yeah. So what was all that about last night?'

'I'd had a bit too much to drink. You know that. I'm sorry if I said or did anything to offend you. I miss him as much as you do.'

'I very much doubt that.'

'I want us to be friends, Isis. Now Dionysis has gone we need each other for support.'

'I don't need you, Indra. I've already got a special friend – someone to look after me while Dionysis is away.'

'Who? Tell me who he is. Who else have you been talking to?'

'Someone who respects me, that's who.'

'Another warrior? Tell me who it is.' His fist is clenched, both his faces screwed up with…. what? Hatred? Jealousy? He takes her by the shoulders and lifts her off her feet until her face is level with his two. His four eyes stare at her.

'Let me go. You're hurting me.'

'Not till you tell me who it is.'

'OK, OK. I'll tell you, but put me down first.'

'No, you tell me and then I'll let you go.'

She pauses a moment and then bursts out, 'It's Odysseus. He's the only humanoid I trust, apart from Dionysis, because he's the only one who really cares for me.'

I am so surprised by this admission that I have to put my hand over my mouth to stop them hearing my quick intake of breath. I am way back in the shadows but a sudden sound could reveal my presence.

Indra is dumbfounded. 'That old man? What can he do for you?'

'He listens to me, that's what he does. He respects me.'

'Respects you? What exactly is that dirty old man to you?'

'Don't you dare call him that,' spits Isis. She manages to release her little arm and scratches him down the side of one his faces with her long, silver-painted nails.

He lets go his hold on her and pushes her away. She lands smack on the floor. It's as much as I can do to stop myself rushing to her aid.

'You sad bitch. ' Indra looks down at her. 'So all this time you've been two-timing Dionysis with that old man. You wait till I tell him.'

Isis gets to her feet and laughs in his face. 'Tell him what you like. He won't believe you. He knows about my relationship with Odysseus. He knows what you don't know.'

'Oh really? What is that?'

'He knows that I love Odysseus. Know why I love him? Because he's my father, that's why!'

Back in the histo-lab I sit at my compu. Too early to go to my bunku. I won't be able to sleep, but I can't work either. I think about what she said – that I'm her father. Maybe she means that I've always been a father to her just as Kali was a mother to Mercury. Or does she mean that I'm her real father? It occurs to me that she could have been sent to C55 to live with her father after her mother died but I lacked the perception to put two and two together, too "thick to catch on" as Isis would so graphically have put it. I think back. If I am her biological father there is only one person who could have been her mother.

I was never a person to be promiscuous, never had more than three or four sexual partners in my entire life. For the timescale to make sense, it could only have been Penelope. The memory of her face, as round as the full moon, the face I made myself forget, yet a face remarkably like that of Isis, comes back to me now. Why haven't I made the connection before? Odysseus and Penelope. We laughed about the coincidence of our names, told each other our love was meant to be. I close my eyes and see her face again, the soft, pale cheeks, the bright quizzical central eye, the little snub nose, the long fair hair, pinned up during the day, free-flowing in our bunku at night. We were so happy together. But she asked to be transferred to another sectoid, abandoned me. At first I had hopes that she would return, that "absence would make the heart grow fonder" as the old adage goes. It didn't. I didn't hear a word. I tried to find her but without success. And, as the months passed, I convinced myself that she didn't want to be found and put her out of my mind, locked the memories of our precious days and nights together in a dark treasure chest never to be opened.

But suppose, just suppose, that she left because she was pregnant and thought I wouldn't welcome the burden of a child? Didn't she know that no child of hers could ever be a burden to me? Why didn't she tell me and why didn't she contact me after she'd left? Why that terrible silence?

After she'd gone, I shut myself up in the histo-lab and devoted myself to research. There were no further intimacies with female humanoids and no deep feelings for anyone else. Until Isis came along.

From the very beginning I had a soft spot for her. Could it be that on some subliminal level I did see in Isis a resemblance to Penelope? If I am her father that would account for the special relationship that has developed between us and the ambivalent feelings I have about the young male mutants who, in my opinion, are never good enough for her. The sight of Heracles and Isis having sex on the floor of the histo-lab released emotions I didn't know I had. The sacking of Heracles became a pleasurable revenge, a response so alien to my nature it shocked me and continues to shock me. If Isis is my daughter and, on some subconscious level I was aware of that, I suppose it goes some way to excuse my behaviour.

Isis turns up to work on time the next morning and starts sorting through the clothes chest again. Her obsession with making different costumes for herself intrigues me. Who is she trying to impress? Not Dionysis/Osiris. He's gone off to war. Surely not Indra. I don't like the idea of her with any male mutant humanoid, but better an absent warrior than the ever-present Indra.

I pluck up courage and ask her if she remembers her mother.

'Course,' she says, 'Why do you ask?'

'What was her name?'

She looks at me as if I'm weak in the head. 'You're not going senile, are you Ody? You know her name.'

'Was it – Penelope?'

She gives a little smile. 'Not quite brain dead yet then,' she quips.

So it's true. Isis is my daughter. I berate myself for not realising it before. That's why she was sent to C55 after her mother's death – to be with me, her father. But why didn't anyone tell me? Has Isis known about our relationship all along and assumed I knew too? Why didn't she mention it? Did she think I was to blame for Penelope leaving?

I long to ask Isis about her mother, not least about why and how she died, but when I approach the subject she says, 'Give it up, Ody. That part of my life is well over. I'm looking to the future now.'

Isis spends more time with me in the museum, takes an

interest in the paintings, particularly the ones from the golden age of the Renaissance in Italy. Apart from Raphael's Sistine Madonna, the inspiration for the blue dress and silver hooded cloak, she admires several other depictions of the Virgin including an earlier work, *Madonna della Vittoria* by Mantega. I tell her that this was dated circa 1496 and was transferred from wood to canvas for Francesco Gonzaga, that it was originally in the Cappella della Vittoria in Mantua, hence its name, but was acquired by the Louvre in Paris. I try to explain about the formalisation of the surrounding figures and how they are not as naturalistic as representations in the later years of the period but, once again, she isn't listening. She's staring at the Madonna.

'Look at the colour of her dress, Ody, and the way it hangs in folds over her arms and legs. I'm going to look for some material that colour,' and she's off, diving into the old chests again.

It isn't until a few days later when I hear her gasp at Correggio's *The Holy Family*, known as *Madonna della Cesta* that I begin to realise how obtuse I've been yet again. "Thick as a plank, Ody." I'm referring to the painting in which the male child's chubby legs are exposed and his genitals lie spread out on the mother's thighs, while the mother clutches her breast, ready to feed him.

'That,' says Isis, 'is totally the most beautiful painting in the world.'

I begin to talk about Correggio's use of light and dark to highlight the central personas; but something makes me stop and look at Isis. Her face is ecstatic. Her eyes are shining and her moonface gleams. That's when I realise.

'You're pregnant,' I gasp.

'I wondered how long it would take you to catch on,' she laughs. 'Isn't it marvellous?'

'Marvellous,' I repeat, but all kinds of thoughts race through my mind. Will the foetus survive? If it does, will she be allowed to keep it? What mutations will it have? I also realise how I have underestimated Isis. I thought her interest in making new garments was purely aesthetic, to prettify herself. I was wrong. The gowns are maternity clothes, designed to accommodate the bump that contains her expected offspring. How perspicacious of Isis to turn to the Renaissance painters for inspiration.

'Give us a hug then, Ody,' she says, bringing me back to reality.

I put my arms round her and hold her close, but not too close. I don't want to hurt her precious cargo. She snuggles up and rests her head on my bony shoulder. A moment to cherish. I take a deep breath.

'Have you told anyone else about this?' I ask her.

'No. I thought it only fair to tell you first.'

We will have to decide what to do and who to tell. There's no way we can contact the prospective father. He's still missing and Durga has not been seen lately either.

We must find a doctor but I have the feeling we must proceed with caution.

I think of Penelope. She must have been pregnant before she left, but maybe didn't desert me voluntarily. Having a baby was rare even then. She might have been taken away to give birth in a controlled environment. Why wasn't I informed? Didn't she want me to know? Or was it someone in authority who refused to let me know? All these possibilities are buzzing around in my mind.

One comforting thought is that Penelope must have told her daughter about me. Otherwise how would she have known that I was her father?

As Isis stands here in my arms a great surge of emotion rushes through my entire body. If this is love, an emotion I haven't felt, or at least acknowledged, for years, it's a good feeling, but a terrifying one too. I find myself trembling.

Isis must feel it too, because she looks up at me, questioningly. 'You are pleased for me, Ody?'

'Pleased?' There's a lump in my throat that I'm trying hard to control. 'It's – wonderful.' I swallow several times. I'd like to tell her that I love her, but I can't do that. Not yet. She'd stick a finger in her throat and make vomiting noises. Or tell me to get over myself.

'I wonder what he's going to be like?' she asks. 'Beautiful of course – just like the child in that picture. Just imagine it, Ody. I'm going to have a son. Think of what we can teach him – how to walk and talk and feed himself. And you can teach him all about the past.'

I nod, too choked to speak. Something very special has happened. I want to laugh and cry at the same time. After all, it isn't a common occurrence in this day and age for a mutant humanoid to realise that he is going to be a grandfather.

Chapter Seventeen
Dreams and Schemes
(according to Heracles)

Sati lies back on her huge bunku, the oyster-coloured satin sheets smooth against her ivory thighs. She seems to be asleep. I zoom in for a close-up. God she's beautiful. For a moment I'm tempted to satisfy my growing erection with a bit of self-help, but, annoyed that the bitch still has power to arouse me, I minimise the screen and hone in on Compound 37.

There is Kali, looking more animated than I've seen her for a long time. She's speaking to someone on the intercomfone. I turn up the sound. This eavesdropping device I've installed is proving most useful. Hacker Heracles doesn't miss a trick.

'You bet I'm ready,' Kali says. 'Just say the word and I'll be there.'

Who's she talking to? I tune in and hear two other voices in the conference call. Durga and Jaga. I bring up the videolink and maximise the three screens. There they are in all their glory: golden Durga, red hair cascading way down way past her shoulders, charcoal eyes smouldering: blueblack Kali, fierce face surrounded by head-hugging plaits, Hugo's sleek body coiled round her neck: yellow Jaga, halo of straw-coloured hair sticking out like blades of wheat, green eyes gleaming. Three sister-wives engaged in plotting the overthrow of the fourth sister-wife now reclining so indolently on her day bunku.

'My warriors are on red alert,' says Durga. 'When I give the word, teleport yourselves to C98 and we will attack in force.'

'It's not necessary for me to come to your compound,' Jaga argues. 'I'll stay here in C55 and let you in.'

'Just do as I say,' Durga retorts. 'There can be only one leader in a battle and I'm the best qualified. I need you both here to detail you as to strategy and to fit you out with appropriate battle gear, weapons and chariots.'

It's Kali's turn to protest. 'Chariots? Is your plan to travel through the wilderness to Compound 55?'

'That's exactly what we are going to do.'

'Is it safe?'

'You don't think I'd undertake such a project if it wasn't? I've sent out several forays to investigate the contamination levels. They are now low enough to ignore.'

Jaga pouts her full red lips, as if she finds this statement difficult to believe. 'Then why are we still shut up in compounds?'

'When my – our – objectives have been reached, we will all live differently. Until that happens the compounds must remain and they must be run efficiently. That is why Sati must be eliminated and Kali's regime restored.'

'What do you mean, eliminated? Is Sati to be assassinated?' Jaga asks.

'To start with I'll imprison her, put her in a bare cell with no creature comforts, but in the long term it will be better to subject her to some intense brainwashing, reduce her sex-drive, make her into someone who could be useful to us.'

'You have the technology to do that?' Kali asks.

'Technology will come into it, but psychoanalysis will probably prove more effective.'

'Good luck with that,' Jaga says. 'Sati doesn't respond to the talking cure. I've tried it, believe you me.'

Durga shakes out her red mane. 'I'll be the judge of that. I have all the latest psychiatrists in Compound 98.'

'For when your warriors get war fatigue syndrome?' That's Jaga being nasty.

'Have they ever been to war or do they just play games?' Kali's turn to twist the knife.

Durga glowers. 'You don't know all my secrets.'

'Never mind about your secrets,' Jaga says, 'What I want to know is why do you think Kali should take over C55? What about me? I've worked hard to change things in that sectoid. It doesn't seem fair that Kali should be reinstated.'

'Just a minute,' Kali bursts out. 'As I remember it, Jaga, you turned traitor and joined Sati against me.'

'Ra made the decision for me to be co-leader. Not me.'

'You were only too happy to go along with it. I saw you waltzing off arm in arm with Sati.'

'Enough,' Durga snaps. 'No internal squabbling. We're all on the same side. Both of you need to trust my judgment.'

She narrows her eyes.

'You've done a reasonable job, Jaga, I'll grant you that, but I'm sure you'll agree there have been one or two fiascos during your time in C55 that you couldn't control. Turning the basement into a brothel, for example, not to mention the riot in the RR when the large screen was smashed to smithereens. It would be difficult for you to remain in C55 once Sati's gone. For one thing the workforce have split into two camps, those loyal to you and those, for whatever reason, loyal to Sati. In the past Kali was able to keep the workforce united and I believe she could do it again.'

'No trouble,' says Kali, 'I'll soon whip them into shape.'

'An unfortunate word "whip", Kali,' reprimands Durga. 'You should take a more conciliatory course. Have you learnt nothing from your time away from C55? You will find everything there very different now. The new facilities are in place and your colleagues are used to plenty of leisure time. This practice should continue. Under your guidance the workforce should be able to reach their targets while maintaining the better standard of life they've become accustomed to. That's one reason I want you to come to C98 – to see how we do things here. C98 is highly organised with the correct balance of work and leisure activities.'

'What about me?' Jaga complains. 'If Kali is to be chief administrator for C55, what am I going to do?'

Durga pauses. 'How would you like to be chief administrator of C98?'

'That's your position.'

'It is indeed, but I'm going to be very busy with military affairs for the next few months and I need you to manage things while I'm away.'

'So – it's only a temporary post.'

'Not necessarily. I can't reveal all my plans at the moment, but put it this way, I'm very ambitious.'

'What?' says Jaga. 'How much further up can you go?' She gives a little gasp. 'You're not thinking of making a play for Ra's job?'

'Ra is one of the aspects of this venture we need to discuss. For now, that is all I'm willing to say. I will keep you informed. Prepare yourselves both physically and mentally for the changes that are to come. Wait for the summons.'

I click off the three screens and think about what I've overheard. Durga is more devious than I'd thought. She's planning, not just the takeover of C55 but also, it seems, the replacement of Ra. That's my objective too, but she has an army to support her as well as her sister-wives. She intends to put them in key positions just as dictators of the past relied on members of their families to support them. Think

Muammar Ghadafi and Saddam Hussein. Pity I have no family.

It's the old question. Which is stronger – a leader backed by the military or one backed by intellect? If I'm to thwart Durga's plans and instigate mine I shall have to use my not inconsiderable brainpower and act quickly.

I wonder how much of the information I have learnt today I should report to Ra. By tapping this conference call I have proof of Durga's traitorous intentions, but little idea how or when she will act. If I tell Ra what I have discovered, it will demonstrate my loyalty and with Ra's backing I have more chance of counteracting her plans. Ra is in Hos-sat. There is little he can do from there apart from give orders. He has told me to give my findings directly to him and I can do that, of course, by intercom-net, but in his absence, should I share what I have discovered with Athene?

As if in answer to my question, there is a knock on the door. I sing out, 'Come in,' and in she comes, Athene, the ersatz goddess, her face as inscrutable as if carved out of marble. To my surprise, the marble cracks a little. She smiles at me.

'You look happy. Does that mean Ra's health is improving?'

'Not really. The news is he'll have to stay in Hos-sat for quite a bit longer.'

'What have you got to smile about then?'

'I've come to a decision.' She slips on to the shaper facing me. 'I think it's about time we stopped being in competition with each other and worked together.'

'What exactly has led you to that conclusion?'

'It was Ra's idea actually. In his absence he's made me chief administrator. I'm to use his office and his multi-compu – I now have the code key – and you are to report directly to me.'

That's why she's smiling. She's gloating. Why has Ra done

this? *I* am his second-in-command, not Athene. It should be me sitting in the main office.

I say as serenely as I can manage, 'Congratulations on your *temporary* promotion.' I tap my fingers on the desktop. 'I'm not sure about reporting to you. Ra specifically told me that I must report directly to him.'

'We're on the same side, Heracles.'

'Are we? Until Ra informs me directly, I shall keep to his original instructions.'

As if in answer, there is a click on the screen informing me that I am about to receive a personal inter-mail from Ra. I open it. It confirms what Athene has just told me. To all intents and purposes she is now my boss and I should share all my research with her. I don't tell her the contents of the personal inter-mail, but I'm aware that she knows. For a moment I wonder if she has sent it herself. Maybe it's not just Durga and myself who have aspirations to be CEO of Worldwideculture. Athene may be a contender too.

I lean forward and look her straight in the eye. 'How loyal are you to Ra?'

She doesn't blink. 'The real point is how loyal are you, Heracles?'

'I'm totally loyal,' I answer. 'You have failed to answer my question.'

'Because it doesn't need answering. OK, here is your answer: I have always given Ra one hundred percent of my time and effort and intend to do so in the future.'

'Even though he fired you and appointed me.'

'That's not what happened. Your appointment was my idea.'

'You really expect me to believe that?'

'Believe what you like. It's the truth.'

I sit back, cross my arms and think about what she said. I already know that Ra is a paraplegic and that's he's had a heart attack. Athene would have been aware of his poor health and my appointment could have been part of her plan for the future.

If indeed my being given this position was her idea, her intention must have been to groom me to be her number two when Ra stepped down because of ill health. She becomes CEO over my dead body, I think, but I'll play along for now.

She curls up in the shaper, waiting for me to react.

It won't hurt to show her my latest hacking effort, the conference call between three sister-wives of Shiva. I switch on the recording and watch her, carefully judging her reaction to Durga's schemes. Her first response is to sit up straight and open her eyes wide. 'You're able to eavesdrop on personal intercom-fone calls? That's really cool.'

'Child's play,' I yawn, stretching languidly, though it's a feat I'm proud to have achieved.

'You'll have to teach me a few tricks.'

I don't think so. I need to keep my expertise to myself or I'll be redundant. 'Don't you think you should stop admiring my compu skills and listen to what they're saying?'

She shrugs. 'I've heard it all before. They're always plotting. Attack C55, reinstate Kali, compensate Jaga by finding a token post for her, put Sati in solitary…. Am I right?'

I could switch it off now, but I want her to hear it to the end, to realise that I really have discovered something new and that Durga's ambitions are far from innocuous. I'm not disappointed. The end of the conference call provokes a frown on Athene's usually smooth forehead. She asks me to play the last few exchanges again and I note her complete concentration as she listens and watches the replay.

As it finishes, she gives a short laugh. 'Over-confident bitch,' she says. 'She's heading for a fall.'

She rises elegantly to her feet and offers me her hand.

'Good job, Heracles,' she says, 'you've done well,' and she glides to the door as elegantly as an old-time film star.

Over-confident bitch yourself, I think as she closes the door neatly behind her. *You're the one heading for a fall.*

Not more than a couple of days after this, I find what I'm looking for. The portal to Oasis. Up it comes and I maximise the screen to see the full image.

It's quite a place: green parks, wide avenues lined with mansions, immaculate gardens bursting with exotic flowers and public buildings that seem to be made entirely of glass. A city-paradise. A few people are walking about, but no cars, no transport of any kind as far as I can make out.

From what I've read, Oasis is the best of the satellites, the flagship, just as C99 is the flagship compound for mutant humanoids. Only completes live on these specially constructed satellites. There are about fifty to date, including Hos-sat and Pris-sat, but more can be built as needed. Each satellite houses human beings of the same nationality or at least those who speak the same language. There are several for English speakers, Oasis one of them.

The camera focuses on a group of small humans playing in the park and there under a tree sits a female with a pram. Children. So, the completes are still able to give birth. We are not. Or only rarely. When mutants of my generation die there will be no more of us. Have we been deliberately sterilised as the "final solution" to the mutant problem? If so, is there an antidote? I doubt I can find the answer to that, however much hacking I do. Even this superior machine is unlikely to reveal secrets of that nature. Mutant humanoids are not permitted to know too much.

What I need is a satellite of my own. Forget my previous plan of building new cities here on Earth. A brand new satellite in the sky will be better. The mutant humanoids were left on Earth to stagnate in these compounds while the uncontaminated were whisked off to live in a series of utopias. Bloody discrimination. Just because we have physical mutations doesn't make us less intelligent or less worthy of enjoying the same luxurious life-style as them. This prejudice has gone on long enough. I haven't got an army but I do have my wits. What Durga intends to do by force, I will achieve by negotiation.

Thor knocks on my door, a more tentative knock than usual. Even he has come to realise my importance in the hierarchy of Worldwideculture. I haven't much time for him any more. I'm focused on my future and any spare time I allow myself I spend with Athene, when she's not visiting Ra in Hos-sat. She's become more amenable and often suggests we dine together, sometimes in the intimacy of her cube. It's not a regular dormo-cube. It has a living area as well as a sleeping space. She calls it her aparto-cube and I suppose it is rather like the apartments in American filmograms. Her living-cube is furnished simply with a low table and several shapers, one of them a double, but we always sit in the singles, and I've never ventured into the dormo-space. I don't want to push my luck. I'm learning to control my urges. I'm no longer the impetuous, randy young mutant humanoid I used to be.

Another knock. I stand up, stride across the work-cube and open the door. Thor's grinning face greets me. 'Hungry?' he asks.

Aware that I've been neglecting him lately, I sling an arm loosely round his shoulders as we stride out in unison to the dino-cube. He's a good mate, the one humanoid here I can really trust. Worth keeping him sweet in case I need his assistance.

We collect our food packoids from the bar and choose a table in the corner. I think of the images I've just seen of Oasis and can't help contrasting the lightness of the glass-walled buildings there with the gloominess of this dark prison. The artificial pools of neo-lite here seem cold and harsh in contrast. Depressing.

I glance at Thor who is munching a huge sandwich in his lower mouth. I wonder how far I can trust him. How much should I tell him? Not much, I decide.

'How do you fancy an adventure?' I ask him at last.

His face lights up. 'Oh man, how can you ask such a thing? You know I'm with you whatever you decide to do.'

He tells me he's bored sitting at the compu all day and that it's no fun going sharking without me.

'A lot of the females have left and their replacements are not as hot as the others. There are one or two specials, but they're out of my league, if you know what I mean.' He touches me on the arm. 'But not out of yours. You should come to the disco-cube tonight. It won't take you long to fix yourself up.'

For a moment I'm tempted, but somehow it doesn't appeal any more. I've moved on. 'Can't, I'm afraid. I'm having dinner with Athene.' It's true, but why do I have to boast about it? A bit of the old Heracles swagger coming to the fore, I suppose.

He raises his eyebrows. 'Wow. You've made it then.'

'Not at all,' I tell him. 'Just business.'

'Oh yeah.'

He doesn't believe me and part of me – the reckless, arrogant part – is pleased about that.

Athene wanders in, nods at me, goes to the lunch-bar, takes her food packoid and sits down at a separate table.

'Have to go,' I say to Thor. 'Keep an eye on your personal intercom-mail. Read it, delete it and follow the instructions exactly.'

'Sure, Mr. Bond,' drawls Thor.

'Believe you me, James Bond is nothing compared to me,' I assure him.

He looks after me as I leave, grinning all over his face.

I touch Athene lightly on her shoulder as I pass, but don't speak to her. We're playing a cat-and-mouse game at the moment, but who is the cat and who the mouse?

I click on Oasis and see a huge Plaza. It begins to rain a little and all the humans run for shelter. They must be weaklings, not able to put up with a trickle of water. A sudden change. The rain comes down in force, huge sheets of the stuff, splashing over the ground. Brutal. No wonder they scuttle for shelter. They know how swiftly the weather can change. I make a mental note of that: useful information for a prospective space traveller.

My eye falls on a small figure in one of the shelters. I zoom in to take a closer look. There is no doubt about it. It's Mercury. Kali's suspicions are justified. Mercury vanished the day the complete in a suit came to talk to us. But why would he take Mercury, a mutant humanoid, to a satellite designed for completes? My first thought is to contact Kali to tell her that Mercury's safe but change my mind. She'll want to know where he is and there's no way I can tell her that. Not yet.

The rain stops and everyone comes out of the shelter. Mercury too. There is something odd about the way he moves. No, I've got that wrong. There is nothing odd about the way he moves, no little jumps, skips or jerks. He is walking the same way as everyone else. Either it isn't Mercury or he has learnt to control his movements. I zoom in again. I'm sure it's him. What a smart little mutant to learn to walk so that he can mix with the inhabitants of Planet Oasis! Mercury has few mutations. He does have extra large ears but I can't see them, his hair longer than it used to be. It would be more difficult for me to pass as a complete with my extra eye and three legs.

I think of that word "pass." I once saw a filmogram in which a lightly coloured female with a black mother decided to "pass" for white in order to get a white husband. It ended in tragedy when she gave birth to a black baby and her husband turned her and the baby out. It seems that Mercury is passing successfully as a complete. Good luck to him.

I zoom out to see where he's going. He walks under an arch with a sign over it: Oasis University.

He always was a clever little chap. Like me, he's a wizard on the compu. He must be studying at the uni. He winds his way smoothly through a throng of other students but doesn't stop to chat to any of them. He always was a loner. How useful it will be for me to have an accomplice on Oasis. Mercury will know how everything works, who's in charge, the right completes to talk to. We've never been close, but he's a good little man and I'm sure he feels the injustice of only allowing completes on the satellites and will help me to initiate change. If not, why is he there? I must contact him. I've tried before, sending out random messages, but he's never replied. I tap into the university compu system and try out various possible electro-addresses, mercury@unioasis. inc being the most obvious, and send a series of personal intercom-mails asking him to contact me. Should I send them or not? I don't want to do anything to compromise my proposed mission. We were never friends. I regret not being nicer to him at Headculturedome, but surely he wouldn't betray me, a fellow mutant humanoid. I make up my mind, click *SEND* and off it soars into the ether.

It takes me the rest of the afternoon to find the teleport co-ordinates from here to Oasis. At last I have them. Tomorrow, while Athene is visiting Ra on Hos-sat, I intend to make a little trip of my own.

Chapter Eighteen
Games People Play
(according to Heracles)

Dinner with Athene. She's going to cook for me, she says. I shave, shower, change my clothes and squirt some perfume behind my ears. One advantage of being on C99 is that there is plenty of everything: clothes, toiletries and food. Adjoining the RR are some outlets. I suppose you could call them shops except no money changes hands. We are free to take what we like. There is a bit of a scramble on the day new merchandise arrives and some good-natured squabbling about who saw a favoured item first, but no serious arguments. My latest acquisition, picked out today, is a two-piece blue jog-suit, which I believe accentuates the blue of my central eye. Athene beware. I'm irresistible.

She is waiting for me, dressed in a long white gown. A cover-up job but then she always dresses discreetly. She looks as beautiful and untouchable as ever. Dinner is simple, a selection of sweetmeats arranged with finesse on silver plates. We sit on our separate shapers and eat in silence for a while. I take a mouthful of cold Chablis.

Athene's cool grey eyes narrow. 'I see you've made contact with your old friend.'

For a moment I think she has discovered my personal intercom-mails to Mercury but as she continues speaking, I realise she's referring to Thor.

'He's a bad influence on you, takes you away from your work.'

'He's a good mate, helped me to settle in when I first came.' I pop another sweetmeat into my mouth and relish its sweet-sour taste.

'I noticed. Took you clubbing to meet females. Sharking I believe it's called. Is all that nonsense about to start up again? Is that what your reunion was about?'

'I had lunch with him today because he asked me. I've neglected him lately. I spend all my time working, as well you know.'

'So?'

'I'm a loyal humanoid. Once I have a friend I stand by him – or her. I feel I should see him sometimes if only for half an hour.'

Those cool grey eyes never leave my face. 'That's all there is to it?'

'That's all.' I can't resist adding, 'He did want me to go to the disco-cube tonight but I told him that was impossible, that I had a hot date.'

My eyes don't leave hers and finally hers are the ones that look away. She gives a little laugh. 'Is that what you think this is – a hot date?'

'Not at all. I told him that to get him off my back.' I pick up another sweetmeat but change my mind and put it down. It's delicious but I'm not hungry. 'What makes you think he's a bad influence? He seems harmless enough to me. A regular guy.'

She smiles. 'They're the worst. Still, it's up to you who you choose as friends.'

'Yes, it is.'

She stands up suddenly and holds out her hand. 'Come, I want to show you something.'

I'm not sure if she intends me to take her hand or not.

She reaches out and clasps my wrist, pulling me gently along behind her into the adjoining cube. I feel out of place, massive and clumsy, in the prettily decorated dormo-cube with flowered wallpaper and matching curtains around the double-bunku, a four-poster.

'Lie down,' she says.

I hesitate, unsure what she intends to do. If this is a seduction it's a strange one.

'On your back. That's right. Now – put your arms above your head and spread your legs wide.'

I grin and sit up.

'I said lie down. Do as I say.'

She takes a piece of silk and ties first one wrist, then the other, to the posts at the top corners of the bunku and binds my two outer ankles to the posts at the bottom. My middle ankle she ties to a horizontal pole in the middle. I allow her to do this without question.

What kind of sex game is this?

I think of the bondage porno sites that Jason and I used to giggle over as teenagers. We would jerk off together and see who could hold out the longest. The difference between those filmograms and this real life episode is that I am fully clothed and so is Athene. She tests the knots, making sure they are secure and that I cannot escape, presses a button and the top half of the bunku rises up to support my back, so that I'm in a sitting position.

'Is this some sort of sex game?' I ask.

She gives me a disdainful look. 'If you can't keep your mouth shut I shall have to gag you,' she says.

She turns to leave and it crosses my mind that she intends to leave me here, tied to her bunku, while she teleports herself to Hos-sat to see Ra or to somewhere more exotic. I wriggle a bit, but she's done a thorough job. The bonds stay in place.

She is back almost immediately without her robe. She seems to be wearing a tight-fitting leotard that covers not only her torso but also her legs and arms. It takes me a moment to realise that this is no leotard or body stocking. She is naked. Her body and limbs are covered with what I take to be tattoos. Whenever I've imagined her naked (quite often) she has been marble white all over, like a classical statue, but in reality only her face, neck and hands are white. Every other centimetre of her skin gleams with opaque, rich colours. That must be the reason she wears long dresses with a neckline almost up to her chin and long sleeves covering her wrists – to keep secret her richly decorated body. Is this body art the way she earns her creative points for Worldwideculture targets?

She stands at the foot of the bed, her back to me and, very slowly, revolves to face me. A spotlight directly above her increases in intensity to illuminate the intricate patterns that make up her body art: an exotic jungle of trees, plants, birds and animals. Incredible. A creative wonder.

As mystical music kicks in, Athene begins to move. Her lithe body twists and turns, flexibly, gracefully, her arms and legs bending and stretching in time to the music.

Now she's on the floor, curling herself into a leafy ball of undergrowth. Uncurling, tendrils reach out, sinuous, sensual, flowing and transform themselves into a tall willowy plant.

The pace of the music quickens and the jungle springs to life.

I no longer distinguish body from limbs, no longer aware that this dance is being performed by a humanoid. I see only the jungle and the jungle's story. The wind charges through the branches and thrashes its way through the leaves. The trunks of the trees creak and bow down, almost touching the ground. Jewel-coloured birds of turquoise, amethyst, ruby and jade, speed through a sky of midnight blue. Tigers with stripes of yellow, orange and burnt sienna, prowl through the undergrowth.

The music rises in pitch and volume. The storm breaks. Thunder growls, lightning cracks, the wind howls, twigs and greenery break up, whirl and spin in every direction. A tiger hurtles through the jungle, demented, parrots squawk and race ever upward, soar higher and higher, desperate. The racket of wind, rain and thunder swells, animals collide and crash into each other and birds screech, trapped in the topmost branches. A huge tree groans and uproots itself. The entire jungle crumples and collapses. Silence, darkness, oblivion.

Tears are streaming down my face. I have just witnessed a dance that showed me every curve of Athene's body, a dance that by all the usual rules and regulations that determine the susceptibility of the male body to the female should excite me sexually, but I know there will be no sex with Athene. The performance was not foreplay, not an aperitif, but the main course. Her body the vehicle for an exciting, unmatchable phenomenon: the depiction of the jungle storm. Forget sex. Forget ambition. Forget power. This is totally something else. The most exhilarating, mind-blowing experience of my life.

Athene stands before me, dressed once more in her white cover-all gown. She notes my tears and sees only too clearly my emotional response to her performance. There's no need for words. She starts to untie me. I remain inert on my back.

'Come,' she says. 'Let's go back to the living-cube and have a celebratory glass of champagne.'

We raise our glasses and drink to our future partnership, to our loyalty to each other, to Ra and to Worldwideculture itself. Athene leans her head back languidly on the shaper and closes her eyes in an expression of satisfied lassitude.

She believes she's got me now, that I'm in her power, that I'll always be loyal to her, no matter what.

She feels confident enough to leave me alone tomorrow while she visits Ra. She is quite sure I won't do anything foolish.

Why are females so gullible? They think that sex, or in this case an exotic dance, will bind us to them forever, when all it does is give us a momentary thrill. I think of the rumours that Athene is Ra's mistress. Is this dance the nature of the sex between them? I get a kick out of the idea that Athene has been unfaithful to him tonight – in her fashion. For a humanoid in a wheelchair this display might be sufficient – or at least better than nothing – but, fantastic as the experience is, it will never be enough for me. I may never have sex with her painted body, but there are plenty more females on offer. I think of the pledge I made to Thor not to be beguiled by one female again but to "love them and leave them". Nothing that has happened tonight has changed that resolve. For a moment or two I was bewitched, yes, but it was a temporary diversion. Nothing more. It won't take me long to get back on course.

Back in my office, I check the intercom-mails I sent to Mercury. They have all bounced back, unopened. It makes no difference. I'll find him.

The following morning, as soon as Athene has left to visit Ra. I summon Thor and we go to the teleport where I show him what to do. As soon as I've gone, he must cancel the co-ordinates on the coder machine so that no one will know where I am. He nods agreement. I've chosen well. He's a reliable accomplice. I tap in the numbers, take a deep breath and off I speed to Planet Oasis.

My head and body feel as if they are splitting into millions of particles, a quite terrifying sensation, much stronger than the other transportations from compound to compound. This time there is an impression of elevation accompanied by a whirring noise and I seem to be spinning, my body completely out of control. Not pleasant at all. When the whirring and spinning stops I can scarcely stand. I feel dizzy. Disoriented.

I must have arrived.

I take a quick look around but only have time to note that I'm in a kind of metal container before a stinging pain attacks my head. I fall to the ground and everything turns black.

When I come to, I find myself on the floor of a cube. No furniture in it – no shapers, bunkus or workstations. I stand up and note that one wall is transparent. I peer out through the glass but it's dark and I see nothing. I turn round and note that there are two doors, one on the right hand wall and one at the back. I turn the handle of the side door, but it's locked. The door on the back wall does open and reveals a lavat-cube. I go in, close the door, use the facilities and return to the main cube.

A prison cell, that's what it is. They must have shot me with a stun gun on arrival, hence the pain, captured me and locked me in here.

A light comes on above me, a very bright spotlight that hurts my eyes. Another light floods the corridor outside the transparent wall. Some completes appear, ambling along, jostling each other.

They stop outside my cube and stare at me. I stare back at them. They seem to be talking and laughing but I can't hear a thing through what must be toughened glass. I knock on it. They laugh their silent laughs and knock back – silent knocks, mocking me. They point at my three legs, my extra eye, my big square face and double over with laughter. I lift my hands and arms up in the air like a gorilla and roar at them. I beat my chest. If they want to laugh, I'll give them something to laugh about. They stretch their mouths into a monkey grin, put their hands on their heads and wriggle their fingers.

Think they can scare me? I start to walk about on all fours and bare my teeth. They copy me. That's when I realise how small these completes are. These are not adults but children. A taller complete arrives, their teacher perhaps. From the look on his face he's giving them a good telling off. Good. The group shambles off and I'm left in peace for a while.

I sit on the floor and think about the situation. I didn't come to Oasis to be shot, arrested and put on show like an animal in a zoo, but there's not much I can do about it.

Hours pass. Other visitors, young and old, troop by to gawp at me. I scream, bang on the glass and the side door, demand to be released but when I realise this has no effect, I give up. More people arrive and gawp at me. What kind of place is this? Why have I been put on show?

Some of the visitors are reasonably polite. Others less so. The polite ones point out my mutations and discuss them amongst themselves, some have the grace to look a little embarrassed. Others are less subtle. They pull faces and shout and try to provoke me to react. So I do, giving them as good as I get, make threatening gestures, some of them vulgar ones, screw up my three eyes, clench my fist and give the glass wall a mighty punch. They pretend to fall down and play dead, poking fun at me, or collapse laughing. I've become a freak show. It makes me angry that my adventure should come to this. I sit down and turn my back on the spectators, not giving them the satisfaction of responding to their taunts.

A hole in the side door opens and a packoid of food and a plastic bottle of water plops through and lands on the floor. I'm so hungry I snatch up the packoid, tear off the wrapper and stuff the sandwich into my mouth.

This action seems to attract some passing youngsters who stare at me. Feeding time at the zoo. I ignore them, finish the tasteless sandwich, throw the packaging on the floor, retrieve the bottle, which has rolled to the edge of the cell, unscrew the top and guzzle down every single drop of the water.

More time passes. More visitors arrive to stare and make remarks. The side door opens. Two completes enter, force my hands behind my back and handcuff my wrists. They bundle me out of the cell and take me to another cube with a wooden table and two chairs – not shapers – nothing comfortable about them. An interrogation room. One of the men, the bald, thin-lipped one, sits behind the table and gestures for me to sit on the other side, facing him. The other man, a huge bully type, stands behind me. I've seen enough filmograms to be wary of this man. He's the torturer, should torture be needed. As if to prove my theory, he moves forward, kneels down, ties my ankles to the chair legs and fixes my manacled wrists to the bars at the back of the chair.

The man behind the desk begins to ask me questions. What am I doing here? Who sent me? How did I find out about Oasis?

I tell him that I came because I felt like an adventure, that no one sent me. It was my own idea. The interrogator nods at the bully who promptly whacks me on the head with some sort of wooden club. I can't see it, but it hurts even my thick skull.

He asks me the same questions over and over again. I give him the same answers and am treated to a series of clouts round the head that I hope will not affect my ability to think clearly. When he asks me who told me about Oasis, I can't resist boasting. 'No one told me. I found out for myself by hacking into the auto-put.'

Baldie frowns and holds up a hand to stop the bully from whacking me again. 'Hacking, you say?'

'Yes. I'm the best hacker in my sectoid. The best in all the compounds.'

He thinks about that for a moment. 'Are you indeed? I'm afraid I'll have to detain you a little longer Mr – er – '

'Heracles. But really, if you must detain me, can't you keep me somewhere else? It's disgusting being in that cage having everyone staring at me as if I'm a freak in a circus or an animal in a zoo.'

Baldie pushes his thin lips together. 'I'm afraid you'll have to stay there for the time being, but I would like my colleague to meet you. We need to talk a little further about this – hacking – you've been doing.'

Shit. Damn. Fuck. I shouldn't have opened my big mouth. This tendency to brag will be my downfall.

Back in my cage, I spend another few hours as a zoo exhibit, before being taken to the interrogation room again. The same bully stands behind me but two men sit behind the table, Baldie and someone who is obviously a complete of a higher grade. His black hair is sleeked back from a high forehead. The nails on his long fingers are tapered to needle-thin points. He raises a hand to stop the bully from strapping my ankles to the chair and orders him, in a voice as suave as polished mahogany, to undo the handcuffs.

'Good morning, Heracles,' he says in a soft but deadly voice. 'Let me introduce myself. I am Orlando Wolfe, the Minister for Foreign Affairs in the Symposium of Planet Oasis.' I store up this information for future reference. He's clearly a high-ranking politician and could prove a useful contact. He asks me what I know of Oasis.

'Only what I've seen on the internet.'

'And what is that?'

'Green parks, plants, trees, a sparkling lake and fantastic

buildings that gleam in the sunlight. Do you wonder I long to see more of this wonderful place?'

'Impossible – without the proper permit.'

I decide to take a chance. 'This permit – how can I obtain it?'

'You can't – unless you are invited by the Symposium.'

I push my luck. 'Could you organise an invitation for me?'

His lips push themselves together in what I take to be a sarcastic smile. 'Why the hell should I do that?'

I take a deep breath. 'From what I've seen Oasis is a perfect place, a Utopia. I have dreams of building such a city myself one day.'

He looks down at his pointy nails, considering this. 'It's good for a young man – human or mutant humanoid – to have ambition.' He looks directly into my central eye. 'Where would this proposed city be built? On Earth?'

'That's one possibility.'

'And the other?'

'On a satellite designated for mutant humanoids.'

He gives a short laugh. 'You've got a lot of cheek I'll give you that. Are you an architect?'

'No, I'm an ideas man. But we do have architects and….' I hesitate, '…I thought you completes might give us the benefit of your experience to help me achieve this objective.'

'Did you now. Are you rich? It takes money to build a city in the sky.'

'We don't use money in the compounds.'

'Because we supply you with all your needs.'

'Maybe you wouldn't have to do that if we had our own cities. We could enter the monetary system ourselves and be self-sufficient.'

He taps his pointy nails on the table. 'I understand there's some restlessness in the sectoids.' Orlando Wolfe narrows his eyes. 'Especially now some of you have found out about the satellites. You envy us our lifestyle and want it for yourselves.'

'Of course we do!' I consider what to say next, how far to push it but this may be my only chance to make an ally. 'There are those who think war is the answer.'

'Ah yes, Durga and her golden warriors.'

I'm a little taken aback that he knows about the warriors.

'I don't agree with her,' I assure him. War never solves anything.' I lean forward and sense the bully getting ready to grab me. 'If Oasis could help us establish our own satellite, that restlessness would not be directed against you. We would have a new project to work on and….'

'And live happily ever after in a utopia of your own.'

I risk a grin. 'That's about it. Yes.'

'Are you speaking on behalf of a particular sectoid?'

'No. This is solely my idea. But I'm sure there are lots of humanoids – everyone really – who would support the plan, especially if we had the backing of Oasis. Living in compounds is not all it's cracked up to be.'

'Not ideal, no, I understand that. What's wrong with building new cities on Earth?'

'As far as I know it's still contaminated.'

'I'm sure with a little help from us that problem could be rectified. Would you be happy to build your cities there on Earth – if it were safe to do so?'

I think about that. 'It's a possible solution but I think a satellite….'

'The satellites, Heracles – that is your name? Right. The satellites are for completes.'

And that, it seems, is that.

He gets up ready to leave but I have to try to stop him. This is the only chance I may have to persuade him.

'If that is the case, why is there a mutant humanoid living here on Oasis now?'

He turns, walks slowly back to his chair and sits down. 'A mutant humanoid living here on Oasis, you say?'

He didn't know. I feel as if I'm betraying little Mercury but I can't backtrack now. 'I saw him on my screen, in the Oasis portal, walking in the park.'

'Where exactly?'

'Near the university.'

'How mutant is he?'

That's an insulting question but I answer it all the same. 'His mutations are not obvious. He looks like a complete.'

'How do you know he's a mutant?'

'I know him. I recognised him.'

'What's his name?'

I hesitate. How can I possibly answer that question?

He stares at me, stands up, walks up to me, puts his face near mine. His breath smells. He had garlic for lunch.

'Tell you what I'll do. You return to your cell now and the guard will provide you with an electro-pad. You write down everything you know about this mutant humanoid, including his name. If I'm satisfied with the information you give me, I'll think about releasing you and allowing you to return to Earth.'

Chapter Nineteen
Museum Pieces
(according to Michael)

Jonathan pops his head round the edge of my compu-cube and asks me if I fancy a break. 'All work and no play make Michael a dull boy,' he tells me.

'You think I'm dull?'

'Not at all,' he grins, 'but you could lighten up a bit. There's more to life than studying.'

'You're a fine one to talk,' I say.

Jonathan Dowell is a fellow student, a diligent worker, almost as keen on his studies as I am. He works in the next compu-cube to mine and we attend one or two of the same lectures. He's a lanky fellow, as tall as I am short, and has wispy fair hair, which he never bothers to cut. It's continually flicking over his eyes and he's continually trying to push it away, a habit I find both irritating and endearing. My hair is longer now too, a rebellion against convention, perhaps.

Or maybe I'm just copying my new friend. For that's what Jonathan has become. For the first time in my life I have a friend. Apart from Isis, but that was different. We weren't on the same wavelength, whereas Jonathan and I are incredibly in tune with each other. Most of the time anyway. Wow, look at those mixed metaphors! A good example of what I mean, actually. Isis wouldn't have a clue what I'm talking about. She wouldn't know a metaphor from a metacarpal. Jonathan would.

We must look odd together as we roam the streets, Jonathan stooping a little to speak and listen to me, me looking up at him. I'm about half his height.

'How did you manage to grow so tall?' I ask him.

'How did you manage to stay so short?' he asks me.

We thrive on teasing each other.

He believes what I tell him about my past, that my parents separated years ago and that my mother brought me up on another satellite until her premature death when my father brought me here to join his new family. It's the story I always tell and no one has ever questioned its validity.

Having been born here, it's logical that Jonathan is much more knowledgeable than I am about what goes on in Oasis. He takes pleasure in showing me around and he's good at explaining how things work. He's a good teacher and that's exactly what he wants to be when he finishes university: a teacher.

We share a passion for reading. I belong to the university library, of course, but Jonathan introduces me to the city library and endorses my membership. How thrilling it is to find, not just e-books, but real books made of paper with cardboard covers. I love the feel and smell of them. Some of them are very old. The knowledge that other humans have held and read the same book, curled up in a shaper like me, is a comforting thought. Good too that I've met someone who feels the same way about books, reading and compus as I do. We talk non-stop about our courses and the books we read. Intrigued by the theories of Freud, Jung and Lacan, we indulge in psychological analyses of the novels and have heated discussions about leaders of the past: Mao, Napoleon, Hitler, Mandela and Assad. We're interested in the machinations of our politicians in the Symposium: sleazy

Orlando Wolfe, the Foreign Minister, misguided Harold Smythe in charge of education and pompous James Allen at the Home Office. (Adjectives we conceived to describe them, I should point out.). Jonathan thinks it's cool that my father is the Minister of Culture. We're both lefties, intent on improving the world.

It's in the spirit of progress that Jonathan takes me to the area where the underprivileged people live. It's not a shantytown or a slum but is comprised of row upon row of identical terraced houses.

'Cheap to build and maintain,' Jonathan informs me. 'Those who have failed in their careers and lost their jobs have been given these houses by the more successful people – such as our parents. Amazingly philanthropic, don't you think?'

'How does the system work?'

'Those who have done well try to help those who have failed by providing basic living conditions – houses, food and clothing – to give them a kick start to help them try again. They even help them find jobs. It's called The Oasis Social Project.'

It's a rather bleak place with none of the style and opulence of our part of the city.

The streets are nearly empty. A few older people peer out of the windows and some young people lounge about on the pavements, smoking and playing some sort of game with cards and dice.

A girl in a sky-blue dress is trying out a few dance steps with an elegant nonchalance that I find fascinating. I stop to watch her and she smiles at me. There are dimples in her cheeks and her eyes match the blue of her dress. I can't stop looking at her. She's the most exquisite creature I've ever seen. I'd like to talk to her but Jonathan pulls at my arm, keen to move on.

'Come on,' Jonathan whispers, pulling my arm. 'It doesn't do to loiter in this part of town.'

'I wonder who she is,' I say as he continues pulling me along. 'Hang on a minute, I'd like to talk to her.'

He starts taunting me, saying I'm in love with her or some such crap. I feel myself blushing and allow myself to be hustled away.

'The Oasis Social Project is a good idea, Michael,' Father says when I tell him about our visit. He sits in the salon after dinner, his long legs stretched out in front of him. 'But it doesn't always work. Some of the people re-housed there take advantage of the situation. They'd rather live off us than work themselves. Some are just plain lazy. Others start to look for an easy way to make money without declaring it. However hard we try to make a perfect society there are always people who will find a way to buck the system. There are some rough types there. Better for you not to venture into that area again.'

Father is over-protective of me, as usual, but I know I will go back. Alone. I have to get to know the blue-eyed girl.

I respect Father and Stella, but often these evening sessions after the children have gone to bed lead to heated discussions about my continued interest in the compounds on Earth. Since those early visits to Stella's study, she has never invited me in there again. I've tried to discover for myself what is going on in the various sectoids, but Worldwideculture.inc is a private site and Stella refuses to give me the code.

Father promised me unlimited access to the world-wide-web but, in this case, he supports Stella and obstructs my access. It's censorship. There's no other word for it.

I understand their reasons: Father and Stella want me to be fully integrated in my new life and not to look back. I try to make them see that it is not natural for me to dismiss my past, that my past is an important part of me.

I feel, too, that I have much to offer my fellow mutant humanoids by being instrumental in improving the conditions under which they live. I'd like to work alongside Stella to contribute to these ideas, but she doesn't appear to want my help. The truth is I was too outspoken during those early sessions with her. I shouldn't have lost my temper; but her belief that the creative targets give a focus to the lives of the mutant humanoids makes me furious. I believe this insistence on meaningless targets is a patronising method of control. I know I should be more tactful and keep my opinions to myself, but I know more about life in the compounds than Stella does. Or Father or any other complete for that matter. And I'm not afraid to say so.

When Stuart and Bella have gone to bed the conversation between us three adult members of the family all too often reverts to the same subject.

'If I am to be a liaison officer between the sectoids and Oasis, I must keep up to date with what is going on,' I protest.

'Just concentrate on your studies at the moment,' Father advises. 'When you graduate you may decide you are better suited for a different career.'

'You promised me that job when I agreed to come here.'

'Things change, Michael. We will review the situation when you've finished your studies. At the moment, it's important to keep an open mind and become fully integrated with life on Oasis so you can look at life in the compounds from a different perspective.'

From his perspective, he means, from the viewpoint of completes. There is still a lot of the mutant in me. He's lived his entire life as a complete. For me the period is much shorter: a matter of months. I can't help thinking that to be a good liaison officer it is important to see both sides in any dispute, but Father only wants me to see things from his side.

What does he mean by saying that I may decide I'm "better suited" for a different career? What is he afraid of? That I will be biased in favour of the mutant humanoids? It's true that I will listen sympathetically to any ideas they put forward and give them a fair hearing. Who else on Oasis could promise to do that?

Sometimes I think Father's fear of people finding out about my past makes him try to control my life as surely as Stella tries to control the lives of the mutant humanoids in the compounds.

When Jonathan suggests a trip to the museum, I agree straightaway. I've been meaning to visit it for ages but somehow or other haven't got round to it. The museum is an imposing building in white marble, the entrance seemingly supported by slender fluted columns in the Corinthian style with ornate capitals of acanthus leaves and scrolls.

As we enter, I am overwhelmed by the size of the interior, its height, its width, the skylights, the spacious galleries and the way the paintings, statues and artefacts of all kinds are arranged both logically and aesthetically. How Odysseus would love this place. I flit about from one room to another, gasping at the use of light in the portraits by Rembrandt, the subtle use of *sfumato* in Leonardo da Vinci's paintings, the elegance of the Art Nouveau furniture and the delicacy of filigree jewellery. I am drawn into a room where a reconstruction of ancient Babylon makes me hold my breath in awe. This imposing piece must have come from the Pergamon museum in Berlin. The cobalt blue walls with its line of huge lions that form the approach to the palace are amazing. Mind-blowing stuff.

Jonathan is at my heels. 'Come on, Michael. You can

come back here any time. Let's find the new exhibits that everyone's talking about.'

I'm in a daze. The exhibits I've seen already are quite enough for me. 'What new exhibits?'

'Why, the mutants, of course.'

I pull up short. 'Mutants? What do you mean?'

'You really don't know? Oh, have you got a treat in store. Come on, we'll try to get near enough to see the golden warriors first. Bound to be crowded though.'

I can't move. It's as if my feet are stuck to the floor. 'They have statues of mutants?'

'Not statues, no. Like everything else here, these are originals. Genuine mutant humanoids.'

I can't believe what he is saying. 'Dead ones?'

'Good Lord no, that would be totally gross. They're very much alive. Come on. Don't you want to see them?'

My feet feel like dead weights but I manage to lift them off the ground and follow him as he moves purposefully through the galleries to a special exhibition hall at the back.

There are a lot of people here, as Jonathan said there would be. Being short, I can't see much at first. I peep through the gaps between the bodies in front of me. Encased in a huge box, with glass at the front, a group of golden warriors is marching up and down as if on parade. I've heard of them, of course. They come from C98, Durga's compound, but I've never seen them.

A stir of excitement from the spectators. 'Look, that one has two heads!'

'And that one three eyes. One in the centre of his forehead. See it?'

'Just look at that one on the left. He's got three legs. Yes, really, three legs! Can you believe it?'

My hand flies to my throat. I think I'm going to be sick. These beautiful warriors have been put on show like animals at a zoo. It's obscene. A gap in the bodies as some people leave, Jonathan gives me a little shove and there I am at the front with a good view of these beautiful mutant humanoids: Durga's legendary golden warriors. There are ten of them. They march proudly, heads held high, circling, splitting into two groups, circling again and joining up in one solid formation, stepping out in unison, always impeccably in unison, as if putting on a parade was the most important thing in the world. Their faces are expressionless as if it is beneath them to show any emotion in front of these crass so-called completes who gawp at them and point out their mutations.

I'm proud of their resilience, of their dignity and of the way they are determined to keep fit, ready for the moment when they will fight again.

After a few minutes of marching they split up into pairs, take up some foils stored at the side of the glass box and begin to spar with each other. They take it seriously, competing to see who can make the most hits.

They act like automatons but these are no robots. Now and again a look of frustration passes over a warrior's face as he fails to hit his target and I can see the sweat from their exertions rolling down their cheeks.

I could stand here all day admiring them, but the jeers and catcalls from the crowd at my side make it impossible. I don't want to be associated with this vulgarity.

I will come back another time when it's less crowded and try to make contact with the warriors.

A burly man next to me yells, 'Fucking mutants! You think you're so fucking clever with your fancy marching, but what good does it do you, stuck in here?'

This offensive remark creates a huge guffaw and even applause from one or two of the spectators but no response at all from the warriors. I don't think they can hear the comments through the toughened glass. I hope not, but I can stand it no longer.

I turn and push my way through the *voyeurs* and dash through the main galleries without looking at a single painting or artefact. I'm in such a hurry to escape that I start to revert to my previous little skips and jerks, darts and flits, until I realise people are staring at me. I'd better be careful or I could end up an exhibit in a glass cage too.

I slow down a little and try to "walk like a man." I manage to control my movements and arrive back at the entrance hall without mishap, march down the steps to the Plaza, not caring if Jonathan is following me or not. I pace round the square, trying to think about what I have seen but it's unthinkable.

I'm so angry now I want to throw rocks and smash windows, scream, shout and lash out at these completes who think themselves so superior. They consider themselves civilised, but civilised people don't kidnap other humanoids, lock them up in glass cages and put them on public display. I'm ashamed to think that I have opted to be of the same species as such brutes. I want my stunted wings back and my over-sized ears. I want my integrity. I don't want to become like them – selfish, unfeeling and cruel.

The citizens of Planet Oasis have not only looted the best artefacts from collections and galleries all over the world, but have captured live mutant humanoids as exhibits too. It's sickening.

In the charter of the Symposium of Oasis, there is a whole chapter on human rights. Father told me about it.

My father prides himself on his humanitarian beliefs, and his compassion for underdogs. He professes to believe in egalitarianism and decries unfair treatment of anyone of whatever race or creed.

But he must know about this abuse of human rights. If

he knows, it means he condones this treatment of mutant humanoids and, if so, how can I possibly go on living under his roof?

The more I find out about this self-professed utopia called Oasis, the angrier I seem to become.

I sit down on the bench in the middle of the Plaza, put my head in my arms and weep for the fate of Durga's warriors, trapped in a glass box, reduced to a tourist attraction. It's a travesty. I weep for myself too, for another travesty, my transformation from mutant humanoid to human being.

It's in that position, on that bench, that Jonathan finds me a few minutes later. 'Michael, what happened? Whatever made you dash off like that?'

I stare at him. This is my mate, Jonathan. We have talked about so many things in the last month or so and are generally of the same mind. How can he not understand why I'm so upset? I thought he and I were on the same page. Another metaphor. Obviously not.

He sits down beside me. 'You found it disturbing?'

'That's putting it mildly. How can this "perfect society" treat people like that?'

He looks at me questioningly. 'They're not human beings, Michael. They're not like us.'

'They are. They are. They have the same sensibilities as we do.'

He looks at me and screws up his eyes. 'How do you know that?'

'I just do. What gives us the right to treat them like freaks? We call ourselves civilised human beings but we've learnt nothing.'

He thinks about that for a moment. 'Would you rather they were sent to Pris-sat with the other criminals?'

'They're not criminals!'

'What would you call them then? Terrorists?'

I'm quiet for a moment. I've obviously missed something.

'What would you call an army that teleports itself to Planet Oasis with the express intention of attacking us? If not criminals?'

I think about this. If the warriors were arrested on arrival, this puts a slightly different complexion on the matter, but it still doesn't justify their treatment.

Why would Durga send ten warriors to attack an entire city-state? The answer must be that she didn't. This was the advance party, meant to demonstrate her power. A kind of warning shot. She knew Oasis wouldn't destroy them. Such an action would have provoked a real attack. But I'm sure she hadn't imagined that they would have been put on show to be ridiculed.

'What exactly happened?' I ask Jonathan.

'What always happens when uninvited guests try to enter our sat.' He looks at me oddly. 'How come you don't know?'

'Oh you know me, I'm so immersed in my studies I rarely read the daily bulletin.'

'Everyone's been talking about it in the common room.'

'You know I don't go in there much.' He's looking at me strangely so I add, 'I don't know any students, apart from you. I've never bothered to get to know them.'

He gives me a little punch on the shoulder. 'Nerdy,' he says and laughs, and the tension between us eases a little. 'OK. Want me to fill you in?'

I nod. 'Please.'

He flicks his hair out of his eyes and begins. 'They just turned up in the teleport, with no permit. Anyone can teleport themselves here as long as they have the correct code. These warriors weren't expected, so as always happens – I expect you have a similar system on the sat you came from – they were shot on arrival. Don't look so shocked, Michael. There are auto-stun-guns set in the walls of the teleport set to go off when uninvited visitors appear. They undergo what we call a "little death" which lasts for about twenty-four hours. When they wake up they're questioned about their motives in coming here. During the last few months there have been quite a few illegal visitors, some of them mutant humanoids. How mutants find out about the existence of the satellites we don't know. They do have computers on Earth but with very limited access. I suppose there's always some clever dick able to hack in, find out about us and break the code. Some of these visitors are just tourists, curious to know what life is like here.'

'What happens to them?'

'We bounce them straight back to where they came from.'

'They didn't do that with the warriors.'

'No. According to rumour, these warriors were so well-trained, they refused to say a word during the interrogation no matter what methods were used to encourage them to talk – if you get my meaning.'

'Are you saying they were tortured?' I'm horrified.

'Oh Michael, you should see your face.' He gives me another friendly punch. 'The police have their own methods of dealing with these situations. We don't call it torture. We call it protecting our satellite from terrorists.'

I must have turned very pale because Jonathan says, 'Are you all right, old chap? Shall we go for a caffeine intake or something?'

I shake my head. 'No thanks. I'm fine. So – they don't know why the warriors are here?'

'Nope. Not yet. Dressed up like that they're not innocent tourists, for sure.'

'But why put them in the museum?'

Jonathan shrugs. 'They do that sometimes – especially with mutants. They hold them for a while. If they find incriminating evidence against them they're sent to the Pris-sat – there's a special section for the re-education of mutant humanoids. If no evidence is found – it's back to the teleport and return to sender.'

'That doesn't explain why they're in the museum.'

Jonathan looks a bit uncomfortable and shrugs his shoulders again. 'As far as I can make out, the objective is the same as for other items in the museum. To educate the public. We've all heard about the mutant humanoids living in compounds on Earth and, rather than lock them up in cells at the police station, we give completes the chance to see them for themselves – ourselves.'

'That crowd today didn't come to be educated. They came to mock humanoids less fortunate than themselves. You can't approve of that.'

'I certainly don't. The abuse and the language used was the height of ignorance. Those people should have been removed by the warders.'

'Yes, they should, but they weren't. There wasn't a warder in sight.'

'Don't get angry with me, Michael. I agree with you. Their behaviour was disgusting. The trouble is, there was such hype about the ten golden warriors that people who don't normally go to museums came to look at them. Uneducated people.'

'The warriors shouldn't have been put on show like that in the first place. It encourages people to think of mutant humanoids as freaks.'

'I entirely agree with you, Michael,' he assures me, but there is something about his manner that tells me he's not completely comfortable with my outburst.

He studies his hands for a moment and then adds, 'I just wondered if there is some special reason you feel so strongly about this.'

He knows about me. Or at least suspects. He's been my

teacher in our trips around the city and is aware how little I know about Oasis. No wonder he's suspicious. I'm not sure what to do and am tempted to come clean and tell him the truth, but that's not possible. It's not just my secret. Father, Stella, the doctors, the nurses and the therapists are all involved.

'Jonathan,' I say, turning to him and looking him straight in the eye. 'Can you keep a secret?'

He nods, anxious to hear the confession that he is sure is coming.

'It's not general knowledge, you understand, and if I hear gossip about this I will know it has come from you.'

'Michael, you can trust me not to tell a soul.'

So there, on that bench in the Plaza in front of the marble-fronted museum, I tell Jonathan that Stella Jameson, my stepmother, is the controller of Worldwidecuture.inc, an organisation that has been instrumental in creating a better standard of life for mutant humanoids in the compounds.

It may not have been the news he was expecting, but he's impressed. 'Wow! So that's how you know so much about them.'

'Stella has a multi-screened computer and can watch everything that happens on Earth. I've seen inside the compounds, Jonathan, watched the mutants at work and at play. Apart from their physical differences, mutant humanoids are just like us, with the same variety of human characteristics, good and bad. They have – how can I put it – the same sense of self as we have. That's why I was so angry and upset about what I saw this afternoon.'

As we walk back to uni together, Jonathan asks me lots of questions and I try to answer them as truthfully as I can. Before we part to go back to our compu-cubes, I tell him that, like him, I have an idea of what I to be when I graduate.

'You are passionate about being a teacher. I want to be

some sort of liaison officer between Earth and the satellites. I want to improve conditions for the mutant humanoids and make sure that we all – completes and mutants alike – learn to treat each other with respect.'

He gives me a punch on the shoulder. 'Good thinking, Michael,' he says, but he gives me an odd sideways look as if he thinks I'm a little crazy.

Once back at my computer, my ideals become grounded in practicalities. I make a list of things to do. I intend to pay another visit to the museum later to see if there are any other captives on show. I need to know the extent of the problem before tackling it. My other task involves something I've resisted doing before. I must become a hacker. If Heracles can do it, I'm sure I can. I'm not a deceitful person, but Father has censored my computers after promising me unlimited access. I must keep up to date with what is going on in the compounds before I can hope to negotiate the release of the warriors. Because that is what this first year university student, Michael Court, intends to do. That is my justification for the illegal action I am about to undertake: hacking into the Worldwideculture.inc website.

A few hours' work and I've managed it and can open the portals of each compound. I click on the portal for C98, Durga's compound, and see golden warriors at the shooting range, wrestling and practising archery. Others sit at computers playing war-games. I guide the camera to other areas in the compound. There is Odysseus in the histo-lab sorting through some papers. If only he could see the collections of artefacts we have in Oasis museum, how excited he would be. And there's Isis, sewing. She's looking well but has certainly put on some weight. I'm pleased to notice that she looks happy enough. I swing the integral camera round to explore every corner of the compound, the dino-cube, the RR, the compu-centre and Durga's private office.

Of Durga herself there is no sign.

I glance at the time. If I want to go back to the museum this evening to see if there are any more mutant exhibits, I must go now before it closes. I log off my compu and dash straight to the special exhibition hall where I saw the warriors. No crowds here now. I am the only visitor. A guard stands near the entrance to this section. Where was he this afternoon when he was needed? The warriors are still there, a few still sparring with foils, others practising their stance with bows and arrows but most are resting. A small group sit on the floor playing a game with dice. They take no notice of me as I pass. Why should they? They're used to being looked at.

An adjacent box contains two more mutant humanoids, one male, the other female, leaning against each other dozing. I've never seen them before.

In the next box a huge three-legged mutant humanoid is loping up and down, shoulders slumped. He turns towards me and I see his big, square face almost puce with fury, his extra eye flashing in the middle of his forehead. He stops pacing and peers at me through the glass. It doesn't take me long to recognise him. Or him me. He thumps on the glass and yells. I can't hear him. As I suspected, the glass is soundproof, but I can make out the word he is forming. My name. Or rather my ex-name. Mercury. 'Mercury!' he mouths over and over again, in long silent wails of anguish.

The warder has followed me and tells me it is time to leave, that the museum is about to close. I try to signal to Heracles that I'll try to help him and that I'll come back tomorrow, but he's frantic, begs me not to desert him. Tears roll down his massive cheeks. I can't help comparing his lack of control with the quiet dignity of the warriors. To be fair, the warriors have each other for support and Heracles is alone. He must be terrified.

But what's he doing here? Why has he come to Oasis? A dreadful thought occurs to me. Heracles is a hacker. Has he found out I am here and come looking for me? On Kali's behalf, perhaps?

He thumps on the window, mouthing that horrendous silent yell, 'Mercury, Mercury!' in a desperate bid to keep me from leaving.

I turn my back on him and rush out, pushing past the warden, my mind in turmoil.

Heracles and I have never been friendly. In a way we were rivals for Kali's affection – or at least for her attention. His behaviour at Headculturedome made me distrust him and at C55 there was some sort of problem between him and Isis. I don't know the details but I know he made her unhappy. The thing is I don't like him at all. I consider him arrogant and ruthless.

But he's a fellow mutant humanoid and, whatever he's done, he doesn't deserve to be banged up and put on show like this. I have to try to help him.

Chapter Twenty
Murder and Mayhem
(according to Michael)

I storm into Home-Court-Jameson. Father and Stella are in the kitchen. He's cutting up some meat and she's chopping vegetables.

'What's the matter, Michael?' Stella asks, her voice as serene as a cat's purr. Her red manicured nails stretched over the handle of the knife remind me of cat's claws.

I come straight to the point. 'I've been to the museum and seen the live exhibits. It's absolutely disgusting putting them on show like that.'

'Ah, I see,' says Father. He and Stella exchange a look. 'No wonder you're upset.'

'Upset doesn't begin to describe how I feel. It makes me sick to think that the Symposium of Oasis condones such treatment. What about human rights? What about respect, what about compassion? What about....'

'It's all right, Michael, we understand your response and agree that is wrong to put humanoids on view like that but....'

'How can there be any buts? You are the Minister of Culture and you should not allow such a thing to take place.'

'Sit down, Michael. I'll make you a cup of mint tea,' Stella says.

I ignore her. Father puts down the cleaver and gives me a weary smile. 'You credit me with too much influence,

Michael. Sometimes, however much I object to something – and I assure you I do object very strongly to this particular initiative – I end up on the losing side.'

'How can you stand there and call such a travesty of justice an initiative? Father, it has to stop. Tell him, Stella, explain to him that mutant humanoids are real people and cannot be treated like artefacts in a museum.'

'I don't need to tell him. Your father already knows.' Stella lays her hand on Father's shoulder.

'What I object to is that you didn't tell me about it, that I had to find out for myself. That hurts.'

'We didn't tell you because we knew it would distress you,' says Stella. 'We try to protect you from the knowledge of certain – unsavoury aspects of life.'

'I don't want to be protected.'

Father sits down at the kitchen table and motions for me to sit too, but I'm far too angry. I continue to pace about.

Father clears his throat. 'Let me explain how Oasis is governed. It's a democracy. The public elect the Symposium. The ministers are elected internally. We have no Prime Minister and no Cabinet. It's non-hierarchical. Everyone is allowed to express an opinion on any issue and then we vote on it. One vote per person. That's how our policy is shaped. Sometimes we disagree with the result of the vote, but we are bound to accept it.'

'Sounds to me as if there are some very nasty people in your Symposium. How can they justify putting mutant humanoids on display? You should get rid of these perverts.'

'It's not easy to get rid of powerful politicians, Michael. You are young. You don't understand.'

Why is it that older people invariably accuse the young of not understanding and ridicule them for being idealistic?

'I understand only too well,' I tell him. 'One of the subjects I'm studying at uni is history. The ruthless quest for power has been the downfall of many societies. I know that. But we have to fight this, Father, not buckle under and accept such things.'

A little smile plays round Father's lips. 'Well said, my son. It's good to know you care, but you have to realise that the world cannot change overnight.'

'We can make a start, Father. We can start by reversing this travesty of human rights that is taking place in the museum.'

'What is it you think I can do, Michael?'

'For a start you can use your influence to let me talk to one of the imprisoned mutant humanoids. I know him, Father. He came with Kali and me from C55 to Headculturedome and now he's done something stupid, come here uninvited and landed up as an exhibit in the museum. His name is Heracles.'

'This is all about Kali, isn't it?' Stella shakes her head. Her mouth turns down at the corners. For a moment she looks quite ugly. 'You're still looking back, thinking about her.'

'Of course I want to know about Kali. She was my mother for sixteen years. It's natural I want to know how she's getting on. It would make it easier if you gave me the code to the website.'

And there we are. Back to the same old argument. That's good in a way, because now they will have no reason to suspect that I've hacked into Worldwideculture.inc. I'm as devious and corrupt as some of the politicians in the Symposium.

Father lifts a hand to stop this diversion. 'This – Heracles. You say he's in the museum? You recognised him?'

I nod.

'Did he see you?'

'He saw me all right, banged on the glass, called out my name – Mercury, not Michael of course – and begged me to help him. Not that I could hear him through the toughened glass, but it wasn't difficult to lip-read. Father, let me speak to him. I stand more chance than anyone else of finding out why Heracles is here.'

'Leave it with me. I'll see what I can do.'

'Tomorrow. I promised him I'd talk to him tomorrow.'

'I'll make a few phone calls now, see what I can arrange.'

He looks genuinely worried as he goes to his study to start phoning, but I can't help feeling that his main concern is not the caging of mutant humanoid exhibits but the fact that someone could find out that his son is – or was – a mutant.

At uni the next day I keep all my communication lines open waiting to hear from Father. When the message comes, it's not exactly what I expect. A personal coded intercom memo, a completely private device that no one else can read. I've never received one of those before. I feel like 007. It's easy to decode. I expect it to be a summons to the museum to interview Heracles. Instead it informs me that Father has already fixed things and Heracles has been teleported back to C99. I can't help being disappointed that I wasn't needed but now realise that was never Father's plan. He wouldn't want me involved.

He rings almost immediately, an innocuous call from father to son, asking me if I'm free for lunch. You bet I am. I can't wait to find out exactly what has happened.

Meanwhile, I tap into Wordwideculture.inc, bring up C99 and sure enough there is Heracles standing somewhat awkwardly in a huge office. Behind a large workstation sits one of the most beautiful females I've ever seen. Her dark hair is scraped back in classic style to reveal a white face with a huge extra eye in the centre of her forehead. I tune in to their conversation.

'Do sit down, Heracles. I need to talk to you.'

He sprawls on the shaper opposite her, legs splayed wide, as if to convince her, or perhaps himself, that he's relaxed, but an involuntary pulse in his neck tells a different tale. She seems to be in charge and he is no doubt afraid of being questioned about his trip to Oasis. Whether she knows what he's been up to or not I have no idea but she doesn't challenge him about it.

'I have some sad news, Heracles. Ra, our beloved chief controller, the CEO of Worldwide culture, died this morning.'

Heracles sits up. 'I'm sorry to hear that, Athene. I hope he didn't suffer.'

Athene. She's called Athene. Very apt. So Ra is dead. This is news indeed.

'Thank you for your sympathy, Heracles. Much appreciated. Ra and I were very close. I shall miss him. His death was not altogether unexpected. He's been ailing for some time. He passed away peacefully in his sleep early this morning.'

Heracles is watchful, unsure what to say next. 'If there is anything I can do….'

'Thanks. I'll let you know. The cremation has already taken place at Hos-sat, but his ashes are to be returned here. I would like to plan some sort of memorial event for him. A celebration of his life citing his achievements, that sort of thing. Maybe you could help with that.'

'I'd be only too pleased.'

They are both being extremely polite, but there seems to be some underlying tension between them.

'Thing is, Heracles, I think we should keep quiet about this for the time being.'

'I agree. When a leader dies there is bound to be a period of unrest as everyone wonders who will take over and what effect the change in leadership will have. I remember when Ra took over, how fearful my colleagues were of his power to hire and fire at will. Some of us survived and have done rather well under his regime.'

She looks him straight in the eye. 'I'm glad you are appreciative of what he has done, Heracles. Would you like to make a speech in his praise at the memorial ceremony? When the time is right for it to take place.'

'Yes. Why not?'

There's a fleeting cunning look in his central eye.

Athene must have noticed it too. 'I'd need to vet it first, of course.'

'Why? Don't you trust me?'

Athene smiles, a tender, knowing smile, one that reminds me of Stella. 'What we don't want to do is create an atmosphere of panic. For the moment, everything should continue as usual while we take stock of the situation.' She stands as if to dismiss him and adds, as if an afterthought, 'I hope you enjoyed your extra-terrestrial trip. I expect a full report by the end of the day.'

Heracles's face is a picture: his jaw drops, his face reddens. She's a cool one, this Athene. I wouldn't fancy the chances of anyone who dares to cross her.

Jonathan pops his head round my wall-divider. I click off the screen. I'm lucky to have my own workspace. You could hardly call it a room. It's a hole in the wall, just big enough to house a compu and a shaper, designed to allow students to concentrate on their studies without interruptions from others. There's no door so, in theory, anyone could look over my shoulder and see what I'm doing, but that's not likely. We don't take much interest in each other's research – too busy with our own – and anyway, we respect each other's right to privacy.

Jonathan looks a bit sheepish. He probably regrets taking me to see the warriors and thinks I will think less of him now. He asks me if I'm ready for a break but I tell him I must do some work as I'm having lunch with my father.

He pulls a face. 'Trouble?'

'Not at all. Just a friendly chat.'

'Oh yes. I know all about those,' he says as he leaves.

I wonder what he means.

Father has chosen a rather special restaurant for lunch. It's at the side of the lake and we have a table in a corner by the window.

I've never really got over the lush greenness of the trees, plants and grass on Oasis and here I have a view of an emerald green lawn sloping down to the side of the water. It's flanked by a profusion of exotic ruby-red flowers. Fantastic. Stella is not with us today and I'm happy about that. There are times when a twosome is better than a threesome, especially when the two people concerned are father and son.

We decide what to eat and drink. Or, rather, Father decides, because I still don't take much interest in food – the result of those formative years in C55 eating the tasteless contents of food packoids. I can't wait to ask Father questions and, as soon as the waiter has taken our order, I blurt out three of them at once.

'Why didn't you send for me? Did you talk to Heracles yourself? What was his excuse for being here?'

'Hold on a minute. Let me catch my breath,' Father says, but he's smiling that special intimate smile that won me over the day I first met him. 'Firstly, I didn't send for you because it wasn't necessary. Secondly, I didn't speak to him because that wasn't necessary either. Thirdly, I don't know why he came here but I made up a reason acceptable enough to get him released and packed off back to C99. That was all achieved with one phone call to the right person. Aren't you proud of your father?'

I can't help wondering, if it was easy as that, why he couldn't have done something to stop this insulting voyeurism before now, but I decide to keep calm, play the game and nod.

'What reason did you give for his visit?'

'I said he was a known hacker – which is true – and that he'd found out about the existence of Oasis and decided to check it out for himself. In other words, he was a tourist.'

'Unlikely to be true, though.'

'Very unlikely. He'd already been interrogated and admitted that he'd come to Oasis specifically to meet another mutant humanoid.' Father's cool grey eyes meet mine across the table. 'Have you been in touch with this fellow?'

'No.' He goes on looking steadily at me so I feel compelled to add, 'But he has sent out auto-mails, random ones, trying to find out where I am. On Kali's behalf. One or two of them landed up on my computer. I didn't reply, just deleted them.'

He nods and seems to accept what I've told him. 'If anything happens like that again, Michael, please let me know. There are things I might be able to do to prevent further trouble. No one must know where "Mercury" is. You do understand that?'

'Of course I do. I just didn't think it necessary to tell you. I dealt with it myself. I don't want to run to you for every little thing.'

'I realise you want to be independent and I respect that, but in matters of this kind I'd rather be kept in the loop.'

'OK. I promise to keep you informed if anything like that happens again.'

'Good. Here's our food. Come on – eat up. Enjoy.'

Fillet steak, mushrooms and chips. Delicious. I'm

developing taste buds at last. I even try the wine but not too much. I have somewhere I intend to go before going back to uni. 'Why do you think Heracles was here?' I ask him.

'Doing a reconnaissance. Ready for a possible attack.'

I shake my head. 'I don't believe that. That's what Durga's golden warriors are here for, not Heracles. In my opinion, Heracles was looking for me. He may have had some half-baked idea that if I – another mutant humanoid – was enjoying the benefits of living on a satellite, maybe it would be possible for him to live here too.'

Father looks horrified. 'Looking for you? How would he know you were here?'

'I'm not sure, but you once told me that the computers in C99 were more advanced than those in the other sectoids. Maybe he hacked in, found out about Oasis, remembered that I hadn't been seen since the day you visited Headculturedome and put two and two together.'

Father stares at me. 'You have a quick mind, Michael, but this time I do hope you're wrong. If he can work out that you disappeared the day I was there, others can put two and two together and come to the same conclusion.' He frowns. He seems permanently worried that someone will find out our secret.

'What about the golden warriors?' I ask, finishing the last chip. 'Did you manage to get them teleported back?'

'No luck there, but the couple in the adjacent cubicle was sent back: a young male showing off, taking a young female on the trip of a lifetime. The warriors are a different matter. I was told their very presence was an act of war and…'

'Ten soldiers to attack a city? They were the advance guard. A show of power. Nothing more.'

'A bit of sabre-rattling, I agree, but what sort of message does it send to Durga if we let them go with no assurances in return?'

'What sort of message does it send to Durga if we keep them here? In my opinion holding them is an open invitation to Durga to avenge their capture.'

Father looks uncomfortable. 'There are some people in the Symposium who, I'm sorry to say, would like Durga to launch an attack. She has no chance of winning. We're not warriors, but we do have some very advanced weaponry against which Durga and her warriors wouldn't stand a chance. They'd all be slaughtered on arrival. There are some members of the Symposium who favour that option. They think it would send a definitive message to all the sectoids not to attack the satellites. You could call it the ultimate deterrent.'

'You can't agree with that?'

'Of course not. It would be a massacre. A blood bath. Some think that would be a small price to pay for our security. I disagree. It would be a denigration of everything we stand for, of everything it means to be a human being.'

'It would send a message to the mutant humanoids that no one cares whether they live or die. All the work Stella has done over the years would be destroyed in one fell swoop.'

Father pushes his plate away. 'What do you think is the answer, Michael?'

'There's only one answer. Negotiation.'

Father is quiet for a moment as he thinks this through. 'Now the mutant humanoids know about the satellites they naturally want what we have. Suppose we gave them a satellite of their own? How would that suit?'

I laugh. 'Sounds like another prison to me – except it's in the open air. A ghetto.'

'They're already ghettoised. They wouldn't be happy living side by side with us, any more than we'd be happy living side by side with them.'

'Why not? It might work better than you think.'

Easy for me to say. I remember the jeers and insults thrown at the golden warriors by some of the inhabitants of Oasis and the taunts of 'mutant' I received from the boys in the park, and know that the success of such an experiment would be far from easy to achieve.

'You and I seem to get on all right,' I say to lighten the mood.

He laughs then, that rich laugh that I'm learning to appreciate. 'Two reconstituted completes! Well, we can't decide on the future of the world over lunch. What would you like for dessert?'

I enter the narrow streets of the Oasis Project. They are deserted again apart from one or two youths hanging about on a street corner who give me odd looks as I pass. I make for the red brick building where I saw the little dancer in the blue dress. I've only gone a few steps when I realise the boys are following me. I stop and look around. They pull up and huddle together. When I start walking I hear their footsteps behind me again. I circle the streets, trying to give them the slip. A bit stupid, because they must know these streets better than I do. Sure enough they jump out at me and one of them grabs my arm and drags me into the porch of a house. I struggle to get free, but a blindfold is tied over my eyes and my pockets emptied. They don't find much. I haven't any possessions to speak of apart from my mob-fone kit, a present from Father that I haven't yet had fitted. If I'd taken the time to have the chip put behind my ear they wouldn't have been able to take it. What a bummer to have lost that.

'Give it back to him,' says a high, clear voice. I hear the mob-fone kit drop and the boys run off. My rescuer unties the rag round my eyes. It's the girl I saw the other day. She's wearing the same blue dress.

'Hello again,' she says, grinning, and I see again the bright clear blue of her eyes. 'What are you doing here?'

'I came to find you,' I say with a boldness I'm far from feeling.

She leans down, picks up my mob-fone kit and taps into it. 'There. That's my number. You should get that fitted pronto.' She smiles. 'My name is Elizabeth – Lizzy. Next time, please call me before you come and I'll make sure we don't have company.'

She glances down the street where the youths are still watching us. 'What's your name?'

I'm just about to say "Michael" when I change my mind. 'I'm Edward Darcy,' I tell her.

'Mr. Darcy and Elizabeth,' she laughs. 'Good one. OK Mr. Darcy, I'll buy that.'

She glances down the street again. 'Brothers are such a pain. Over protective. Have to go now. Call me. Don't forget now,' and, with a swish of her skirt, she swirls round and trips into one of the identical houses.

I'm so excited I give a little hop and a skip as I set off to find my way out of the labyrinth of streets. Another adventure is about to begin. Her brothers snigger but don't follow me.

Lizzy. I can't stop saying her name to myself. She's bright, beautiful and, as a bonus, a Jane Austen reader. I have no idea how she's landed up in the Oasis Project but I'll find out and see if there's anything I can do to help her. Maybe I can find her a job or a grant to study at the university. My imagination soars, my mind full of this girl. I realise I must keep her a secret from Father and even from Jonathan. It won't be difficult. I find that I don't want to tell anyone about her. I want to keep her existence private. She's someone just for me. I'm Darcy and she's my Elizabeth Bennett. I call into a tech shop on the way back to uni and get my chip fitted. The guy in the shop shows me how to use it.

'This is the latest model, a real state-of-the-art cell,' he tells me, impressed. 'The sort that members of the Symposium use.'

I don't tell him my father gave it to me and he's the Minister of Culture.

'You need to import your favourites from your old mob here,' he explains.

'I'll put them in later,' I tell him.

I haven't an old one and I haven't any favourites – only Lizzy. I suppose I could add Jonathan but I see him everyday so there's not much point. I ring Lizzy's number straightaway. There is no reply. I don't leave a message. I want to talk to her and hear her voice and make what I suppose is called a date.

I'll make myself wait until tomorrow. Or perhaps later today.

Back at my compu, I open the portal that reveals the wilderness and the outside of the domed compounds, a similar scene to the one that Stella showed me once before. The wind blows dust balls mixed with plant life over the barren ground. Still barren, yes, but I can see signs of life: green shoots pushing their way up through the packed-down soil – and surely that's a tiny animal scuttling across, searching for food. A field mouse, a rabbit? A weasel? Some creature that has survived underground and propagated despite the plague. How resilient life forms are, whether plants, animals, humanoids or human beings. Every living creature is programmed to fight for survival. I think of Lizzy and wonder about her life.

A humming noise as a survey-drone cruises over the wilderness. In the distance a golden mist comes into view. A mirage? I zoom in for a close-up. Out of the swirling haze emerges a glorious sight: two golden chariots flanked by a battalion of marching warriors. No horses or golden calves to pull the chariots. They must be power-driven. I can only speculate on the fuel that has been used to run them. All kinds of alternative energies were explored in the twentieth and early twenty-first centuries but I rather suspect that present-day scientists have discovered new sources of power. I must remember to find out what they are. It's important to keep up with research. The chariots do not move very fast but give an impression of speed, as they churn up the dust.

A close-up reveals Durga in the first chariot. Her red-gold hair flows out of her golden helmet. Spectacular. Slightly behind her, in the second chariot, stands a figure that makes my heart beat faster. Another zoom in and there is no doubt about it. It's Kali, her blue-black face glowing under her helmet; my old mates, her snakes at neck and wrists, extend their sleek, shiny bodies, their mouths open wide, revelling in this bold ride. The warriors march in step on either side of the chariots, their golden breastplates, shields and weapons gleaming. How magnificent is that! Seeing a group of them in the museum is nothing to this, but I do have a twinge of conscience. I'm a voyeur, just like the visitors to the museum. Just like Stella. Computers have imposed on their privacy. But this is only a fleeting thought. I don't let it stop me watching this drama that is about to be played out.

I don't need to be told where they're going. Not to Oasis but to Compound 55 – to reclaim it for Kali.

I am so privileged to be able to see this, but it's a privilege I've taken for myself by hacking into a computer owned by the university. I must take care that my subversive action is not discovered. As if to remind me of that fact, Jonathan appears again. I minimise the screen and tell him that I'm in the middle of something important but could take a break in a couple of hours. There's no way I can leave now. It would be like switching off an action movie in the middle and missing the end.

Durga, Kali and the warriors are streaming across the wilderness towards C55. The effect is like a huge bar of solid gold. Unstoppable.

Outside a dome – it must be C55 – Durga pulls up and raises her hand. The warriors halt. Durga and Kali line up their chariots, side by side. The warriors stand in formation on either flank. Resplendent, forbidding, terrifying.

Durga calls out 'Advance party – forward march!' and ten warriors step forward. What next? How are they going to break down that door? I don't need to wonder for long. The captain of the advance guard is holding a huge key. Resourceful Kali didn't leave her beloved compound without making sure she could re-enter when she wanted to. The captain unlocks the door and the advance guards, rifles at the ready, enter the sectoid. Durga, Kali and the others remain in position, perfectly still.

I zoom inside my old compound. The warriors point their rifles at the shocked workforce of C55. Jason and Apollo exchange looks and step back. Merlin pulls a face. Damocles squirms and recoils. The females cringe. The warriors indicate that everyone should stand up, leave their workstations and line up against the far wall of the compu-centre. They don't have to be told twice.

All the workers scramble to their feet and make an uncoordinated dash towards the wall, with a variety of jerky movements. I've forgotten how this lack of control leads to misjudgement of space. My ex-colleagues bump into each other and into any object that gets in their way. I stare at them, pitying them. Was I as clumsy as this? I hate myself for my reaction and begin to understand, for the first time, how easy it must be for completes to look down on mutant humanoids.

'No need to worry,' says the three-eyed captain. 'We do not intend to hurt anyone. Don't oppose us and you will not be harmed. We have come for Sati.'

A few more exchanged looks but no one volunteers information as to Sati's whereabouts. They cower against the wall, hands in the air, too frightened to move or speak.

The captain details six of his team to seek out Sati and to round up any other stray members of the workforce. The warriors, although mutants themselves, are so much more coordinated than the humanoids in this sectoid. I conclude that it's the training they've received that have made their legs and arms perform the exacting movements needed to march, hold their weapons and fight. I remember my own excruciating training with Janey and realise how hard they must have worked to achieve such control.

Some of the warriors return with a few more members of C55's workforce. They prod them with their rifles and herd them against the wall with the others.

Following them down the silver cylinder march four more warriors, Sati between them. She floats along on the tips of her toes between her cohorts as smoothly as ever, her two heads turning effortlessly from side to side taking in the situation. She sees her intimidated workforce pressed against the wall and smiles. Full marks to her for trying to look unconcerned. She's certainly keeping her dignity; but she's waiting for something. If it's for her workforce to rebel, she's going to be disappointed. They clutch on to each other, cringing, and one or two of them are whimpering. The warriors lead her to the open door. She looks outside, sees her two sister-wives in their chariots and the block of warriors on either side of them.

'Quite a show, Durga,' she says. 'You and your toy soldiers.'

'I've come to take you away from here, Sati,' Durga declares.

Sati smiles. 'Where do you intend to take me, Durga, my beloved sister-wife?'

'To my compound, C98.'

'And what do you intend to do with me there?'

'That's for me to know and you to find out. I will do exactly what I like with you. Throw you in prison or kill you. Or – I might empty out your brain of all those silly ideas and give you another chance. Depends on how you behave yourself.'

'As you offer me no assurances, I must decline your kind invitation to accompany you.'

Durga laughs deep in her throat. 'It's not an invitation, Sati. It's an order. I don't think you have any choice but to accept.'

'Oh yes, I have.' Sati turns to the warriors who hold her. 'Take your filthy hands off me.'

They are soldiers accustomed to receiving orders and her voice is nothing if not commanding. They let go and, in that moment, she slips back into the compu-centre and addresses her workforce. 'What do you think you're doing, cringing against that wall? You don't really think these toy soldiers will hurt you?' No one moves. 'Jason. Aren't you going to help me, after all I've done for you?'

I see Jason hesitate a moment before charging towards her, falling over his feet and bumping into a workstation in an attempt to reach her. A shot is fired. Jason falls to the ground.

What's happening? Mutant humanoids killing each other? This is beyond belief. The warriors look shocked themselves and that is probably why Sati's disparaging, 'Now look what you've done,' prevents them from stopping her when she kneels down beside Jason and kisses him, first with one mouth and then with the other. Kisses she hopes will bring him back to life. She takes Jason's hand in hers and feels for his pulse. She looks up at the warriors, 'You morons,' she says. 'This is not what Durga intended. She didn't tell you to kill anyone. Now – get out.'

The warriors look at each other but don't move.

'Sisters,' Sati calls. 'You will pay for this. You have committed murder. It is you who will be going to prison. Not me.'

I hear Durga commanding the advance party to keep control. The two nearest to Sati exchange a look and take a step forward. They halt as Sati leans over Jason and speaks to him. 'You were the best, Jason. You always were the best and you have given your life for me. I appreciate that so much that I've decided to join you,' and, before the warriors are aware of what she is doing, she slips a tablet into each of her mouths and falls on top of Jason's body. The warriors stand dumb-founded. None of their training has prepared them for this.

In stride Durga and Kali, followed by a cohort of warriors.

Durga addresses the captain. 'Captain Theseus, get these bodies removed. Put Sati's body in my chariot and that of the male humanoid in the other. You, Captain, will drive the second chariot back. Kali will stay here and take charge of this pathetic group of humanoids, as is her right.'

More warriors enter and lift up the bodies of Sati and Jason and take them outside.

I am pleased that Kali has her sectoid back. She deserves to be in charge again. I'm sure she'll soon lick the workforce into shape. But I have to admit this is not an altogether successful attack. Sati's comment about Durga's toy soldiers is not far from the truth. With such an army, Durga must not attempt to invade Planet Oasis. It would indeed be a blood bath.

Time to ring Lizzy. This time she does answer and my heart beats faster as I hear her lively voice agreeing to meet me by the obelisk that marks the border of the Oasis Project, at midday tomorrow. She seems as keen to see me again as I am to see her.

Chapter Twenty-one
Insurgence
(according to Stella and other watchers)

The golden army streaks through the wilderness. Durga and Captain Theseus stand in the front section of their chariots, the dead bodies in the back. The drone overhead records their progress for anyone with the correct passwords to view.

The voyeurs with access to the Worldwideculture website interpret the events on screen as they unfold. Stella in her study, Michael in his computer-cube at the university, Athene and Heracles on separate auto-puts in C99 and Jaga in C98, all watch.

Sati stirs, rubs her eyes and sits up. Maybe the jolt of the chariot has dislodged the tablets she didn't actually swallow, like the piece of apple on Snow White's tongue. Or perhaps, like Juliet, Sati has taken a superior kind of tranquilliser to simulate a little death. At any rate, she is alive now. Carefully, she dislodges the rifle that Durga has slotted into a groove at the side of the chariot and places it on the floor at her feet. She grabs Durga's long red hair, forces her head backwards and lifts up her chin. The stretched neck chokes any sound of protest. Sati unclips the helmet, removes it and throws it out of the chariot. She picks up the rifle without releasing her grip on the hair and whacks her sister-wife's exposed head with the blunt end. All this happens very quickly. Durga screams and slips to one side. Sati strikes her again with the butt of the rifle. The screaming stops. Durga topples over, hanging half-in half-out of the chariot. With an almighty effort, Sati shoves her over the edge. Durga lies splayed out on the ground.

'Halt!' Sati yells and the warriors obey.

Sati climbs over to the front of the chariot and manoeuvres it alongside that of Captain Theseus. Sati's dark-haired head watches as the blonde one whispers to the captain. How does she persuade him to transfer his allegiance from Durga to her?

What does she promise him? Promotion? Intimate privileges? The watchers can only guess. Sati speaks so softly the drone overhead cannot pick up the sound, but the seduction is clearly successful.

'Forward march!' shouts the captain and the entire regiment moves as one, with not a backward glance at the inert figure of their former leader lying on the hard ground. Sati has decided to leave Kali in C55 and go forward with the warriors to C98.

The watchers at their workstations consider the latest development. Stella, who is considering who should replace Ra as CEO, realises that she must not underestimate the tenacious Sati. Heracles can't help but admire Sati's guts. Jaga looks thoughtful. She must plan some sort of welcome for when her sister-wife arrives at C98. Athene imagines the clash of personalities in the coming leadership challenge and how best to cope with them. Michael continues watching developments, but reserves judgement.

In the Grand Hall golden warriors await the return of their

colleagues. Jaga is not present. The trumpets sound to herald the arrival. All the warriors have heard of the beautiful two-headed Sati but have never seen her. Her beauty surpasses their wildest dreams. She stands upright in Durga's chariot, triumphant in victory, her two heads raised. Blonde curls and smooth dark hair stream behind her.

But where is Durga?

Sati addresses the assembled army. 'I, Sati, am your new leader.' She flutters two sets of long eyelashes. 'I'm afraid that Durga has become one of the casualties of war.'

A communal gasp.

'Not the only one, I'm afraid. One of the members of C55, a brave and loyal humanoid called Jason was shot dead in an effort to protect me. A full military funeral is to be prepared for him. The warrior who killed him, Geronimo, will be tried, found guilty and executed.'

She searches the ranks for any sign of dissent but the warriors stand rigid. Not one protests.

'What about for Durga?' someone calls out. 'Will she have a military funeral?'

Sati smiles. 'Durga tried to kill me. She lies defeated in the battlefield. She does not deserve a funeral ceremony of any kind.'

A few exchanged looks but no real objections. The warriors are trained to accept all decisions from their leader, even a new self-appointed one.

Six warriors enter the Grand Hall, Jason's body on their shoulders. Sati regards the procession with due solemnity until it disappears through a side entrance.

'Jason's body will lie in state in the chapel and warriors will be detailed to keep vigil day and night, under the command of the Brahmin.'

The Brahmin bows his two wobbly heads. Odysseus and Isis exchange looks.

Jaga appears at the opposite end of the hall, looking magnificent in a simple straw-coloured gown that matches her hair. 'Sati. What a surprise. Welcome to my sectoid. I'm delighted that my sister-wife survived the attack on C55. I invite you to take sanctuary here with us.'

Sati steps neatly down from the chariot with the help of two willing young warriors. 'No need to invite me as if I were a guest,' she says sweetly to Jaga. She looks up at Captain Theseus and he jumps down from his chariot and moves to her side. The regiment follows his lead and the warriors she has acquired during the march line up in unified formation behind her. 'I assure you that your days in this compound are numbered.'

'Now sister-wife, there's no need for such talk. I saw everything that happened on the compu-screen and am prepared for your arrival. The contingent of warriors that escorted you here may remain loyal to you – at the moment – but I have my own supporters.'

As she speaks another regiment of warriors appears and stations itself behind Jaga. Impasse.

Jaga breaks the silence. 'No use trying to threaten me, Sati. I know you too well. Let's calm down a little and assess the situation. Come…. ' She holds out her hand. Sati pauses for a moment before moving forward through the hall in her usual smooth, feline manner. She links her arm through Jaga's, giggles and off they waltz together.

The watchers are all aware that peace is by no means restored. This is a standoff. Another internal battle is about to be played out. The watchers flick to C55.

Kali begins to take control of the workforce. She uses the well-worn technique of the carrot and the stick. She promises to keep the new leisure hours as long as the targets are met.

'Same old, same old,' grumbles Merlin under his breath. 'Targets, targets, targets.'

'The new facilities such as the gym and the disco-cube will still be available to everyone – but not in working hours. We will start each day with a meeting in which you will all be invited to suggest new initiatives. I will consider every single one of them seriously.'

She asks if anyone has any questions. At first there are none, but then Apollo blurts out, 'How can you justify Jason's death?'

His colleagues study Kali's face, keen to hear her answer.

'I want you to know that Jason's death is as big a shock to me as to all of you. The very idea of mutant humanoids killing each other is an anathema. It's not acceptable.'

'What are you going to do about it?' Damocles asks. 'It's murder. Are you going to let Durga's warriors get away with it? They must be brought to justice?'

There is a buzz of agreement. Jason was never popular but the members of the workforce are testing Kali.

The watchers know that if she doesn't handle this situation with care there could be a rebellion before she's even taken control.

Kali pauses. She studies the faces in front of her. 'Those who know me well will appreciate that I never make snap decisions about important matters. The present situation is no exception. Although we all feel angry about what has happened, our response needs to be carefully assessed. If anyone has any ideas on how to deal with this matter I will be happy to consider them but the ultimate decision will be mine.'

There are a few murmurings but her answer appears reasonable to most of the listeners.

Kali springs into action and directs the repositioning of

the workstations in the compu-centre, making sure they are spaced further apart to ensure more concentration, less chat. When this has been done, she selects a workstation for herself in the middle and indicates that her colleagues should start work.

The expression on her face tells them that she is in charge and not prepared to leave them unsupervised. Soon the hum of the auto-puts is the only sound to be heard.

No point watching them work, think most of the watchers. The main action is over for the moment.
Michael zooms into Compound 99.

Athene is at her desk, Heracles opposite her, stretched out on a shaper.

'I've decided to release the news of Ra's death and invite the other top mutant humanoids to a meeting here in C99.'

'What's the point of that?' Heracles asks.

'To keep the lid on the unrest that is bubbling up as they vie for the leadership. I'll chair the meeting and emphasise the fact that it is necessary for us all to work together in order to achieve better conditions for mutant humanoids here on Earth.'

'Very altruistic, Athene, but what do you think such a combined effort will achieve?'

'Now that we know about the satellites, we will have to work together to devise a strategy to persuade the completes to share their resources with us. As it's the richest and most influential English-speaking satellite, I think we should concentrate on Planet Oasis.'

'I get your point, Athene, but how do you intend to achieve this?'

'Certainly not by force as I'm sure Durga would propose if she were still with us. By negotiation.'

'Again I'm in agreement, but first and foremost we need a good negotiator. The obvious choice is myself.'

'Are you sure about that? Have you forgotten your disastrous attempt to infiltrate Oasis?'

'It was not disastrous. I made some good contacts there.'

'Your interrogators?'

'The politician I told you about, for example. Orlando Wolfe. And….'

'And who else? Is there something you're holding back, Heracles? Something you haven't told me?'

'No, of course not.'

'There's no of course about it. What else did you discover while on Oasis?'

'It's all in my report.'

'Is it? Tell me, who else do you know there?'

'Now you're interrogating me. One minute you ask for my help as a colleague, the next you're treating me like a criminal.'

Athene sighs. 'OK. Let's start again. Let's assume we're on the same side. For the moment. How willing do you think Oasis will be to share resources with us? How should we approach them?'

Heracles leans back in his chair. 'To negotiate we must have something to offer in return. What we have to offer them, Athene, is security – an assurance that we will not attack them. That is why using Durga's army as a threat is not such a bad idea.'

'If there is an attack, her warriors will be annihilated on arrival. Or at any rate stunned and captured as you were. They showed us what would happen by taking the ten warriors as hostages.'

'That won't necessarily happen the next time.' Heracles stretches his huge arms above his head and flexes the muscles of his massive three legs.

'What have you found out now, Mr. Super-Hacker?'

'Nothing definite yet, but there is a way to overcome this device and I'm working on it.' He grins and pulls himself up on to his three feet.

Typical Heracles, thinks Michael. Such a know-it-all. Always thinks he knows better than others. Stella considers what kind of leader Heracles would make. He has a good brain all right. There's no doubt about that. Nor is there any doubt that he's determined to get to the top and cares very little who is hurt in the process, but is this really the kind of person she wants in charge of her company? As for Athene's plan to hold a meeting of key personnel, that's not a bad idea. A joint enterprise such as that might reveal insights as to the suitability of each candidate's leadership skills.

Heracles is on his feet ready to leave, but Athene calls him back. 'Before you do anything else, Heracles, I'd like you to investigate the vicious rumours going around that I am responsible for Ra's death. Bring me the name or names of the culprits tonight.'

'That might be difficult.'

'Don't give me that, Heracles. For someone who believes he can solve the problem of Durga's warriors not being assassinated on arrival, this task should be child's play.'

Michael punches the air. That told him, all right. Athene is not just beautiful to look at but has a quick brain to match.

Stella too admires that final jibe and realises, not for the first time, that Athene has the measure of Heracles. Athene herself is difficult to read. What exactly is hidden beneath that calm exterior? Was she responsible for Ra's death?

As Stella considers her list of prospective CEOs she has no doubt about their strengths as leaders. Her doubts lie in the philosophy that underlies their intentions. She had no doubts when appointing Ra. She truly believed that, although he could be ruthless, he was not self-seeking. His goal was always to do what was best for the company and for the majority of humanoids in his charge. She cannot be sure that any of these candidates have a similar attitude. They all seem as full of self-interest as many of the politicians in the Symposium on Planet Oasis.

Stella tunes in to C55 again.

And so does Michael. Now, as it is the middle of the night, he watches events from the computer in his room at Home Court-Jameson, interested in Kali's well being as always.

Kali hears a pounding on the door. She is still up, the only humanoid remaining in the compu-centre, maybe loath to close her eyes in case her colleagues should plan to take her prisoner while asleep. Not one of them has protested, but she must sense an underlying hostility, especially from the male humanoids deprived of the benefits of Sati's sexual favours. Kali is pleased to be back in charge and a few hours' missed sleep are nothing to her compared with that satisfaction.

The pounding outside increases. Kali has not expected an outside attack. All her fears have been concentrated on danger from within. Kali clicks on her auto-put and brings up the image outside the door. A dirty, dishevelled figure confronts her but the touches of gold that shine through the torn rags and the trace of red in the long dusty hair leave Kali in no doubt that this is Durga. Kali strides across the compu-centre to let her in.

So now, thinks Stella, we have three pairs of allies. Kali and Durga: Jaga and Sati: Athene and Heracles. There is no assurance that these paired allies will remain loyal to each other but the fact that they are lined up two-by-two must imply a threat to the future of Worldwideculture. Of that Stella has no doubt. Without careful handling, everything Stella has worked for could collapse. She must pre-empt such a disaster from occurring.

A recovered Durga tells Kali that the takeover of the flagship, C99, is vital for their survival. She intends to displace Athene and become the most influential person in Worldwideculture, one step nearer being CEO.

'The wilderness is safe now,' she says. 'We'll march with your workforce and demand entry.'

'My workforce are not used to marching,' Kali reminds her.

'I'll train them,' Durga says. 'I'll train them to be warriors.'

At the morning meeting, Kali tells her colleagues that she has decided what to do to avenge Jason's death. Durga will take charge of the most able-bodied mutant humanoids and train them in the skills of warfare.

Durga does her best to teach them to walk, march and run round the outside of the compound. At first most of them quite enjoy the experience. It's a novelty to be away from their workstations, to be outside, breathing relatively fresh air; but Durga is a hard taskmistress and soon they are puffing and blowing and complaining of aches and pains.

She bribes them with gaudy uniforms in red and silver, tells them how manly they look and praises their efforts.

'Quick march!' she says and off they go again with their awkward jerks, judders and twists.

It's ludicrous, thinks Michael. How can she turn these mutant humanoids into warriors? At C98 she was given less damaged mutants to work with, the pick of the compounds, but these recruits will never be able to keep in step when they march and the thought of them trying to fight is a joke.

Durga sends them out to find twigs and tendrils from the plants and bushes that have now begun to sprout. Some they shape into bows and arrows, others they sharpen to use as swords or daggers. All are makeshift weapons, as clumsy and unwieldy as the mutilated humanoids destined to use them.

Kali watches their efforts and shakes her head. Her snakes uncoil themselves and hiss but she has no choice other than to agree to Durga's crazy plan. A fair exchange for Durga's help in retrieving C55.

As the bizarre training continues, Stella switches her attention to Jaga and Sati.

They too intend to attack C99. The difference is that they have ready-trained warriors to help them. Jaga suggests that Sati lead the attack on C99 with Captain Theseus and his battalion of warriors. 'They're loyal to you and will not be tempted to change sides at the last minute.'

'No chance of that,' agrees Sati. She puts her heads on one side and winks at Jaga. 'I've made quite sure of their devotion to me.'

Jaga shrugs. 'If your unorthodox methods work for you, who am I to complain? You will proceed with the attack. I'll stay here and organise things from this end. Once you're in the compound, I'll join you with backup.'

Sati pouts. 'So I do all the work and you reap the benefits.'

'Sati – I could lock you up in a cell now and throw away the key. You know that. Count yourself lucky that I'm trusting you to do this thing.'

So there they are, two disparate groups of warriors marching across the wilderness, hoping to capture and occupy C99.

Neither Stella nor Michael believes that either group has much chance of success. Stella is concerned that the proposed tactics could result in a power shift quite different from that she plans. She watches and waits. And so do Michael, Jaga, Athene and Heracles on their respective computers.

Durga, Kali and the raggle-taggle army arrive outside C99, only to find Sati and her battalion of golden warriors already there. Durga strides up to Sati, swings her arm back and gives the blonde head an almighty slap on the cheek before striking the dark head with a stinging backhander which knocks her sister-wife over.

Durga barks out, 'Forward march. Halt. Present arms.' The warriors obey and are Durga's to command once more. So much for Sati's confidence in their loyalty. Under Durga's command they face the entrance of the flagship compound, ready to attack.

A huge figure looms large in the doorway of C99, a giant protecting his castle, three muscular legs wide apart, a rifle aimed at the intruders.

Sati crawls towards him, kneels, grabs his legs, begs for sanctuary. 'Heracles, you have to help me. Remember how good we were together. We had good love sex together once and could again. Please Heracles, let me in.'

He doesn't look down at her but kicks her out of his way. She lies on the ground, doubled up in pain. With the same decisiveness he shoots Durga in the head and she falls to the ground. With a quick gesture, Heracles summons Thor to come out, tie her up and carry her inside.

Not dead then, stunned, the observers decide.

Kali, aware that her turn may be next, calls out, 'Heracles, wait! I only came with Durga because I owed her a favour

– because she helped me reclaim my compound. You know that's all I've ever wanted. Please allow me and my workforce to return to C55 in peace.'

Heracles looks at the motley set of clowns in their garish makeshift uniforms and grimaces. 'OK, off you go, then,' he grins and Kali and her careworn excuse for an army begin their long march back to C55.

Michael breathes a sigh of relief. He can now look forward to his date with Lizzy, assured that Kali will soon be back in her rightful place.

It's the turn of Heracles to give the order to the fickle army: 'Forward March!' he yells and the golden warriors change their allegiance yet again and march inside C99. Heracles strides into C99 after them and closes the huge door.

A moment later he reappears, takes hold of Sati's long, dark tresses with one hand and her blonde curls with the other and drags her unceremoniously inside. The door slams shut.

Stella has to admit that Heracles has dealt with a potentially dangerous situation very well indeed. She wonders what Athene has been doing during this coup. She flicks to Athene's office and sees Athene watching the proceedings on the screen. She's watching and waiting, as calm as ever. And Jaga? Stella flicks to Compound 98. Jaga is at her workstation too, watching the same events. She looks far from distressed by Sati's defeat and the loss of a regiment of warriors. On the contrary, her little smile of satisfaction as she leaves her workstation to begin a tour of C98, shows Stella that Jaga is as content as Kali to have her position as head of a sectoid confirmed. Never mind that it's at the expense of her sister-wives, Sati and Durga.

Back at C99, Athene is sending messages, calling for the proposed meeting in the conference cube of C99.

Stella notes that Athene's list of invitations is almost identical to her own shortlist of candidates for the post of CEO. Durga, Sati and Heracles are already in C99 and the others are to be teleported to join them. Stella is still not sure how sincere Athene is in her wish to cooperate with her colleagues. Does she genuinely want their input? If so, it is the sign of a good leader; but if her intention is to take the opportunity provided by the gathering to seize power, that is a dangerous ploy. The clash of personalities involved could lead to an inappropriate takeover. A disastrous power shift.

Stella has no intention of letting such a coup take place. The appointment of a new CEO is her prerogative, a right she will not relinquish. It's not a post that is up for grabs. Normally Stella doesn't interfere with what is happening on Earth, but this time she must. An intervention is necessary.

Chapter Twenty-two
Power Games
(according to Heracles)

What satisfaction it is to pleasure myself with a pliant Sati. She's so anxious to please there's very little challenge. I pump up and down on top of her, bored out of my brain. The thought that so many mutants have been in this intimate spot before makes me consider her worthless. I get pleasure from telling her that. 'You're a worn-out old tart,' I tell her, 'a wrinkled old whore.'

I change the ground rules, am less active myself, make her pleasure me. Yes, that's the answer. Let the bitch do all the work while I relax. She's only too willing. The new strategy works for a while but then palls. She's putting on an act, pretending to be my slave but in reality gloating over her hold on me. And then, suddenly, it's over. She really has lost her appeal, sexual vengeance not so sweet after all. I chuck her in an empty cube with no bunku and lock the door. Let her rant, scream abuse, bang on the door, exhaust herself. Let her turn on the waterworks with tears and sobs. Who cares about a spoilt bitch permanently on heat for any male who fancies her? Not me. Not Heracles the Great. Not any more. I'm satiated with Sati.

I mooch down to the RR and chat to Thor. I need him to do something for me – go the sci-lab and find a drug, not strong enough to kill, but strong enough to act as a sedative.

It's not intended for Sati, but I will try it out on Sati, mix it in her food packoid and see what effect it has. At least it should put a stop to that screeching. Thor agrees to help me. He's a good chap, completely loyal to me and I shall think of a suitable reward for his loyalty when I achieve my goal.

Something else occurs to me. Why not try out the seda-drug on Durga as well?' She's locked up in solitary in the dormo-cells in the basement. She likes to exercise her vocal chords whenever anyone approaches. A dose of the seda-drug should keep her big mouth shut for a while.

On another tack, I ask Thor if he has found the source of the gossip about Ra's untimely death. He understands that it doesn't matter if the humanoids he hits upon are the genuine instigators of the rumour as long as they are willing to take the blame.

What methods he uses to achieve this result is up to him. The truth is not important. The important thing is that a couple of scapegoats are found to take the rap for the gossip about Athene.

'It was no problem at all,' he assures me as he hands me the names of a couple of dodgy mutants who, 'with a bit of persuasion,' as he puts it, confessed willingly enough.

'Good chap.' I give him a manly slap on the back. 'You're sure they will keep to their story when confronted by Athene?'

'Trust me. There's no way they'll crack. I've made sure of that.'

We shake on it. I'm well pleased with Thor. I have no idea what Athene will do with the information I'm about to give her. That's not my concern. I've fulfilled my part of the bargain – to give her the names of the culprits. It's up to her how she deals with them. I suspect she'll let get them away with a warning. Not my way. When I'm in charge anyone who opposes me, any potential enemy, will disappear, never to be seen again. It doesn't pay to be soft. Think Pinochet. Think Mao. I won't stand any nonsense once I'm CEO.

Athene is becoming a real pain. She has called the meeting of those she calls "top mutants" and is determined to chair it herself. She's becoming far too officious and it won't be long now before I'll have to do something drastic and show her who's really in charge.

'What we need to do at this meeting, Heracles, is to demonstrate that – with you at my side – I am the right person to be CEO of this company. That's why we need to be really organised. We mustn't permit any deviation from the agreed agenda.'

Who is this "we"? Does she really think I'm her pet puppy dog, trained to obey her every demand?

The list of invited delegates is supposed to consist of prospective rivals for the post of CEO. It's a deeply flawed selection. For a start, Athene has included Durga and Sati, my captives, without, I may say, asking my permission. How insulting is that? How can either of them be prospective candidates for CEO when I've arrested them and banged them up?

Secondly, she's included two old men, Odysseus and Brahmin, scarcely able to put one foot in the front of the other. Their minds are stuck in a rut in the past. Why should they be consulted about the Earth's future when they have so little time left?

As far as Odysseus is concerned, he has made some bad errors in the past, not the least being to fire me and keep that airhead, Isis, as his assistant. He also stole some precious artefacts and secreted them in his dormo-cube. Ra should have fired him for that. No way should he be considered as a potential leader. It's ludicrous.

The final names on the list, apart from Athene and myself, are Jaga and Kali. Much as I respect Kali, I can't think why she's been invited. She's already achieved her ambition, to regain her position as chief administrator of C55. That's as high she can fly. As for Jaga, she's proved herself willing to change sides at the least provocation, so hasn't earned her place at the conference table either. The final humanoids on the list, Athene and myself, are, in my opinion, the only genuine contenders for the post and I have no doubt, when push comes to shove, about who will win that contest.

Athene sits at the head of the table in the confer-cube; I lounge on her right-hand side, playing with my auto-pad. Athene is subdued, her eyes dull. She passes a hand over her forehead as if her head aches. The seda-drug appears to be working. Good job I tried it out on Sati and Durga first to assess the required amount.

The dose we put in Sati's food packoid led to her sleeping for two whole days. I was a little worried that we'd gone too far, that she might never revive, but she did. And how. With her energy renewed, she started ranting again, demanding to be let out and treated in the manner she deserved. I grinned, told her that she was being treated in the way she deserved and left her banged up. We gave Durga a reduced ration which didn't send her to sleep, but certainly quietened her down for a while.

From Durga's reaction I assessed the amount to give Athene. I realise that everyone's metabolism differs so I can't be sure of Athene's response.

What I intend is for her to lose her edge and be incapable of controlling the meeting. When that happens, it's my chance to take over.

On the other side of me sits a seemingly chastened Sati, my spoil of war and concubine. She's behaving herself at the moment, looking quite sweet and demure in fact, but I don't trust her.

Next to Sati sits Odysseus and, next to him, Brahmin, both looking somewhat surprised to be there.

On the opposite side of the table sits a disgruntled Durga, a smug Jaga and a formidable-looking Kali. Colleagues, sister-wives, allies and adversaries: an unlikely collection of collaborators.

Athene calls the meeting to order, welcomes everyone and asks for ideas about the future direction of Worldwideculture.

Durga demands to know who gave Athene permission to take charge of the meeting. A provocative start.

Athene looks her calmly in the eye. 'As the chief administrator of C99 and your host for the day I automatically assumed….' She pauses and runs her hand over her forehead. The seda-tabs are beginning to slow her down.

'It doesn't do to assume,' pipes up Jaga.

'Quite right, sister wife,' says Durga.

Athene takes a deep breath. 'But I am quite willing to relinquish my position. Maybe we should take a vote on it.'

Odysseus coughs. 'I don't think that will be necessary. As you point out, this is your sectoid, Athene, and you are within your rights to chair the meeting. You have asked us for our ideas, a strategy which seems to me to be perfectly fair. Perhaps you, Athene, would like to start by presenting any thoughts that you have about the future of Worldwideculture and Planet Earth.'

I have to hand it to Ody. With one fell swoop, he has taken charge. I may have underestimated him.

But Athene is not beaten yet. She throws the question back to him. 'Far be it from me to dominate the meeting. Why not give us the benefit of your wide experience first, Odysseus.'

Oh my Zeus, she's opened the floodgates, let us in for one of Ody's long-winded speeches. I close my eyes and lean back in my shaper.

Odysseus clears his throat and begins, predictably, by suggesting that history has much to teach us and away he goes launching into an account of the past, regretting lost knowledge, lost treasures and stressing the importance of recording memories.

Durga interrupts. 'Forget the past, old man. This meeting is about the future. We must take back what is ours by right, the resources and treasures that the completes on the satellites have stolen from us.'

'We mustn't steal them back,' says Brahmin. His voice is reedy, like the scraping of an old bow on a viola. 'An eye for an eye and a tooth for a tooth is not the way. We must tread carefully.'

'Being cautious never achieved a thing,' snaps Jaga. 'We must be bold.'

'Too right,' agrees Durga. 'We must fight for what is ours.'

'No more warriors sent on a fool's mission, though,' says Jaga reminding everyone that she, not Durga, is now in charge of the army in C98. 'We can't afford to risk losing more warriors. By the way, Heracles, it's about time you returned the ones you stole from me.'

'He stole them from me, not you,' bursts out Sati.

Jaga gives a contemptuous smile. 'But you have no power, Sati. You allowed your warriors to be taken from you and now you're a captive yourself. They belong to me.'

'All the warriors are mine,' shouts Durga. 'I am the one who nurtured them, trained them and taught them how to fight.'

'A captive can't be the leader of an army,' scoffs Jaga. 'And anyway, who lost ten of our best warriors to Oasis without checking that they would be safe?'

'Not lost,' Athene says quietly. 'Just misplaced. Believe me, we will get them back. Their return must be part of any treaty we make with the completes.'

Everyone turns to stare at her. 'Treaty? What kind of treaty can we make?' asks Jaga.

'What kind of treaty would you like?' Athene asks.

She's very calm. *The seda-capsule is not doing the job I'd hoped for. Her speech should be slurred, her head nodding like a puppet. She ought to be making a complete fool of herself. The seda is taking longer to take effect than I thought.*

What they have to say is predictable. The olds advise negotiation for the return of artefacts, Durga suggests the threat of outright war is the only answer. Sati says we must have our own satellite, Jaga says we must persuade the completes to help us build new cities on Earth. Athene and I keep our thoughts to ourselves.

Voices rise and overlap as they argue. 'They're not planets but man-made satellites.' 'Don't be pedantic.' 'We should attack Oasis, capture it for ourselves.'

'Impossible.' 'We should share Oasis, share their cities, live side by side with them.' 'You must be joking. We'd be second class citizens.'

'We should stay on Earth. Rebuild cities here.' 'How the hell do you think we can do that?'

'Get them to help us.' 'Why should they do that?' 'To recompense us for contaminating Earth.' 'For locking up us.' 'Now you're being unrealistic.'

A cacophony of sound fills the confer-cube as they continue to argue.

Just as I'm about to make my presence felt, bring this motley crew to their senses and show them who is boss, a huge screen behind us lights up. For a moment I think Ra is about to appear, risen from the dead, but instead a woman appears on the screen. She's a complete, power-dressed in a Dallas blue suit with padded shoulders sporting gold epaulettes. Matching blue shoes with gold-spiked heels complete the outfit. Her voice, smooth, sweet but cold, resounds throughout the confer-cube.

'My name is Stella Jameson and I live on Planet Oasis. I believe that by now most of you have heard of this satellite. At least one of you has made an attempt to visit it.'

She appears to look directly at me, but I do not react. As far as I know only Athene knows of my abortive trip to Oasis and I don't want the others speculating on what happened there.

'We are still holding your warriors hostage but I want you to know that they are in good shape. We are taking care of them until we feel the political climate is favourable to release them. One of the purposes of my visit today is to make it clear that uninvited guests are not welcome on Oasis.'

At that moment, an amazing thing occurs. This Stella Jameson steps forward, out of the screen into the confer-cube. We all gasp. How can we not? It's a miracle far beyond our technology. Is this a hologram or a real person? She seems real enough and smiles at our incredulity before continuing to speak to us.

'I do realise that I am an uninvited guest here today and apologise for interrupting your meeting, but please allow me to explain why I feel justified to be here. I am the Owner and Managing Director of Worldwideculture.inc and it is in this role that I wish to address you.'

She has our undivided attention now and begins to tell us the history of Worldwideculture, about her ancestor, Rebecca Harfield, the members of her family who succeeded her and their continued aim to improve and enrich the lives of the humanoids in the compounds.

This Stella Jameson talks about the initial fight to get permission to install computers and the setting up of targets to encourage creativity and innovation. She explains that it has long been the philosophy of the company to encourage self-rule and that she wishes that practice to continue. The Chief Executive Officer and the heads of each sectoid have always been and continue to be mutant humanoids. It is not her policy to interfere with the decisions made by the CEO, but she is always available for consultation if needed.

Stella Jameson's face darkens and her voice deepens. 'Following the death of Ra I have noticed that there's been considerable unrest among you, a jockeying for power, which I will not, cannot tolerate. It must stop. The new leader will not be determined by a wrangle for power, a takeover or even a majority vote. The appointment of Chief Controller, the CEO of Worldwideculture, has always been and will continue to be the right and the responsibility of the Managing Director, in this case myself.'

This statement causes a bit of a stir and there are a few mutterings, but Stella raises her hand and silence prevails.

'I wish to assure you that I intend to be as fair as possible in my choice of CEO. I have the advantage of being able to judge objectively who would best serve the interests of Worldwideculture and of your fellow humanoids. The CEO I select must have a clear philosophy based on solid values,' she glances at Brahmin, 'whether religious or secular, and should have a clear vision about how to deal with future changes.'

She pauses. 'I am offering you a chance to talk to me individually about your ideas. I say again, it is my job to choose the Chief Controller but whosoever I choose will have complete autonomy. I have no desire to interfere with the running of the sectoids, although, as I said before, I am always available for consultation if needed.'

A few more murmurs. Stella raises her hand again. 'If you have any concerns, please discuss them with me, face-to-face during our private meetings. I am happy to consider any one of you as a candidate for CEO. If you do not wish to take on this very demanding position, please inform me now, before we start.'

I look round the table at my colleagues. No one speaks. I think Odysseus is about to say something, to tell her that he thinks he's better suited to be curator of the museum than CEO, but he does not say a word. Neither does Brahmin, nor Kali. I thought Kali might be content to stay in charge of C55, her beloved compound. It seems I have underestimated the appetite for power inherent in all of us, whether mutant humanoid or complete. Stella herself seems to be enjoying her power over us and it seems that all the assembled delegates want to put their names forward as prospective replacements for Ra.

Before installing herself in Athene's office for the interviews, Stella assures us that she will listen to what we say and consider carefully who will be best suited to take on this important post. We will have her decision in twenty-four hours.

I have no idea what transpired during the other interviews but Stella was certainly thorough, spending a long time with each of us. She certainly listened carefully to my two proposals: the building of new cities on Earth and the alternative plan of creating a satellite of our own. She nodded to express her understanding of what I was saying but made no comment as to the viability of either scheme. It was near the end of my session that she managed to surprise me.

She stood up, moved round the workstation, perched herself on the edge of it, her legs neatly crossed at the ankles. A very confident woman. 'I understand that while you were on Oasis you thought you saw a fellow mutant humanoid.'

'I did see him and he saw me. In the museum.' I could add, where I was caged and gawped at like an animal in the zoo, but I resist the temptation to provoke her. I have the feeling that this Stella is a woman it would be better to have as a friend than an enemy.

'You are sure about that?'

'Oh yes, quite sure. It was Mercury. I believe he was instrumental in securing my release. I was sent back to Earth the very next morning. If you happen to see him please be kind enough to thank him for me.'

'I'll do that – if I ever meet him.' She looks at me closely and at that moment I realise that she does indeed know him but wants to hide that fact from me.

'I can't help wondering,' I say, 'if Oasis is just for completes, why he is there.'

'I have no idea.'

'My interrogator wanted to know that too.'

A flash of fear flicks on to Stella's face but her calm exterior returns quickly enough. 'You don't happen to know the name of your – interrogator?'

'He said his name was Orlando Wolfe, a member of the Symposium of Oasis.'

Her lips push themselves together in what I take to be apprehension.

'May I ask what exactly you told Mr. Wolfe?'

'Nothing at all. I had no idea why Mercury was there. I hadn't actually seen him then – only caught a glimpse of him online, going into the university.'

'Did you tell Mr. Wolfe that?'

'No. I didn't tell him anything. He lent me an auto-pad and asked me to write down his name and anything else I knew about him and said he'd collect it the following morning. That didn't happen because I'd been transported back here by then.'

'What happened to the auto-pad? Did you bring it with you?'

'No. I must have left in the cell.'

Stella thinks about that. 'Had you already begun your notes about this humanoid – Mercury? I wouldn't like it to fall into the wrong hands.'

It's my turn to think. 'I might have written something. Are you suggesting that you wouldn't want this information to land in this particular politician's hands?'

'It's better that no one knows. My concern is for the safety of your colleague. All of you are my concern.'

But particularly Mercury, I suspect, and wonder how they are connected. I determine to find out.

'That's good to know,' I tell her. 'We need someone to be on our side.'

She gives me an odd look, stands up and shakes my hand.

'It was very interesting talking to you, Heracles.'

'And to you too – Stella.'

'I'll be in touch soon.'

'I'll be in touch soon,' she said. I have a gut feeling that she's impressed with me and that she won't have too much difficulty making her decision about the appointment of the next CEO.

Chapter Twenty-three
Brave New World
(according to Michael)

Journal Entry

Guess what? Jonathan Dowell is in love. He spends more time with that lanky Susie than he does with me. To tell you the truth I'm a tiny bit jealous. Not that I fancy her or him for that matter. Please don't think that. It's just that I miss him. I've never had a friend before, someone to chat to, exchange ideas with and now I'm back to square one. On my own. When I suggest a walk in the park or even to see what's happening in the Projects he says he's busy. Oh well, I'm used to my own company. I don't care. So, dear Journal, you remain my confidante.

That's not altogether true. About being on my own, I mean, because I have a girlfriend too. Well, she's a girl and a friend and I like her very much. I'm not in love with her. Not yet. But I like her very much and can imagine a day when....

The first date. I wait for her at the arranged meeting place. She's late. Or perhaps I'm early. I don't think she's going to turn up. She arrives, a small figure skipping along towards the Obelisk on the edge of the Project. I'm convinced she's a born dancer, the way she swings along, her body as flexible and fluid as running water. There. I'm becoming quite lyrical. When she sees me waiting for her she slows down to an easy, casual walk. She's wearing the same dress as before but it looks different. As she gets nearer, I suspect she's washed and ironed it, especially to meet me. I feel chuffed about that. We're both a bit shy. I have no idea what to talk to her about or where to go. We stand looking at each other. Neither of us can stop smiling. It's going to be all right.

'Shall we go to the park?' I ask her at last.

She doesn't answer.

'It's my favourite place. I'm sure you'll like it.'

'I'm not supposed to go out of the Project,' she says. 'Not unless I've got a job interview or something.'

I frown. I didn't know that. 'Do you have a park in the Project?'

She shakes her head.

'Or any open space with plants and trees where we could walk?'

'Nah. Nothing like that here. Only boring streets with rows and rows of houses.'

And her brothers, watching us, I think.

'Can't you pretend you've got an interview?'

'No papers,' she says and when I look puzzled she adds, 'you have to have the right papers to prove where you're going. In case you're stopped.'

'You won't be stopped,' I say with all the brash assurance of a young male with his girl. 'Not if you're with me.'

She laughs, a pretty, trilling laugh that makes me feel good. 'They'll still know where I'm from if they look close.'

I haven't a clue what she's talking about. She rolls up her sleeves, puts her arms out in front of her and on the back of both hands and way up her arms are printed the words OASIS PROJECT in huge letters. She lifts up her fringe and the same words have been tattooed in the middle of her forehead. I can't believe it. She's been labelled as if she's a criminal. I haven't felt this angry since the incident with the mutant humanoids in the museum. I want to crash my way into the Symposium and tell those smug politicians what I think of them. How can they subject people to such humiliation?

'Can't you get rid of them somehow? Paint over them or something?'

'Not allowed. If we do that we could lose our house and we can't afford to do that. My Dad hasn't got a job. Neither have my brothers.'

'Can't they get work?'

She shifts from foot to foot. 'No one wants to employ folk from the Projects, Mr. Darcy.' She gives a mischievous grin.

'My name's not really Darcy. It's....'

She places a finger on my lips. 'You'll always be Darcy to me.'

'OK. Darcy and Elizabeth it is.'

'Lizzy.'

'Lizzy. How long do you have to keep these – whatever they are – tattoos?'

'They erase them in Hos-sat when we leave the Project. If we ever do.'

'You mustn't think like that, Lizzy. Of course you'll leave.' She hangs her head, not wanting to talk about it. 'Are you still at school?'

She nods. 'That red brick building where we met, that's our school. I was on my lunch hour yesterday but today I'm taking the whole afternoon off.'

'Won't you get into trouble?'

She shrugs. 'They can't do much. I'll be sixteen next week and then I'll be finished with school for good. What about you? Are you free all afternoon?'

'I can be. I can please myself, more or less. I'm a student at the uni. Perhaps when you leave school you could apply for a place there.'

'No way. Studying costs money. My family can't afford it. Anyway I'm not that clever.'

'You've read *Pride and Prejudice* and are obviously a Jane Austen fan.'

She grins. 'Not read it. I've seen the film.'

'You should read the book too. I'll lend it to you if you like. Austen's a ruthless writer, highly critical of the society in which she lived.'

'I'd like that. Thanks. And *Emma* – have you got Emma?'

'I have all the Jane Austen novels.'

Her eyes light up in anticipation of a reading feast. 'I wish I could afford lots of books.'

It must be awful to be short of money. On Earth we didn't use money. Food and clothes and even compus were provided and here, on Oasis, Father supplies whatever I need.

'Don't you have a library here in the Project?'

'There is a library here but the only books are instruction manuals aimed at teaching us skills to train us for jobs.'

I think about that.

'What about your father? Maybe I can help him find some work. Has he any particular skills?'

She shakes her head. 'Even if he could get a job he wouldn't earn enough to keep us and rent another place outside the Project. Dad says it's better to have a roof over our heads so he's stopped looking for work. So have my brothers.'

'Lizzy, don't you think it's better to have a job than live off....' Oh Zeus, what am I saying? I've been dependent on others all my life and now here I am telling her what her father should do. He's caught in a trap. He has to think of his children. But what quality of life do they have here in the Project and what happens to his – and their – self-respect? The philanthropy practised by the privileged members of society seems to have turned into something rather sour. Whether by bad management or deliberate sabotage I have no idea, but I intend to find out and do something about it.

Lizzy has noticed how quiet I've become. She touches my arm. 'If you don't want to be friends with me, it's all right. I quite understand.'

'Don't say that. Of course I want to be friends. From the moment I saw you, I…' I find myself blushing and bite my lip. I'm not used to paying compliments to girls or to talking to them. I take a deep breath. 'Today, I'm going to take you to the park in the city centre. That is, if you're up for it. If anyone asks any questions, leave it to me to answer.'

Her eyes light up but then she frowns. 'Dad will murder me if I'm caught. If we lose any more points we'll lose the house.'

'You won't get caught and you won't lose your house. I promise. Do you want to come or not?'

'Of course I do.'

She yanks up the hood attached to the back of her dress and pulls it right over her head, almost covering her eyes to make sure the inscription on her forehead doesn't show. Then she tugs down her long sleeves and plunges her hands deep into her pockets. She looks like a pitiful orphan out of a nineteenth century workhouse. She'll be picked up immediately if she goes on the streets of Oasis looking like that.

'You look as if you're trying to hide something.'

'I am,' she giggles.

'You have to look as natural as possible if you don't want to attract attention to yourself. Come on, off with that hood, keep your head held high, look happy and hold my hand. Then everyone will believe you're my girlfriend. No one will notice your tattoos. After all I didn't see them until you pointed them out. I couldn't take my eyes off your pretty little face and sparkling blue eyes and that's all anyone else will see. Believe me.'

She takes her hands out of her pockets, lifts her hood and lets it rest on her shoulders, pulls her fringe down to hide the inscription on her forehead without taking her bright eyes off my face. My heart beats faster as I feel her soft little hand clasp mine. She looks nervous but I smile at her and she smiles back and we set off for a stroll through the city to the park. No one stops us. A couple of times we rush to shelter from a torrent of rain but that just adds to the fun. She frets that the wet hair sticking to her forehead will expose the inscription but the fringe soon dries, becomes fluffy again and hides it.

Being with Lizzy is not the same as being with Jonathan. There are no intellectual discussions – but I love being close to her and sharing her joy in everything I show her: the flowers, the river, the statues and buildings, things she's never seen before. For once I am the mentor with a student keen to learn.

Lizzy asks if the park has a name and when I tell her that as far as I know it hasn't, she says in that case we will name it. She finds a twig, pointed enough at one end to write in the soil of a flowerbed, and writes the word PEMBERLEY, the name of Mr. Darcy's estate. She looks up at me, her eyes shining, and I nod my approval.

And that, dear Journal, is the highlight of our first date.

Journal

Stella has made an intervention. Not just on screen as Ra did when he stopped the fight between Kali and Sati, but in person. She transported herself to Earth as Father did when he came to find me. She has interviewed all the prospective candidates for the post of CEO and is to announce the name of the new controller tomorrow. I didn't see the private interviews but I do have an opinion.

A quick run-down of my thoughts on the matter. First the definite No-nos: Heracles, too clever by half, a wild card, impulsive, untrustworthy, a danger to his fellow mutants; Odysseus and Brahmin, too old and stuck in their ways; Durga, another impulsive wild card, willing to risk other people's lives for her own glory; Sati, a selfish, scheming alley cat; Jaga, a selfish traitor, not to be trusted. Only two possibilities left: Athene, cool, calm and clever, but I don't really know how her mind works (maybe Stella has found out); Kali, firm, authoritative, straight as an arrow, caring, honest, a good leader....

OK, dear Journal, I know I'm biased and I know well enough that Kali has her faults but I will be thrilled if Stella chooses her. Just think. My two mothers, one as CEO and the other as Managing Director of Worldwideculture. I'd be so proud.

Not going to happen. Can you imagine it – Stella appointing Kali? No way, José.

Journal Entry

A bulletin from the Symposium to all inhabitants of Oasis is posted online. The new CEO of Worldwideculture is to visit us tomorrow. Wow! I'm so excited. Imagine: the first mutant humanoid to be invited to visit Oasis. (Apart from myself, of course, but that's a different story.)

The stun-gun device in the teleport is to be switched off. My father and several other government officials are to escort the CEO to the Symposium building in the main plaza. I intend to be in the crowd to witness the historic arrival and Lizzy is coming with me. Who is to be the new chief controller? I don't know. No one knows. It's top secret. Even though Stella likes to think of herself as my mother she doesn't confide in me. Actually, I'm not sure she really likes me. In fact, I don't think she trusts me. And, to be honest, I'm not sure I really like or trust her.

Journal Entry

The streets are packed. Lizzy and I have a good spot near the transporter. I'm loath to stand too near the front as I don't want Lizzy to be exposed, but we're both short and someone pushes us forward and there we are in the front row. I am so keyed up. I can't wait to see who emerges from the teleport. Lizzy clutches my hand. She has no idea why I am so interested in this momentous occasion but she catches some of my excitement and is happy to share it with me. There's a real buzz in the crowd. I see Jonathan and Susie on the other side of the prom but I don't wave. Better not attract attention to myself. He might remember Lizzy and disapprove of my being with a girl from the Project.

At last the moment arrives. The members of the official welcome party stand by the teleport. Apart from Father and Stella I recognise Orlando Wolfe with his sleek-backed hair and mean eyes.

The teleport lights up, flame-coloured, purple and green. A rustle of anticipation in the crowd and, a moment or two later, out comes – Athene.

She's as beautiful in the flesh as on screen. Tall, classically dressed in a long white gown, she resembles a Greek goddess. Her only mutation, as far as I can see, is the extra eye in the centre of her forehead, but that eye is marine blue and serene and, to my mind at least, does not detract from her beauty. But then I'm used to mutant humanoids. It must be different for the real completes.

Stella greets Athene and introduces her to the other members of the welcome party. Athene shakes hands with each of them in turn.

They escort their guest through the city to the Symposium. Athene moves gracefully with a calm self-assurance that suggests she will be a decisive but balanced

CEO of Wordwideculture. Stella walks beside her, head held high, confident she has chosen well.

The people on either side of me stare at the phenomenon before them – a mutant humanoid on the streets of Oasis – but they are well behaved. I note that there is a substantial police presence in case of an incident. Someone begins to applaud and others join in and soon the clapping becomes louder and there is even some cheering but, thank Zeus, none of the jeering or crude comments that so horrified me in the museum. All is quiet and controlled. For once I can be proud of being a complete.

As Orlando Wolfe passes, I see his eyes scrutinising the crowd. Perhaps it's his job to make sure Athene arrives without mishap. His eyes alight on me and rest on me for a little longer than they should. Is it my imagination? I don't think he and Father get on very well and Wolfe would be delighted to find fault with his son. Pulling Lizzy along with me, I weave my way through the crowd to the back. By the time I look up again, the official group has moved on, Orlando Wolfe with them. It gives me a bit of a scare seeing him gaze at me like that. I believe he was involved in the interrogation of Heracles. Could Heracles have mentioned me?

A big screen has been erected in the Plaza. The conference in the Symposium is to be relayed there and online. What a break-through. Negotiations usually take place behind closed doors, but these are not negotiations, they are opening speeches and, in the name of transparency, it has been decided they will be televised live. How democratic can you get?

Oasis is very proud itself today and so it should be. Lizzie and I make our way to the Plaza to view the events on the big screen with everyone else. We look up and view the modern high tech interior of the Symposium building with its members sitting in a wide semi-circle.

Journal Entry

What is to happen? An enlightening exchange of ideas: the start of a better relationship between Earth and Oasis? Or a revelation of how far the two sides will have to compromise for any changes to take place?

A representative of the Oasis Symposium, Stephen Giles, a tall man with a long face and beaky nose, kicks off the proceedings with some suggestions. I will list them for you, dear Journal, with my comments in italics.

1) To show goodwill, the ten hostages, the captured golden warriors, will be returned immediately to Compound 98 where Jaga is now in charge. *Excellent news.*

2) Certain artefacts and paintings from the Oasis museum will be transferred to the principle museum on Earth, also in C98. These will be gifts, a further sign of good relations. *Excellent again. Odysseus will be thrilled.*

3) The technology in the compounds will be updated and all further technological advances will be shared. *Equality is on its way. Whoopee!*

4) Human beings will keep the satellites for themselves but offer to share all resources and ideas with the mutant humanoids on Earth, provided the humanoids promise not to attack or attempt to infiltrate the satellites. As the air on Earth is no longer toxic, the Oasis government suggests that the humanoids could – should they wish – leave the compounds and build their own towns and cities on Earth. This would be strictly for mutant humanoids. They could use designs based on Oasis if they so wished and receive advice about the construction of roads and buildings including schools, universities, hospitals and theatres. In fact, Oasis is willing to supply any kind of help needed. *Very magnanimous. A bit patronising?*

To summarize: the Oasis government intends to keep the satellites as an autonomous zone for themselves but in return the humanoids are offered their own autonomous zone, the Earth. *Big deal. Very little is being offered here.*

Athene listens to these suggestions in silence, her expression inscrutable. In a clear firm voice she thanks the Symposium of Oasis for the return of the warriors, the gifts for the museum and the offer to share resources, ideas and technological updates with those left on Earth. She pauses, smiles and adds that she can't help comparing the gifts being offered with the brightly coloured necklaces given to natives to placate them when colonising their land. *She thinks, as I do, that it's patronising to suggest that the mutant humanoids can be bought with a few gifts that should have been shared before now.*

She also thanks the government of Oasis for giving them the sole rights to develop Earth, but as they already live there, possession being nine tenths of the law, she suggests it's not much of a concession. *Note my comment above – Big deal. Athene and I are on the same wavelength. Fantastic.*

The help in designing and constructing cities might well be useful, but the Symposium might be surprised to learn that the sectoids have their own talented, skilled architects. *Great. She's proud of the mutant humanoids.*

Her main objection to the ideas put forward is that it will take time for such cities to be built. Meanwhile, all they have been offered – apart from a few token artefacts for the museum – is the status quo, segregation as before with the complete human beings remaining on the satellites and the mutant humanoids on Earth.

A few exchanged looks as the Symposium wonder what alternative plan she is about to suggest. I note the stern set of Orlando Wolfe's mouth as he leans to make a comment to a colleague sitting next to him. Is she is going to suggest that mutant humanoids should have a satellite of their own? Not a bit of it. That would be apartheid. Athene argues the case for integration.

'I understand that we look different from you, that some complete human beings look upon mutant humanoids as freaks, but our mutations were brought about by human error. The inhabitants of the satellites can count themselves lucky that their bodies have remained intact and should concede that part of the blame for our mutations lies with them.

'We mutant humanoids are not asking for pity. All we are asking is to be treated as equals.

'I realise that complete integration will take time. Attitudes will have to change so that people learn not to treat those who look different from them as inferior. A step in the right direction has been made today when I walked down the main street of Oasis. It was my suggestion to do that and you were gracious enough to agree. You could say I asked you to invite me! What I propose is a series of similar experiments for you to become accustomed to seeing us.'
Integration. Exciting news. I squeeze Lizzy's hand. She looks up at me – yes, she's even shorter than me – no doubt wondering why I'm so pleased.

Athene smiles. 'As a matter of fact, we will have some adjusting to do too. We find you strange to look at. Yes, really, but I invite you to visit us on Earth so that we can become used to looking at each other. Why not start with a trip to Compound 99? I assure you we will make you welcome and try not to stare at your lack of mutations!'

A ripple of laughter runs through the chamber. *Witty as well as beautiful.*

'Clearly, you have more amenities here on Oasis than we have on Earth. From what I've already seen today I'm very impressed by your city. Naturally we are a little envious of your facilities and would like to share them. I make no secret of that.

'Now for a couple of specific requests. Firstly, Hos-sat. If we have humanoids in need of special treatment we'd like to be able to send them there. As a matter of fact, this privilege has already been awarded us in the case of our previous CEO, Ra, and I thank you for that. I visited him there and was impressed with the quality of both the staff and the facilities. That Ra died in Hos-sat is no reflection on the quality of care and treatment he received. Ra would have died wherever he was. It was his time. As far as I know there is no one dangerously ill on Earth at present. We are well protected from germs and viruses, shut up as we are in the compounds.

'But we do have a pregnant woman in C98. As you can imagine, this is a thrilling occasion for us. No one on Earth has given birth for years. I would like your permission to allow her to go to Hos-sat to give birth to give her the best chance of a successful delivery.'

I suspect that Athene's request is likely to be answered favourably and that she knows this and so has chosen to ask for this favour first. Her later appeals may be more difficult to grant. My respect for her grows by the minute. I hope this will be granted because the mother-to-be is my old mate, Isis.

Her next suggestion posits that intellectually gifted mutant humanoids should be allowed to apply to attend Oasis university. A little stir of consternation from her audience, but Athene continues regardless. She refers to her arrival today again and says again that the more often mutant humanoids are seen here the quicker attitudes are likely to change. 'Surely in the enlightened world of the university the integration of humans and humanoids would be excepted, if not with ease, at least with respect.' *Fantastic. Having fellow mutants at the university would be excellent.*

Athene finishes by conceding that not all mutant humanoids are of good character. 'We have flaws just as I'm sure some of you have – present company accepted naturally,' another titter of laughter, 'but we are used to communal living and to having consideration for others. I said just now that we are not greedy but, on the other hand, we do envy you your lifestyle – your high standard of living – and would like to share it. It will take time to build new cities on Earth. We feel we've been shut up in the compounds long enough and are entitled to share some of the facilities on Oasis and other satellites. We are the same species as you. I'm sure when you get used to the diversity of our appearance you will find we're not so very different.'

By the time she has thanked Mr. Giles and the other members of the Symposium for listening to her and for their hospitality I believe she has charmed them enough for them to at least give her proposals serious thought.

Oh brave new world indeed if we can really begin to integrate. If this change had only come earlier perhaps I could have avoided those operations and the torture of physiotherapy and speech therapy! But I am aware that it will take a long time for attitudes to change and for the society that Athene envisages to be realised, but it could happen. It must happen.

Chapter Twenty-four
Elizabeth and Darcy
(according to Michael)

Journal Entry

'Did you see the eye in the centre of her forehead? A bit creepy that.' Lizzy and I are walking back along the central prom towards the project.

I realise that Athene must be the first mutant humanoid Lizzy has seen. I'm determined to educate her, to make her see things differently. 'I don't find it a bit creepy. I think she's one of the most beautiful women I've ever seen.'

'More beautiful than me?' Lizzy says, raising her blue eyes to mine. She's flirting with me and I can't help but respond – but not in words. There, in the middle of the prom, I take her in my arms and kiss her. Our first kiss. Afterwards she opens her eyes and smiles at me. 'Oh, Mr. Darcy, that was real special!'

I have to agree that it was and we repeat the experience.

A voice makes us spring apart. 'Excuse me, Sir, can I have a word?' And with that Lizzy is off, running away as if her life depends on it. The police officer starts off after her. He's in no hurry. He knows where to find her.

I promised Lizzy that if the police stopped her I would deal with it, that she wouldn't lose points for being in Oasis City without permission and that her family wouldn't lose the house. But everything happens so quickly. I'm in a state of shock, still knocked out by that kiss. I can't move. I can't say a word.

I come to life at last, rush after the officer, catch up with him and find my voice. 'Please Officer, let her go. She hasn't done anything wrong.'

He gives a short laugh. 'Soliciting on the main promenade of Oasis? That's enough for me. '

'Soliciting? I don't understand….'

The officer stops and looks me straight in the eye. 'Take my advice, Sir. Not a good idea to have anything to do with the prostitutes from the Project. You don't know what sort of diseases you might pick up.'

The colour rushes up my cheek. 'She's not a prostitute. She's a really nice girl.'

'I'm sure she is, Sir,' he says evenly, 'but my advice is the same. Keep away from the Project. Find yourself a nice girl in Oasis City.'

I ring Lizzy about five times before she answers.

'Where are you? Are you all right? Did the police constable catch you?'

'He let me off with a caution. Don't know why. I'm back home now.'

'How are you feeling?'

'Fine.' She hesitates. 'Look, Darcy. You mustn't come looking for me no more. It won't do you no good. Thank you for giving me a nice time and for treating me right. But you must forget me. I'm not for the likes of you.'

'Did the officer tell you to say that?'

'Yes, and my brothers. They saw the cop talking to me on the edge of the Project. I can't see you again, Darcy. Forget about me. For your sake as well as mine.'

'I can't forget you, Lizzy. You must know that.' No answer. 'Lizzy, can you hear me?'

We've been cut off. I ring back but there's no answer. I try again and again. The line's dead. I'll try again later. She can't keep her mob-fone switched off forever.

I sit on a bench and think about what's happened. The officer called Lizzy a prostitute. I'm furious. How dare he say such a thing? I've a good mind to report him for defamation of character but even as I have the thought, I know I can't do it. If I did, Father would become involved and that wouldn't do at all.

Journal

'To Athene,' Stella says raising her glass.

'To Athene,' say Father and I in unison.

Stuart and Bella are in bed. Father, Stella and I are celebrating Athene's appointment and discussing the day's events in the Symposium.

'A good beginning to the new regime,' Stella smiles.

Father and I nod in agreement. 'She made a terrific speech,' I say, 'but do you think Athene's proposals will be accepted?'

'Some of them,' says Stella. 'I feel sure Isis will be allowed to have her baby in Hos-sat, for example.'

'Is it Isis who is pregnant?' I ask innocently. I already know that but I have to keep up the pretence that I have no knowledge about what's going on in the sectoids. I can't help thinking how I dislike this continued deception and hope that Stella will soon relent and allow me legitimate access to Worldwideculture.inc.

'Yes. I forgot you knew her in C55,' says Stella.

'We were brought up together. She's only two years older than me. I can't believe she's having a baby. Who is the father?'

'One of the hostages about to be returned. A young warrior.'

'Great. She'll be pleased to see him again.' I'm sincere about that, but my mind is still on Lizzy. I wonder when I will see her again.

I try to keep my mind on the present conversation. 'Do you think they'll agree to allow mutant humanoids to apply for university courses?'

Father shakes his head. 'I doubt it. Most of the members of the Symposium will think that's a step too far.'

He must see the disappointment on my face as he adds, 'Maybe in the future, Michael. Who knows?'

I can't help wondering if he will vote against integration, not on principle, but because he's afraid that someone will find out about my previous mutant status.

Journal

I call Lizzy before I go to bed and again the next morning. The line is dead. I go to uni, determined to do some work. When I turn on my computer, I find a message from Heracles.

It's more or less a rant. He's furious that he hasn't been selected as CEO of Worlwideculture. He slags off Stella for not appreciating him and complains that Athene is acting in a very high-handed manner. She's taken away his captives, sent Durga back to C98 with the warriors he captured. She's to take charge of the whole army again with Jaga continuing at her post of chief administrator. In addition, she's given Sati control of another sectoid, C77.

'She's rewarded them both and taken away my warriors,' Heracles protests. 'It's not fair. She's told me I can stay as her number two for the time being but any funny business and I'll be out. She's insufferable. So patronising it makes me want to puke. But she can't manage without my compu skills. I know that.'

I skim through more of his grumbles until, near the end, I find the following: 'Thing is, Mercury, you may be able to help me. I need to get in touch with someone called Orlando Wolfe. I have the feeling that he and I could prove useful to each other. Do you know him? If so perhaps you could put in a good word for me. Thanks in anticipation, your good mate, Heracles.'

Good mate? In his dreams! Mind you I suppose I was a good mate to him in getting him sent back to Earth. I'm just about to delete the auto-mail when I change my mind and print it out. I'll give it to Father. I did promise to let him know if I had any further communication from Heracles and meddling with a politician on Oasis could prove disastrous. Father needs to know about this. I was right in my assessment of Heracles. He is dangerous. Not only could he bring down Athene, but others as well – including Father.

Journal
Jonathan puts his head round my compu-cube.

'Susie's dumped me' He pulls a face.

'Sorry to hear that.' I give him a wry look. 'I suppose that means you want to go for a coffee and tell me all about it.'

'I know I've neglected you but you'll find out what it's like when you fall in love.'

'I expect I will but I hope I won't drop you.'

'I've missed you, man. You must know that. Well, are we going for coffee or not?'

'Sure,' I say, glad to have my friend back again, even if it does mean I have to listen to the story of his doomed love affair while I keep mine a secret.

Journal
Here we are again, Father and I. Same restaurant. Same table. Same view, except it is raining hard, sheets of water pelting down against the plate glass and the grassy slope. I wonder if the lake ever floods.

I can't wait to tell Father about the message from Heracles. As soon as we've ordered our lunch, I hand him the printout. He reads it intently, frowning and shaking his head from time to time.

'I think Wolfe was a member of the team who interrogated Heracles. He was not very pleased to say the least when I intervened to have him released.' He looks at me. 'I wonder if Heracles told him about you?'

'I don't know,' I say, 'but something happened the other day that I found – well – unsettling. It may not mean anything but....' And I tell Father how, on the day of Athene's visit, Orlando Wolfe scanned the crowd with those steely eyes of his as if looking for someone and that they rested on me for several moments.

'Why haven't you mentioned this before?'

I shrug. 'I haven't thought of it since. I may have been mistaken and it was just chance he looked at me. I don't know. Getting this auto-mail today reminded me. What's he like? As a man, as a politician?'

'Power-crazy,' says Father and smiles up at the waiter as our plates of steak and chips arrive. When the waiter leaves he adds a few more adjectives to describe Orlando Wolfe, 'unscrupulous and immoral.'

'I take it you don't like him much,' I grin.

'Let's put it this way, I don't think I've ever voted the same way as him on any issue in the Symposium and I certainly wouldn't invite him as a guest to our house.'

We eat our steak and chips in silence for a while. I'm beginning to appreciate different food and this steak is particularly tasty.

'Talking about inviting someone to our house,' I say, 'do you think I could invite a friend home one evening?'

He looks surprised. He has no idea I have a friend. 'Of course you can.'

'His name's Jonathan Dowell and he attends some of the same seminars as me.'

'Martin Dowell's son?'

'I think so, yes. His father's a scientist or something.'

Father looks pleased. 'He's the most eminent nuclear physicist of his generation.'

'Famous then? Like you.'

He chuckles. 'Me? I'm a mere politician. Martin Dowell has a brilliant mind. It's good you're friendly with his son. I look forward to meeting him.'

I can't help thinking what a long way Father and I have come in our relationship since we met. He's taught me so much. And he's a good man, a man I respect and he makes it clear that he respects me too and is proud of me.

That last thought disturbs me. I feel guilty about the secrets I haven't shared with him. I can't tell him about Lizzy. Not yet. But I can tell him about the deception that's been playing on my conscience for so long. I decide to come clean.

'Father, I have to tell you something. I'm sorry about this. I've hacked into Worldwideculture.inc because I just had to know what was happening on Earth. '

His reaction takes me by surprise. He bursts out laughing. 'So my son's become a hacker? I didn't agree with blocking your access to the site, but Stella was insistent. I had to go along with it to keep the peace. You know how it is with women sometimes – or perhaps you don't. Yet.'

'You won't tell Stella what I've done?'

'Not if you promise not to tell her that I know.'

We shake on it, complicit in our deception of Stella, and I feel closer to my father than before.

'I don't regret it,' I tell him. 'It's been so exciting to watch the dramatic events that have recently taken place on Earth. Imagine, if I hadn't accessed the site I wouldn't have known that Kali had been reinstated.'

We begin to talk about the happenings we have witnessed on Earth: the spectacular trek across the wilderness by Durga, Kali and the golden warriors; Jason's death and Sati's mock death; the abortive attempt by Sati and Durga to take over C99; and Heracles's triumph in capturing them both. And about Stella's intervention which led to her decision to appoint Athene as leader.

'Do you agree with her intervention? Appearing on Earth in person like that?'

I see him hesitate but he says. 'Stella is her own person, makes her own decisions. Even I don't know what was said in the individual interviews, but I trust Stella's judgment.'

'Let's just hope Heracles doesn't mess things up,' I say.

'Don't worry. I'll deal with him. And with Orlando Wolfe.' Father's confidence is impressive. He drains his glass of ruby red wine.

I have another question I'm dying to ask him. 'Do you think there will come a day when mutant humanoids and completes will live together in harmony side by side?'

'You might be interested to hear, Michael, that the case for integration is already being explored. I am on the sub-committee looking into various possibilities….'

'That is really good news, Father.'

With my father actively involved what could possibly go wrong?

Journal

Jonathan comes to Home-Court-Jameson and I visit his home, Home-Dowling-Palmer. We spend hours in one or other of our study-bedrooms and have long talks about every subject under the sun. We call it "putting the world to rights." We mean our world, Oasis. We talk about the future a lot. Sometimes we disagree but we always listen to each other's opinion and counteract it with a balanced and intelligent argument. Or so we believe. For example, Jonathan doesn't believe that the integration of mutant humanoids with completes will work.

'I'm not saying it's wrong, Michael, just that it's not practical. You're a dreamer. You spend too much time with your head in the clouds.'

'Naturally. Because we live in the clouds!'

He gives me a punch on the top of my arm to show he appreciates my sense of humour.

I'm incredibly fond of him and we make a pact that if either of us has a girlfriend we will still make time to see each other. It's great to know that our friendship is solid.

He's told me quite a bit about his relationship with Susie – more than I want to know actually – but I haven't told him anything about Lizzy. Not much to tell. I haven't seen her. She doesn't answer my calls or reply to my messages.

Journal

I wake up to find a message from Lizzy, asking me to meet her by the Obelisk at one o'clock. 'That is if you want to see me again.'

Do I want to? Can she doubt it?

'I've fixed my brothers,' the text continues. I assume she means that they won't bother us. I set off, excited at the prospect of seeing Lizzy again. We have many problems to overcome but I'm convinced our story will have a happy ending. After all, Elizabeth Bennett came from an impoverished family and she landed up mistress of Pemblerley – so why shouldn't a girl from the Project find happiness with her Darcy?

I stride out towards Oasis Project and think how l lucky I am. Everything in my life is falling into place. My relationship with my father and my friendship with Jonathan are solid. A beautiful mutant humanoid has become the new CEO of Worldwideculture and has been clever enough to begin negotiations for a more egalitarian world.

I believe that I too have a role to play in the shaping of this new world and that if I work hard enough it will come to pass.... Note the biblical language, dear Journal. I treasure the weight of those words and make no apology for using them. I'm not religious but I am an idealist.

As I approach the Project, I see a beautiful girl dancing round the white obelisk. The blue of her skirt catches the sunlight as she dips and twirls, moving fluidly like ripples of water. I increase my step, eager to be with her, to hold her and tell her how much I have missed her.

The End

About the Author

Brought up in a village in Northamptonshire, Jeannie van Rompaey has lived in London, The United States and Spain.

Jeannie considers herself an eternal student. She trained as a teacher at St Gabriel's College and studied Speech and Drama at Rose Bruford, both London based colleges. She has a BA from the Open University, a Diploma in English as a Foreign Language from the Bell School, Cambridge, and an MA in Modern Literature from the University of Leicester.

Her varied career includes teaching, lecturing and running drama and creative writing workshops. She is also a theatre director, actor and voice-over. As Jeannie Russell she is a senior member of the Guild of Drama Adjudicators and adjudicates drama festivals in the UK and Europe.

Jeannie is married to historian and artist, TJ. They live on the subtropical island of Gran Canaria where she spends much of her time writing and painting. She makes frequent trips to London to see her daughter, Anieka, attend literary events, visit art galleries and go to the theatre.

Acknowledgements

I would like to thank the following people for their support.

Hedley Alcock, my first reader, who read each chapter as soon as I had written it, always eager to find out what the characters would do next. His enthusiasm kept me going when I thought of giving up and his comments were always helpful.

Maureen Blundell writing as Roz Colyer, my fierce but fair editor, who has such a keen eye for detail.

Last but not least, my husband, TJ, who has given me so much help. He deserves thanks not just for his practical assistance but also for his personal support throughout the writing process.

Author's Note: I'd like to invite you to take a look at my website. If you would like to be informed when my next book comes out please leave your name and email on the Contact Page. http://jeannievanrompaey.com/

www.ingramcontent.com/pod-product-compliance
Lightning Source LLC
Chambersburg PA
CBHW031120210626
46816CB00016B/1731